On the coin, in letters as crisp as the day they were struck centuries ago, were the words:

FIRST LAUNCH
NATIVE AMERICAN SPACE AUTHORITY
AUGUST, MMCCCLIV

Marekallian Eks recognized the ancient alphabet. He began to tremble. Verley watched in astonished silence as the Mindrunner clutched the coin, a distant fire in his eyes.

"Urth," he whispered. "Homeworld!" he cried, staring at Verley with wild eyes. "The Areps! They came from Urth! They must have crashed here, lost their technology! Reverted to savagery!"

SPACEWAYS

SPACEWAYS #13

JONUTA RISING!

JOHN CLEVE

BERKLEY BOOKS, NEW YORK

**With megathanks to Victor Koman,
plier of the spaceways**

The poem *Scarlet Hills* copyright © 1982 by Ann Morris;
used by permission of the author.

SPACEWAYS #13: JONUTA RISING!

A Berkley Book / published by arrangement with
the author

PRINTING HISTORY
Berkley edition / September 1983

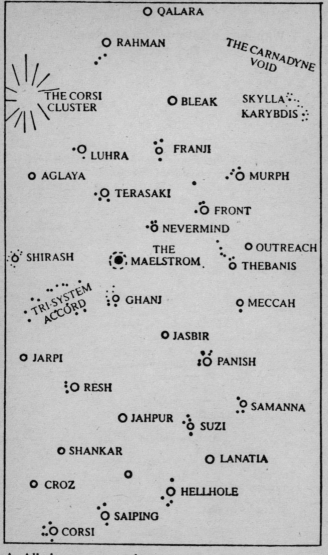

QALARA

RAHMAN

THE CARNADYNE VOID

THE CORSI CLUSTER

BLEAK

SKYLLA
KARYBDIS

LUHRA

FRANJI

AGLAYA

MURPH

TERASAKI

FRONT

NEVERMIND

SHIRASH

THE MAELSTROM

OUTREACH

THEBANIS

TRI-SYSTEM ACCORD

GHANJ

MECCAH

JASBIR

JARPI

PANISH

RESH

SAMANNA

JAHPUR

SUZI

SHANKAR

LANATIA

CROZ

HELLHOLE

SAIPING

CORSI

A: All planets are not shown.
B: Map is not to scale, because of
  the vast distances between stars.

SCARLET HILLS

Alas, fair ones, my time has come.
I must depart your lovely home—
Seek the bounds of this galaxy
To find what lies beyond.

(chorus)
Scarlet hills and amber skies,
Gentlebeings with loving eyes;
All these I leave to search for a dream
That will cure the wand'rer in me.

You say it must be glamorous
For those who travel out through space.
You know not the dark, endless night
Nor the solitude we face.

(reprise chorus)

I know not of my journey's end
Nor the time nor toll it will have me spend.
But I must see what I've never seen
And know what I've never known.

Scarlet hills and amber skies,
Gentlebeings with loving eyes;
All these I leave to search for a dream
That will cure the wand'rer in me.

—Ann Morris

"The closer to the truth, the better the lie, and the truth itself, when it can be used, is the best lie."
—Preem Palver

"You just can't keep a bad man down."
—Kislar Jonuta

prolog

She was a shocking woman. It wasn't just that she was young and shockingly attractive. She was unique: *une type*. Thus her very appearance was shocking, in an altogether positive way. The sort of woman who collected stares—and ignored them.

Among the sprawling star-worlds settled by people calling themselves Galactics, eyes were uniformly shades of brown. Hers were the color of pearls seen through shimmering water. Among Galactics whose natural skin color ranged from that of toasted corn chips or darkish beige to jet—not too much of that, since centuries of intermingling had paled it as it had completely swallowed up pale skin—her color was that of carnations at sunset.

Furthermore her cheekbones were not especially high or prominent and her nose showed no hint of downward turn.

She was short and she just had to be shapely. Unfortunately she was entirely enveloped in a full robe held out from her in a sort of cone by the tiny "hoop" repellor units built into its hem and her anklets. (The units had to be there, although not even her feet were visible, much less her ankles.)

The hoop-robe's rich ultramarine color was quietly and tastefully patterned all over in an arabesque of silvery gray. An off-white shawl, opaque but broidered in white lace, covered her from neck to waist, with fringes extending it to a hand's length longer. An exotic young beauty clad expensively and well—too well; clad in the manner of one of those uptight Seks from Sekhar or as if she was pregnant. As if she had no confidence in her figure. Or was so supremely confident that she needn't bother to display it.

1

Those who saw her that day on Lanatia could not help staring, for she was striking. Shocking. Too, they could hardly help wondering about the color of her hair. That was concealed too, under an indigo wig into which were laced glowstones of azure and pale turquoise. Carved gold "sideburns" hugged her head just forward of the ears. They would have been harsh but for the delicate filigree of their workmanship. From her lobes depended ever-swinging strings of cerulean glowstones like falling tears.

Her lips were neither the pale blue of cerulean or azure nor the deep blue of indigo nor again a (natural?) pink. They combined pink and azure, in a frosted lavender.

She was obviously accompanied by three extraordinarily watchful, almost alarmingly lithe "escorts" (only professional bodyguards ready to kill had eyes like those three), and not at all obviously by a fourth. That one was girlish, dressed differently, and kept her distance.

The over-clad beauty carried herself with casual grace, chin high and eyes carefully distant. Her gaze moved over or through people without making eye contact. And she spent stells as if she had inside information that they were going to be declared valueless in about ten minutes.

This was the fourth store she and her wary-eyed, sleekly lithe entourage had visited in Lanatia's capital, and she had spent kilostells. All on herself. Nearly all on clothing or jewelry. Frippery.

Strange, for a woman whose figure was determinedly hidden within the hoop-robe, to buy so much that was of an indisputably exotic-erotic nature! Decorative clothing and un-clothing designed for the delectation of men. Or a man.

Some rich rajah's well-kept pet, more than one clerk thought, but felt more inclined to call her "Countess" than to sneer. They did neither.

She gave no name, ordered everything sent up to spaceship *Hindilark* docked at Dallastation. All was paid for by the huge silent "escort" in whiskey-colored tights and doublet through whose multiple slashes spilled silken folds of gold-hued shirt. He was conspicuously armed. He used currency—local currency—not cred, and paid whatever fee was named for transport up to Dallastation.

He never spoke. The other escorts, a man and a woman, called her "Lady" and so clerks and hastily-importantly onscene managers did, too.

She tried nothing on. She did have this and that tried on and modeled for her when that was possible, and once she laughed aloud at a cybermodel. Her laughter was throaty but surprisingly unreserved.

Her entourage betrayed little interest in what she purchased, no matter how frivolous or bold or positively, licentiously sexy. They paid no attention when such titillating "garments," markedly brief, were modeled for this nameless lady of means. Even the bioengineered model whose lean legs were over 100 sems long* attracted little of their notice; they were Watching, on watch. All ostentatiously armed with stoppers whose grips were gilded. Scanning, ever looking this way and that as if at any moment a dressing room or rack of clothing might erupt with an assassin or horde of kidnappers.

Judging from the sizes she chose, she was quite small as well as short, though with a figure definitely female.

Her bodyguards did take some notice when she showed her enchantment with fitted, crested turbans of an ancient design—the Thousand and One Nights, they were called. She bought one for each of her three escorts. And a fourth, though she did not wear it.

When she departed each store it was to leave behind large awed eyes and delighted smiles and hands clamped damply around generously bestowed largesse. The leanest, lithest, and shortest bodyguard went first and reconnoitered expertly. She also summoned transportation to the door. Then out swept the lady, gliding, seeming to float within that floor-reaching robe that never touched her body below her ribcage. On the instant clerks and managers and shoppers fell to talking, to wondering, to opining. And pining.

Who could she be?

Where might she—where could *she be from*?

Oh, surely the haughty daughter of one of those mighty

*About forty *inches*, Old Style.

(and mighty wealthy) clan-lords of . . . where was it?—oh, Jorinne. Yes. Jorinne. Surely!

Ah, but perhaps more than that! Perhaps a princess of the Blood (a Viscountess at the very least) of Ghanj, whose nobility ruled in an enlightened neo-feudalism (*Ghanjism*, for it was unique in all the galaxy and in all history), and the daughters of Ghanji lords could afford anything.

Some hyper-rich rajah's pampered pet, a starry-eyed clerk said, almost in a whisper. "Oh, just a high-priced whore then," her customer said, and flounced out—wishing, wishing.

But—with that skin? No Ghanji had such skin!

Ah, but with bioengineering or subcutaneous total-dye or both one could accomplish anything, another pointed out. And a certain male clerk at Eltamaraino's swore to have seen an Aglayan, once, and swore that he looked just that way, in eyes and skin—and had nearly-white hair, too! Ah, but all Aglayans off Aglaya were slaves; everyone knew that. No no, the skin must be the product of celldye and the eyes designer contacts or even corneally dyed by simple injection. *No one* had such skin and eyes—it was almost scandalous!

"Well, whoever she is and wherever she's from, she and her spending have certainly made our day!"

"Oh, pos" (and the reply was breathless, wistful) "And would I ever love to be her!"

"Ha! Wouldn't you just! Me now . . . *I'd* like to be the *man* she's going to wear all that sexy stuff for!"

"Hmp. A lot of chance you got for that, Palik! And what if you was him and I was her, hmm? What about *that*, big-eyed Palik?"

"Stop by the stockroom in about an hour when I'm checking the new shipment of mattresses, and I'll show you!"

The three obvious bodyguards moved out around her, forming a barrier, checking, looking in every direction with eyes never still, checking high and low, alleyways and doors, high windows and even rooftops; vehicles moving and stopped. Meanwhile the unobtrusive bodyguard kept her distance while keeping her watch.

They sped to the spaceport area, three of them in snowy crested turbans now, and resumed their watch the instant they stepped from the car. Watching, moving alertly with gold stopper-butts glinting. Scanning like hungry eagles while their regal charge flowed along within her robe with all the serenity of a personage far too regal to consider the possibility of danger to her untouchable self. She moved among them through all the noise and bustle of the busy depot as if she were alone and invisible.

A scheduled shuttle was just about to depart, but they did not try to gain passage on it. They did not deign to. Instead they had actually gone so far as to lease a private shuttle and keep it on standby. A pretentious luxury at staggering cost.

Presumably no one noticed that the unobtrusive fourth bodyguard had brushed past them and boarded the standard shuttle. Presumably no one connected that girlish, unturbanned woman—wearing a loose yet clingy pyjama-like garment in the drab almost-black of winterpine green, and spacefarer's boots—with the stareworthy group.

The quartet took the private launch up to the geosynchronously orbiting docking station. Where, presumably, a richly-appointed spaceship *Hindilark* awaited while steadily receiving packages from the best onplanet shops.

Up went the shuttle; up went the private launch. A pleasant day's shopping on Lanatia had come to a presumably pleasant end.

Even then the bodyguards remained alert, even though they were alone on a private craft with its pilot—whom they had re-checked.

Their charge, doubtless weary from the shopspree on which she had spent so many, many stellar monetary units, plugged her ears with the sounds of the instrumental group Kaleidolon, and napped.

The regular shuttle reached the great wheel in space first, by several minutes. The girlish, distance-maintaining bodyguard checked schedules, checked the chron on her left glove, and hurried into the restroom. She entered a stall, swiftly and efficiently readying herself for a quick answering of nature's call. She locked the door.

She was still seated when someone entered the adjacent cubicle on her left. The cubicles were private only to a height of about two meters, and to within fifteen centimeters of the floor.

From beneath the partition of the leftwardly adjacent stall came a hand bearing a very small cylinder. The powerfully charged minisyringe was loaded with the tiniest of needles. It released its charge on impact with warmth or on being triggered. The hand merely extended the short tube, blindly, until it touched the boot of the un-obvious bodyguard.

Snik, and the needle ejected and injected, through boot and liner into foot.

The little sting brought a muffled grunt of response and a downward glance. That discovered the hastily withdrawing hand. The gloved hand of the unobtrusive bodyguard closed on the butt of her stopper, began clamping, relaxed. The woman in the adjacent stall flushed and left.

She heard only faintly the thump of the girlish-looking bodyguard's seated body collapsing against the wall of her stall. Already she was paralyzed and aware only of numbness and a deep red that claimed her vision; in a few seconds she would be dead.

The killer hurried in the direction of the Customs Office.

She was a dowdy looking woman of no particular age and unfortunate coloration, with hair so dead and drab it should have been buried. She wore a floppy black hat with a sad bow and an indigo coat over loose pants, dark green. The bustling spacefarers and officials, laborers and clerks, inspectors and money-changers in busy Dallastation paid her no attention whatever. She was obviously unarmed and totally unimportant.

The private launch meanwhile docked, the lady having been awakened one minute before. She dispatched one of her trio of bodyguards, the one in the red doublet, to fetch the Customs chief. Not someone from Customs; the official in charge.

Her two remaining bodyguards kept watch, alertly and

with ever-moving eyes. The pilot used a hand-scanner to read a cartridged book.

After a few minutes a man approached. He was nice-looking, medium young, and wore station blues with prass buttons, and an official cap with a badge. The female bodyguard challenged him anyhow. He produced ID without even attempting to look within at the important personage.

"Your, ah, courier asked me to advise that he has gone on to the ship—using Spoke T," the Customs man said.

Both bodyguards gave him sharp looks, then exchanged a glance. The huge man shrugged and said nothing. His companion nodded over the ID she had been handed, which clearly identified the uniformed man before her as the Senior Inspector, Dallastation/Lanatia Customs. She nodded again and handed it back.

"Our packages came up from planetside?"

"Pos. All were scanned without being opened, the first as a matter of course and the second as an accommodation to your employer. They should be on *Hindilark* by now, awaiting you. Would you like to walk out to your berth, or might I offer the totally unobtrusive privacy of an empty baggage-mover? A closed cart, you understand."

"We—"

"I shall walk," a voice said from inside the shuttle.

Although the huge bodyguard frowned, he and the other got out of the way. She hurried to scramble forth and make a quick look-about before her mistress emerged.

The Customs man stepped back as the robe-swathed lady appeared. He was discreet and gentlemanly enough not to glance down when a foot, shod in a pointed-toe softboot, stepped down the few centimeters. He offered his arm only half-heartedly. It was ignored.

"Would you care for a station security escort, Seety?"

"No." She glanced back in time to see her very big escort emerge. The other was several paces away, being alert.

"It will be necessary that I accompany you to your ship," the man in blue said, again adding the respectful "seety."

"I suppose it will," she said, and slipped a white-gloved hand between his upper arm and his uniformed torso. "Well, I shall take your arm thus, and walk serenely on the arm of an attractive man."

"Thank you, Seety, and it is my pleasure."

She smiled back and turned to her huge retainer, who was frowning in obvious disapproval. She said, "Achmet," without vocal expression, and began walking. The attractive man in blue matched his pace to hers. Ahead moved the lithe woman with the crested white turban and the watchful eyes. Behind came Achmet in whiskey-colored doublet, watchful of deep-set eyes under his crested white turban. He stared briefly at everyone they met.

They attracted a great deal of attention in the busy station while they paced the length of the tunnel-forming spoke marked T. Two Jarps passed and one pretended to be staggered by sight of the young beauty on the blue-uniformed man's arm. She ignored all but him, chattering. He answered her queries concerning his job, his family, the traffic at Dallastation both incoming and redshifting, and whether his job was dull or ever had its exciting moments.

(A short distance away, Dallastation's security chief and an aide were talking with a floppy-hatted woman in indigo and green. Their weapons were not drawn, although she stood over the sprawled body of a man in red doublet and small, fitted white turban, with a crest imitating an osprey's feather.)

First the female bodyguard emerged from the spoke leading back to the station's hub; then onto the perimeter-walk of that wheel of a space station came the young woman in the ultramarine hoop-robe, her hand linking her with the arm of the man in Customs uniform. Behind them, looking this way and that (as his cohort had turned to face her mistress, and was looking this way and that), came the wrestler-sized man named Achmet. Stevedores and spacefarers of three races—yes, excitingly, that *was* a HRal!—moved about along the broad areaway, and one security person in uniform.

"Just a moment, Ehri," the young woman said to the uniformed man beside her, and he paused.

They waited until no one was passing between them and the entrance to the umbilical tunnel connecting the station's airconned interior with the airlock leading only to airless space—except that just now it was linked with the airlock of spacer *Hindilark*. They watched the long-legged, lean native of HRalix with high interest; it paid them no mind.

Then they crossed that area of a circle so vast that no intimation of arc was visible. Achmet followed. His cohort remained at the mouth of the umbilical. Alertly watching, watching. Ready.

(Someone in Spoke P hurled a curse after the drab woman who had jostled her, racing toward the docking area. No one was chasing the woman in indigo and green, though. Who would? Must have misjudged and barely had time to make it to her ship before it was cleared to redshift.)

"Well, Ehri, I do thank you, and almost regret that we must take leave of each other now. You back to dull old Customs, I onto a dull old spacer and out into dull old space. Too bad it's not really as exciting as the clichés 'airless void' and 'eternal ether'! Thank you, Ehri."

"May I see you to your door, Daura," he said, for she had bade him call her that.

Again that jarringly loud, too-common laugh throated from her. "Oh, how very *gallant*! Persi—my dear friend Inspector Ehri Taswar is going to accompany me right up to the airlock! Do go ahead." And to Ehri: "Damn! I'll bet you're going to say that you can't come onboard and have a drink with me before we redshift your station."

He chuckled. "I'll bet I am too," he said, watching the ever-alert vision of litheness called Persi go—rather reluctantly—up the ramped umbilical tunnel until its low mouth and upward inclination caused her to disappear. He seemed in no hurry to follow, and his companion's lips twitched in a small smile. Well, that house-sized cargo loader was oncoming; she'd just let it pass before gallant Ehri "walked her to her door."

Persi possessed the code to open the sealed airlock, and remained alert even though two of her employer's people were onboard. (He had sent no fewer than six of them along while he indulgently indulged this whim of his sister's.) The 'lock would open for no one without the code, which was a vocal one: seven digits. Persi spoke them.

The hatch clicked and eased open with a sigh and little other sound. Beyond lay an unusually padded smallish chamber and another hatch—closed—that led into the ship.

Persi glanced back, practiced a dazzlingly fast draw of her stopper, and holstered it as she stepped just into the chamber. She set her back against a sideward wall. Her restless brown-agate eyes stared down the umbilical ramp in anticipation of her employer's capricious sister (and lover, some dared whisper) whom he denied nothing. Ever watchful, ever alert, right up to the point at which Daura was in the ship. Ramesh Jageshwar paid well and punished more than sternly and Persi was happy with her job. It certainly beat watching an azaafrunn sorter on Franji!

(The running woman spurted out of Spoke P, dodged a violently red cargo loader brand-named Leviathan, and swerved left toward the T-berths. She saw no white turbans.)

Persi turned without concern when the inner hatch opened to her left. That understandable lapse of alertness cost her everything.

She had an instant to know that she did not know the man impossibly there, squatting, *inside* the ship. Then with a quiet sort of cough the needler in his hand sped its tiny missile into her breast. He twitched the weapon upward to sink the second needle into her face. A professional's caution sent him pouncing out of sight, just in case Persi managed to draw and get off a shot even with two barahut-coated needles in her.

He counted slowly to three, swung back into the mouth of the hatch, and rushed to her.

Persi was limp but for her shivering. Eyes glazed. She had fallen back against the 'lock wall and was sliding down it. He caught her and swung her up in his arms. At the same time he was wheeling to hurry back into the ship.

"One left. The big boy. Cute bonnets she bought 'em, hmmm?"

Daura, because she was so preoccupied with Ehri, failed to register the absence of Persi. So she had gone on into the ship. It had to be secure. No one could enter a locked spacer without invitation—or a cutter and some time—and of course Persi would not have secured hatch against Daura!

"*Thank* you, Ehri," Daura said, squeezing his arm, and then she turned to offer him her hand.

He took it, bowed over it, and turned away to descend the ramp. Achmet was ascending the gentle incline. Both men were willing to avoid eye contact. Ehri reached inside his prass-buttoned blue jacket just after they passed.

Daura entered *Hindilark*.

Achmet speeded his pace, now a meter beyond the Customs man.

From within the ship came the sound of Daura's voice. Achmet interpreted wordless alarm and lunged into a charge. His meaty hand was a blur as it whipped out the slender black cylinder of his stopper.

The small outcry had also had a catalytic effect on Ehri. He spun back, going into a crouch with both hands swinging up before him. Together, they held a stopper. Leveled at Achmet's singularly broad back, it hummed faintly. The shimmery hint of light was just as faint. Achmet made no sound. He twitched, seemed to shimmer. Since they were in restricted space, Ehri squinted. Just in time. A flash of light announced Achmet's passing. Then he simply was not there; he became microscopic motes of dust; random atoms.

From within the ship screeched the raucous sound of a barmaid's voice in a low dive: "*You goddam sisterslicin' whoremonger! What the blue-balled bitch-bastard vug d'you think you're* Doing, *you rot-slicer?*"

"Kidnapping you, *Lady*."

She whirled to yell even more loudly. "ACHMET! PERSI!"

"Deceased," Ehri announced as he entered the ship, and she spun again. "So are the other two bodyguards. And—the ship is ours, Daura."

Her face went even more pale and she looked as if she'd been shot a stiff finger in the stomach. "Oh . . . oh my . . . my . . ." She was trembling, white, only just able to form the words, badly. "But . . . *dead*? But . . . how . . . how . . . *no one* could get into this ship without . . . without . . ."

"Oh come on, Daura," Ehri said, with a tight and satirical smile. "Someone could, and did. The ship's ours. So are you." He did not glance at Persi's killer, who was moving silently in behind Daura. "Want to be quiet and resigned, my dear foul-mouthed screechy *lady*, or would you rather go sleepy-bye?"

"T . . . Tee . . . Gee . . . Ohhh," she gasped, trembling and low-voiced.

Ehri bowed acknowledgment. "Indeed. Very good. TGO. Ve haff vays to get into docked spacers. The two you left onboard may be presumed dead, too. We don't have that swine Ramesh Jageshwar, but we have his whorish sister now, haven't we?!"

With an unpleasant smile the man—who was not a Customs official and whose name was not Ehri Taswar—turned his back on her. He started along ship's tunnel toward the con-cabin.

Ramesh Jageshwar's sister was too enraged and out-raged to form words. Face working, eyes glaring and ugly, hands curving up into claws, she pounced after him.

"Left," the man behind her snapped loudly, and in-creased her momentum by kicking her in the backside.

Instantly "Ehri" lurched leftward to flatten himself against the spacer's wall—incredibly covered with padded, flocked satin-on-velour in cream and pale gold. He watched the woman sprawl headlong, almost at his feet, saw the unglittering needleknife go flying from her hand on impact (on the incredibly deep-piled carpeting covering the ship's deck in imitation of thick, pale turquoise grass). Her robe's electronic "hoop" made both her garment and her legs bob ludicrously.

"She prefers sleepy-bye," he said, as the other man came pouncing after her.

"Uh-huh." The fellow plopped down astride her back at the waist and each hand came down just behind him, hard. Each on a cheek of her kicked rump. The ring on the third finger of his left hand had already extruded a needle as long as that finger's first joint, though hair-thin. The skirt proved no deterrent. The needle went all the way in.

Daura squealed in new outrage and attempted to kick. The repellors under her skirt turned that into ridiculous horizontal calisthenics until the skirt broke contact by sliding along violet-hosed, calfy legs. (To one was strapped a knife; to the other a ministopper.) She quivered all over in a sort of rictus, twitched while making loose gestures with one hand, made approximately half a moaning sound, and went limp.

"Fun?" the false Customs man said.

Still astride her, hands still on her haunches, the other man looked up at him.

"Absolutely," he said, and whipped both hands up, then down in a loud double slap. He also pushed off her relaxed backside, and rose. The two men stood gazing down at her.

"The so-impressive and high-nosed 'lady'! Did you hear the way her voice changed into a street-hust's screech? —the language she used?"

"I heard. I see lots of armament, too. And I'm not sad about our hands-off orders until we get her into Sinchung Sin-ful hands. Rat probably has big plans for her."

"If he gags her! Too bad Randy isn't in on this one."

The man called Ehri glanced toward the airlock. "Well he isn't, but dammit, Narzha is; she took out the first two and signaled me to start my act. She should be here by now."

"I am!" she called, hurrying from umbilical and 'lock into ship, a dowdy woman in indigo and dark green, under a floppy hat. "Holy Booda save—*what a plush ship*!" Then she caught sight of the sprawled mass of silver-gray arabesqued ultramarine robe. "Ah. Our little girl get tired?"

"Pos. And she's your charge until we get her back to Yao. Tick: pull the big one onboard and zip 'er up while I go get us clearance. Narzha: drag her to the servants' cabin, not hers—and if you think *this* is plush . . .! Open comm as soon as you get there and stand by for redshift. By the time she starts to wake, you're to have her totally stripped and totally searched, inside and out. Then give her another shot. Keep her naked and drugged, all the way. Rat wants her *intact*—she's part of the first mission of the new one he's so up on—Janja."

Despite his military clipping of orders, the woman called Narzha said "Uh-huh," and bent to catch hold of Daura's ankles while Tick headed for the airlock. Narzha turned the limp woman around, cursed, squatted to deactivate the repellor field, and began dragging her in one direction while Ehri hurried in the other.

"Good job, Hasheer," he said as he entered the con-cabin. "All guards placidated and subject in our hands. A few corpses to eject, later. Get us clearance and get off. The local security chief is so damned impressed he doesn't know his ass from his left nostril. But he should have given Control instructions about us, by now. Good lord, even this floor's carpeted!"

"Yowzah," Hasheer said in a distinctly unmilitary manner, and opened the outship comm. "Ahhh, D-station Control, this is *Hindilark* in berth T-2. All onboard and unzipped and requesting clearance to redshift."

"*Ho*, Hindilark, *this is Control. I read you and you are pre-cleared. You are ungrappled in five seconds* mark. *Do have a lovely time and try not to hit a powersat on your way out, all right*?"

"Firm, Control. My board shows grapple-field clear. Ship clear and docking terminated. Easing off. Had a *lovely* time, Lanatia!"

"*Got an incoming ship*, Hindilark. *Have a care now, and do let us know when you're ready to cut in engines.*"

"I'll try to remember."

A few minutes later *Hindilark* had drifted and nudged herself away from the station, with the aid of station repellors. Hasheer, oncon while "Ehri" got out of the uniform they'd brought all the way from stores back at base, alerted his fellows before advising Control that he was ready to cut in engines and depart. Control imposed a sixteen-sec wait, then bade them sweet spacing.

"Sweet spacing," Hasheer muttered, activating *Hindilark*'s drive. "Good lord!"

Then the captured spacer was moving away from the big

wheel, away from Lanatia, faster and faster, away from Lanatia's sun, faster still, to streak out along the spaceways. Hasheer instructed ship's computer—a lovely, fully vocal SIPACUM—to seek a safe point for tachyon conversion and give all notice possible. Then he leaned back and idly watched the play of lights on the big crescent shape of the console.

(Narzha removed Daura's fifth weapon and felt around in there for more.)

Ramesh Jageshwar had sent six people to convey, pamper, and guard his beloved sister in her caprice. Four agents of TransGalactic Order had eliminated four bodyguards and two licensed ship's masters, kidnapped the king slaver's sibling and her ship, and were on their way to rendezvous and her incarceration. They did not know where she would be held, did not care, and did not want to know. This had been a good operation. Four against seven, and in public and with a mandate of secrecy at that. No contest; no sweat.

Somewhere out near the little collapstar called Babydoll, *Hindilark* ejected four corpses. Each was equipped with a booster-pack to push it toward the black hole. After that Babydoll would take over their disposal.

1

The fingers of a Jarp suit it well to the craft of picking pockets. Long and slender, with two opposable thumbs, a Jarp's hand can easily slide in and out of a jacket, cloak, or tunic and come up with all manner of useful items. In the crowded, poorer section of Sekhar's port city of Refuge, a Jarp plied the ancient art of the nimble but desperate.

This Jarp stood tall, as most of its race did. Wearing a shabby Sektent that covered its entire body except for its richly *orange* face, the Jarp tried to remain inconspicuous in following its target. Yet the dirty white garment served to draw more attention to the face. From the smooth rise of its left temple to the rounded point of its delicate chin ran a jagged slash of badly healed flesh.

The fences to whom it sold its stolen goods, and what few cronies it had, called this Jarp Scarcheek.

Head down, gait slow and flowing, Scarcheek moved through the crowd in the heat of a Sekhar afternoon. It received little notice from members of the throng around it.

Sekhar's blue-white, too-close sun did nothing to inspire sharp eyesight in its inhabitants. And those unfortunate enough to be passing through only sought escape from the heat and migraine-inducing light. Sekhar remained innocent of tourists. No travel agent booked flights to Hell.

Through the heat and dust of the rundown plaza, Scarcheek stalked. Its quarry, a middle-aged Galactic in the unstylish garb of a no-nonsense spacefarer, walked quickly a few steps ahead of it. Scarcheek's left hand, inside the Sektent, stroked at its own breast while it decided what its right hand would do. The right hand reached up and pulled the bill attached to its kaffey a sem lower.

16

The Jarp's dark glasses—darkeyes—hid some of its disfigurement behind their oversized lenses.

Scarcheek watched the man ahead of it. Speeding up its gait, it passed the Galactic just as someone else chanced to bump into him on his right. The man slowed a bit from the jostling, only to have the Jarp collide lightly with him at the same instant. An orange hand flashed under the beige cloak and escaped just as swiftly with a bulky gray perspak in its six fingers.

Scarcheek slowed imperceptibly, shoulder to shoulder with its victim, then turned a few degrees to the left and dropped back.

In the shade of a doorway near a stinking pile of garbage, the Jarp paused to let its flow of adrenaline—or what passed for that hormone in a non-human native of Jarpi—slow its rush through its body. The intensity of its excitement made itself known between its legs. Scarcheek's slicer throbbed warm and semiturgid against its thigh, while its stash warmed and moistened. Looking about, it checked for suspicious stares and saw none. The crowd moved as all crowds did—chaotically, yet guided by the individual purpose of each member.

Pulling the perspak out of its cloak, Scarcheek examined its take.

The pak, cheap equhyde from offplanet, had three compartments. The first contained personal papers of one Denverdarian Eks, citizen of the planet Resh. Mentally thanking *Myrzha* Eks for his contribution to Jarp welfare, it opened the second flap. Inside the wide compartment rested three black, unmarked cassettes. SIPACUM cassettes, used for spaceship navigation and control in a Ship Inboard Processing and Computing (Modular) unit.

With an exasperated curse, Scarcheek opened the last flap.

And stared at more stells than it had seen in its life. Enough wealth to keep Scarcheek in the local brothels for weeks.

It hoped.

Most Jarps found sexual partners easy to locate. Physiologically hermaphroditic and psychologically bisexual, a Jarp could serve any sexual function to one of its own kind or to either sex of other species. The sheer exotic nature of a being with breasts, penis, and vagina allowed most Jarps to pick their sexual partners with relative ease.

Scarcheek, however, was different. Years ago, in a bar only a few alleys away, a drunken Galactic toting an ancient cutting weapon called a *kozuka* had so marked the Jarp's face as to render it very nearly repulsive.

Ashamed of its disfigurement and even more ashamed at lacking the courage to avenge itself, Tleewhee'Leeu of Jarpi—now Scarcheek—became a drifter, a drinker, a patronizer of the whores (of both sexes) of Refuge. It headed to one now, all these new stells drawing it to her apt as if by magnetism.

The spacefarer, recently deprived of his perspak, continued on his way, without noticing the slight decrease in his personal cargo. Denverdarian Eks's stocky body stood little more than 170 sems tall, with short, muscular arms. His dark skin and close-cropped, black hair currently lay hidden beneath his beige cloak and dark brown hat—a Wayne. The optic filters perched on his nose concealed his deep-set eyes. He moved through the crowd as anonymously as the pickpocket Scarcheek had.

Almost.

What Denverdarian Eks most wanted was to be off Sekhar, back in his brother's spaceship. He hated the necessary excursions to planets for the purchase of ship's goods. *Shopping*, he thought with anger. Denverdarian hated planets, hated their gravity, foul air, and crowds. Everywhere people pushed, shoved, bumped, and bounced. He was sick of it. All he wanted was to make the connection, get the TDP these damned Seks designed so well, and hit the Tachyon Trail.

Stopping for a moment, Denverdarian cursed the heat, the sand, and the local god Musla while checking his bearings.

Above the buildings rose the fat column of the port's control tower. That was east. Slightly southeast of that lay the berths for private landers. Denverdarian always used one of the ship's landers to come planetside. His distrust of public shuttles ran a close second to his dislike of planets in general. Reoriented now, he turned toward a side street and took a step.

Two pairs of hands grabbed his shoulders. Two powerful pairs.

"Where are they?" The voice was harsh as a sandstorm.

Strong fingers dug into the flesh of his shoulders, pressing into the bones and nerves beneath. They pushed. Taking a sharp, pained breath, Eks moved in the direction indicated. The gravelly voice repeated the question.

"Don't waste your breath, Hashy," a higher-pitched whispering voice said. "Let's just search him." The other set of hands added emphasis with a shove in the direction of an alleyway.

Alleys were seldom clean or well lit; if they were, they'd have been called something else. The four hands threw Denverdarian Eks to the filth-strewn paving of the alley and turned him over. He stared up at two very displeased men.

They wore the loose robes and Sekcaps of native Sekhari. The taller, older man pinning down Eks's right arm wore a light yellow robe with a vague hint of tan pinstriping. The other's robe, Eks saw, was the same color as all the damned sand around Refuge. Almost completely covered from head to foot, the men were nearly faceless but for their jaws and mouths.

Eks struggled against their hold and made one attempt to fight them. Aiming a kick at the one on his left, he shoved his boot toward the younger man's groin.

Swiftly, accurately, the man's right arm released its hold on his shoulder, swung up over the leg, and crashed against his tibia with agonizing force. The sound of cracking bone was lost in the torrent of pain that pulsed through his body.

Dully, in the cloudy world of his terror, Eks realized that the man must have had an impact truncheon up his sleeve. Soft and pliant when bent slowly, it became harder and stronger than a steel pipe when struck against something. Pressure suits worked on the same principle, but as protection from impact, not as weapons.

"Got 'im, Hashy," the younger man said, holding his

arm with the impact truncheon still firm against Eks's throat.

The older man ran his hands through the pockets of the offworlder's cloak. Up close, the face of the older man—Hashy—revealed the lines etched by a lifetime of worry. Through his choking pain, Eks could see only the man's jaw and mouth. His chin had a cleft in it so deep it could only have been put there before birth by cytological engineering. Hashy's mother must have expected him to be an actor rather than the thug he was.

"Not here," Hashy muttered, turning Eks over and running his thick hands over every part of the captive's body.

The younger man's truncheon, detumescent, pressed against the back of Denverdarian's neck, driving the thyroid cartilage into his throat. He pressed mostly with his arm now, scraping Eks's chin against the flat sandstone cobbles.

"Where are they?" the younger assailant demanded in a whisper, holding his lips close to Eks's ear.

Through the dust clogging his nostrils and coating his lips, he breathed slowly, realizing in his shock what they wanted. And painfully aware that he no longer had them.

Four arms lifted him up and threw him against a wall. "Well?" one of the voices whispered.

"Stolen," Denverdarian replied through bloody lips. His breath came in shallow, rapid gasps. Somewhere, the klaxon of a policer wailed, but not for him. "Had them in my perspak," he murmured. "Must've gotten dipped. I'm sorry, sorry." His knees gave way with weak trembles and he slipped forward against their arms.

"Not as sorry as you're going to be," the gravel voice of Hashy told him.

The younger man twisted Eks's body about until he supported him from behind, arms around his arms and up behind his back. Though a lance of fiery pain shot through his broken leg, Denverdarian Eks tried his best not to scream. It might bring help, but it might also bring sudden death,

Through his pained mental fog, Eks detected something strange about the body of the one holding him. His thoughts would not focus for long enough. He knew only that he faced his death.

"Or maybe," he blurted, "I left them at my apt." He nodded wildly, staring at the blacked-out darkeyes of the man with the cleft chin. "That's where they are. Let me—"

Hashy silenced him with a fist in the solar plexus.

"I don't like the idea of having to look for a stolen perspak in a crowded spaceport, flainer." His voice had taken on a sharp cutting edge, less like gravel and more like flint. "Give 'im the speakeasy."

"I've only got one left," came the whispered response.

Eks heard a pouch unseal, felt a slivery stab in his neck. He tried to push back at his captor, using his good leg. His ears rang suddenly, as if he had been struck. Heart pounding and breath accelerating, he watched the alleyway around him begin lurching and squirming.

"Now, little man, *where are they*?"

Denverdarian Eks broke into tears. Shaking his head as if trying to throw it from his shoulders, he babbled out, "Don't have 'em. Had 'em. Gone, now, gone." Leaning against the captor in the sand colored robe, he became aware of what it was the man wore beneath the garment. "Coolsuits," he murmured, in a weak sort of wonder.

Few other than the rich or otherwise influential could afford the portable cooling garments, and they usually advertised the fact by wearing dark, richly-hued robes. Hashy nodded. Clearly, the interview was at an end.

"Right. Fix him."

The man holding Eks smiled a grim smile and held the broken, drugged spacefarer with one arm. Pulling a scarf of red Panishi reelsilk from inside his Sektent, he whipped it swiftly around Denverdarian Eks's trembling throat. Knotted in the scarf lay a coin of some rarity. Now it rested against the cartilage over Eks's trachea.

Its owner jerked the red fabric taut around the Reshan's neck and continued pulling in one smooth, graceful motion.

Denverdarian Eks's death made no more noise than the cracking of a knuckle.

"Where now, Mizar?"

"Nose about the locals, I guess. Put him over there, Tag."

Heels dragged to the trash heap nearby. A heavy load fell to the top of the pile. Footsteps receded into the hot afternoon.

He had seen dozens of worlds in his life, some beautiful—though he could not appreciate them—and some ugly. But as he silently choked on the blood pulsing into his crushed windpipe, the last vision of Denverdarian Eks was that of sandstone paving in a dim Sekhari alley and of a lone Sekhari dung scarab pushing its burden before it.

Verley 2197223SK heard the timid knock at her door. Rising from her amorphous bed, she crossed her one-room apt in less than five paces. Checking her caller's identity on the second-hand Looker, she recognized instantly the face of Tleewhee'Leeu. Opening the door, she let him enter and whistled as best she could a Jarp greeting.

"Good evening, Verley," Scarcheek said in Erts.

Verley jumped back slightly at the sound. "You've got a translator!" she cried, smiling in delight.

The Jarp smiled back, removing its darkeyes, kaffey, and Sektent. On top of its crimson hair rested a thin harness supporting the small collection of electronic components. The translator converted Scarcheek's native language of whistles and chirps into the language of the Galactics—Erts. (Even those Jarps who could understand Erts were physiologically unable to reproduce the sounds. Galactics, on the other hand, could not duplicate the Jarp tongue and few could understand more than a few words. This seeming imbalance of abilities provided a meal ticket for exobiologists, theologians, and other opinionated sorts until the development of the translahelm.)

Verley smiled and embraced Scarcheek, letting her body slide against its. "I can throw out the notepads *and* all the silly sign language and guessing!" She pulled back and looked into its eyes. "Did you get a job?"

"No," Scarcheek said, smiling back and running a hand over her nightgown, feeling the swell of her breasts. "I just came into some money and I could finally afford one. I thought of you when I bought it."

Twin opposable thumbs pressed on either side of one of the soft mounds, eliciting a soft moan of appreciation from the quite young Sek woman. Orange fingers twined through her black hair, pulling back to bend her neck, and expose her mouth in offertory. Though she was tall, Scarcheek was taller. It bent to kiss her. The translahelm interfered.

"Progress has its drawbacks," Scarcheek muttered, reaching up to remove the helmet.

Verley took the opportunity to turn out the lights and slip out of her nightwrap.

"Before you take off the translator, Sweetbabe," she said, calling it by her own nickname for it, "tell me how you want it tonight. I want you to celebrate."

"We'll celebrate, all right," it replied. "I'm buying you through till dawn. I want it every way."

"Oh, Sweetbabe!" she murmured, pulling into its arms. In the darkness, she heard the metallic sound of a translator hitting the nightstand.

Verley husted for money. Pure and simple. On Sekhar, a harsh planet engendering harsh codes of conduct, Verley was considered a wicked woman. She had divorced her callous husband, leaving him with their child, and had sought sex purely for pleasure in the bars around the spaceport at Refuge. Raised in an oppressive environment of fundamentalist Muslimism, Seks developed oppressive attitudes toward all aspects of life, sexuality included. Those such as Verley, who somehow sought more from sex than reproduction and more from life than survival, bore the burden of the outcast.

One year-Sek ago and not yet a hust, though definitely a slut by Sek standards, she had entered the Cosmoasis Bar in the Imperial Hotel. There she met a spacefarer. Tall and exotic, the spacefarer was not a man. Nor was it a woman. The spacefarer, tall and orange, with deep wine-red hair and round, huge eyes, was a Jarp.

Nicknamed Sweetface, it served as crewmember on-board *Coronet*, a spacer owned and operated by one Jonuta of Qalara—a trader of some sort, Verley understood. Sweetface showed instant interest in her. In a night of passion, the sensitive Jarp unveiled for her the secrets of lovemaking. True lovemaking, not the crude pumping-followed-by-apologetic-prayer of unworldly Sekhari men that was exemplified in her husband.

That night Verley changed.

Now Verley husted for money. Money to buy her way off Sekhar. She husted Jarps. She husted as many as she could, resorting to Galactics or Seks only when she needed extra cred. Every Jarp—travelled, experienced, open, and usually well mannered—aroused in her the memory of Sweetface, and of the first time she had felt in her the union of sex *and* love.

Scarcheek had no thought of her motivations. Its ugly mark prevented it from being attractive to any other than husts.

Verley didn't care. Verley always turned out the lights.

Captives of the night, they made love in the hot darkness. Lips sought out nipples, necks, thighs, and other, deeper lips. Softly the woman took the orange pump in her mouth, heard a whistle of pleasure. The Jarp's tongue circled in and around her oasis (in the slang of a planet that was five-sixths desert, the male genital was a *pump*, the female's, an *oasis*). Her mouth gently surrounded the single testicle in her alien lover's crowded genital area, then moved down to its small, hot vagina.

Scarcheek had been her customer for many months. Verley knew when the time was right. Twisting about, she impaled herself upon its slicer and knelt, facing its knees, her hands reaching down below the thrusting rod and fingering the Jarp's other sex. Hands, thighs, muscles, and breathing all worked in unison toward the pinnacle of desire. She felt her ego scatter until she became a being of pure sensation and light. Her lover exploded inside her, then quaked as her deft fingers brought it to a second climax, a female one.

The Jarp, expended and fulfilled, kept moving rhythmically until the gasping woman trembled, trying to take him, yes *him*, deep, deep inside her. She moaned and grabbed his legs tightly, pulling them close to her breasts, burying her face between the orange, musky thighs. Taking care that her lover remain satisfied, she released her hold and lay down next to it with as much of her hot, loveslick skin in contact with its as possible.

After only a few moments of quiet breathing together, she felt the questing, six-fingered hand of a Jarp still horny, searching for the soft channel it called her stash.

"I fully intend to keep you up all night," it murmured.

Verley did not understand the softly whistled words. The translator lay unused on the nightstand. It didn't matter. Verley understood.

Mornings on Sekhar are actually quite beautiful, though the natives' love/hate relationship with their world seldom allows them to admit it. Long before sunrise, the dust high in the atmosphere catches rays of light, refracting them into stunning fields of red, orange, yellow, and sometimes a special green. It was under this canopy of color that Scarcheek walked, returning to its apt from Verley's. It strode with a tired, satisfied, yet almost proud gait.

Overhead, a public shuttle thundered up into the sky, leaving a white trail of ionized air like a thread connecting Refuge to the heavens. About the lone Jarp, the early morning activities of the common Refuger began to manifest themselves.

Scarcheek talked quietly to itself, listening to the equally quiet translation coming through its headgear. It smiled.

"I hope I left her a big enough tip," it said, hearing the same phrase repeated in Erts.

Its footsteps resounded tinnily on the metal of the apt building's ramp. Sand eddied in the space between the cooltrap double doors. Climbing the inside ramp to its floor, Scarcheek felt the night's fatigue catching up. When it punched the combolock, it stared with its wide eyes even wider. The door eased open without unlocking. With a clank, the deadbolt slipped to the floor, rolled a few sems, and stopped.

The apt had the look of a dust hurricane's aftermath minus the dust.

What few possessions Scarcheek had acquired had been opened up, torn apart, and/or dumped on the floor. The apt's small, dingy bed supported stripped sheets and a slashed mattress. Twisting its head to the left, the Jarp looked at the remains of its shape chair. In it, reclining comfortably, sat a man holding a stopper. A man with gray hair and a deeply cleft chin.

"It took us a while to follow up on the dippers in this part of town," the man said in a gravelly voice. "You're the last on my list. Shall we talk?"

Only then did Scarcheek see the younger man step out from behind the door.

2

Look at the night sky. The dark is far more vast than the scattered motes of light that pierce it. Move toward the center of the galaxy. Stars crowd closer together. The night sky glows brightly. Space travel is simpler, distances between habitable planets shorter. Yet the dark still envelops the light, and night skies everywhere have their share of blackness.

Through that blackness, centuries ago, spread the creatures called Galactics. Their planet of origin they called Homeworld; some called it Urth. They did not *colonize* other planets. No empire of any sort could build and hold colonies when, at the first sign of economic exploitation, the colonists could pack up and go elsewhere in a galaxy of billions of stars. The Galactic race did not *colonize* planets. They *settled*. A restless sort of settling, in that the settled planets became themselves springboards for further waves of explorers, traders, and entrepreneurs.

Organizations sprang up, from time to time, here and there, that found ways to extract profits by nosing into the affairs of others. Some of these groups and individuals came to be called pirates, slavers, and would-be tyrants. Others, through some miracle of public relations, became known as peacekeepers. Not that the latter were any less despised than the former. They simply had better slogans.

One of the popular slogans expressed a sentiment concerning the "undeveloped" planets occasionally discovered.

The people of such a world usually existed in some pre-spacefaring stage either because they simply had not yet evolved that far, or because the planet had once been settled by Galactics who had then lost their ability to get back into space. Interplanetary accords gave these worlds the status of Protected Planet, and Aglaya was one of them. In order that the inhabitants be allowed to progress at their own rate, to avoid culture shock, Protected Planets were technically off limits to everyone. Technically.

Fragile flowers in their planetary display cases, Protected peoples lived, grew old, and died, never knowing that among the points of light in the darkness of the night dwelt others such as they.

It was on one of these Protected worlds, hundreds of light years away from Sekhar, that Marekallian Eks squatted on his haunches and spoke quietly to Rakhin Oualama Q'yaba, Elder of the clan of T'yaba. Marekallian Eks, a tall man of about 190 sems,* spoke in Erts to the dark, regal humanoid opposite him.

The native of the Protected planet Arepien answered in Erts. Fluent Erts.

"The people still worship you as a god, Mayekalliah. Sometimes I feel they are correct. You bring us so many–"

"No," Marekallian said, cutting the Elder's words off with a quick gesture. "I am no more than a man raised on a world where more things are known. We are just further along than you. But that's no reason you should lag behind us."

Shifting his legs so that he knelt on his left and leaned on his right, he looked across the village oval. Huts of wood and grass, cut from the abundant jungle foliage, squatted outside the oval. Beyond their roofs, saddle-shaped and thatched, the deep blue and indigo of the forest rose with imposing majesty.

Tall, deciduous trees stood above the tangle of thick jungle vines like purplescent giants wading through snakes, all frozen in motion. And silent. The early evening air held suspended the smells of food and people, mixing them with the scent of the jungle. Somewhere, a wood cony shrieked its chittering love call.

Marekallian nodded. A peaceful land.

He turned his gaze on Rakhin Oualama Q'yaba. The Elder's skin, red as cinnabar, gleamed with a thin coat of perspiration. Probably about fifty years old and looking it,

---

*190 centimeters: about six *feet*, three *inches*, Old Style.

the humanoid's high forehead and gaunt cheeks added a thoughtful regality to his imposing mien. Eyes like black holes gazed back at Marekallian's own of deep brown. Marekallian Eks, though chronologically almost the same age, possessed the body of a thirty year old, thanks to the technology with which he planned to gift the Arepienese.

They were able to speak to each other in Erts due to the same technology. Drugs that increased mental acuity and supplemented memories comprised the main cargo of Marekallian Eks's small lander. The encephaloboost that Eks had given Rakhin Oualama Q'yaba had implanted in him knowledge of the Galactics' language as well as a rudimentary understanding of chemistry, physics, medicine, mathematics, history, and mechanical engineering. And Eks's own particular brand of social philosophy.

Marekallian Eks smuggled the most valuable commodity in the Galaxy. Knowledge.

The peacekeepers of the spaceways had a name for his kind—*Mindrunner*. In secret, with caution and cunning, Marekallian Eks violated the post-imperium accords to bring knowledge to primitive people. He had been a Mindrunner for six years-ess and (having been raised on Outreach) took an inordinate pride in both his work and himself.

With pride, he listened to Rakhin Oualama Q'yaba question him, as he questioned Oualama.

"So, by cutting slots into wheels of different size, and making them fit together, the rotational—of course! The rotational work of one revolution can be increased in either force or speed by . . . why, Mayekalliah, this is marvelous! It is as though I remember something that I have never learned, and remember it when I need it!"

"That's how a brainboost works. The memory RNA is encoded with the necessary matrices which are recalled at the moment your thinking triggers part of a matrix." He leaned back. "Simple, really. But of lifesaving importance to you and your people, at this stage of your development."

He shook his head, his short queue of raven hair at the base of his neck whipping back and forth in contrapuntal motion. "I can't understand the people who try to retard your progress."

"Perhaps they fear the competition."

"They should welcome it! Competition is the handmaiden of cooperation."

He turned his eyes from the red man and watched the setting of Arepien's second sun. The first had set hours ago as this one had crossed the zenith. "Do your own gods have laws that keep certain people from talking to other people?"

Rakhin Oualama Q'yaba sat quietly for a long moment, struggling with a brainboosted memory. His eyes narrowed, as if gazing at some far horizon.

"I see," he said, "that many people have worshipped their stars in much the same way as we do. Their histories have been just as bloody. This is very sad."

Nodding in agreement, Eks paused a moment before asking, "Is there any shrine that your people have erected to your gods? Any rituals that an outsider might witness?"

The Elder turned toward Marekallian, accusation in his eyes. "It is called sentenology, is it not? The study of other intelligent beings. You wish to study us?"

"I wish to understand you." His dark eyes smoldered with eagerness. Unconsciously, his hands moved to emphasize his speech. "You know that I'm running a great risk to bring you this knowledge—"

"I know that you tell me this. I—ahh, yes, the post-Imperium planetary accords. As if I'd always known!" He shook his head in wonder, light glinting off his shaven head.

"Then you know that I hold freedom and progress as my highest ideals. It stems from my desire to *know*. I've been to a dozen Protected worlds, doing the same thing I'm doing here. I think the risk is worth it. No one else knows what I know about those dozen worlds, about their people, their culture. I've seen rituals that involve an entire continent of people. I've been initiated into mystery cults that know more about the workings of the human mind than most psychoneurologists. All people have something to offer the Galactic community. I would take great pleasure in being a friend to your people, both a teacher and a student."

Marekallian smiled gently. His hands, callused and strong, ceased their motions.

Rakhin Oualama Q'yaba nodded slowly. "Night is here. I detect great sincerity within you. May your god have sexual congress with you." He rose at the ancient words of greeting and leave-taking, then smiled. "I see that other faiths have gods that behave in similar fashion."

With that, and a vague smile, Oualama extended his hand to Marekallian.

Taking the offered hand, he pulled himself up almost to eye level with the Elder, who also possessed the second most honored sign of superiority on Arepien—height.

"Thank you," Marekallian said. "We shall meet tomorrow, Rakhin Oualama Q'yaba?"

"Yes. Then I shall tell you something of our gods. And you may boost as many of the clan T'yaba as you wish."

Marekallian smiled. Often, he would not initiate the reigning high priest or king into his mysteries but pick someone else of influence. Priests and rulers usually had their own reasons for keeping their people from progress. The Elder of T'yaba did not rule, however, but merely advised by benefit of his years. Surely, Marekallian thought, walking out of the village, one of the least worst forms of societal control.

But tight-lipped elders could be a pain in the back of the lap.

In the twilight, Eks followed a path through a grotto and into a small clearing. There, painted a dull black, stood a slender needle—Marekallian's lander. Twenty meters long, eight wide amidships, the lander contained all he needed for his onplanet operations. He signaled the door open and powered up the equipment from its trickle-on state.

Checking the telits, he noted that Denverdarian still had not returned *Eris* into orbit about Arepien.

Damn him anyway, Marekallian thought, running through his standard routine: scanning the sky for TransGalactic Watch ships—or any other intruders who might object to his presence.

Nothing. A sky as clear as Homeworld's must have once been.

And no Denverdarian. *Probably's having trouble getting the TDP device. Damned Seks and their petty rules.*

He sighed. Punching a few buttons on the SIPACUM console, he retrieved the files on what little information he had gathered concerning the Areps' religion. Not much to go on.

The two stars, referred to merely as the Mother and Her Lover, served as the focal points of the local form of sun worship. Though many of the men and women wore small medallions depicting twin starbursts, these ruddy-skinned Galactoids showed no evidence of being an idol-making race. Marekallian flipped his fingers in the ''who knows?'' gesture of spacefarers.

This could take months of research, he mused. *But sooner or later, I'll know what I want.* He smiled. *The Mother and Her Lover willing*!

3

Verley awoke well after noon with the scent of sex in her sheets and the taste of morning on her tongue.

Head throbbing a little, she rolled over on the bed and stared at the chron. Next to the readout plate, in a neat stack, lay a number of large-denomination stells. A few sems away lay a bulky equhyde perspak. Focusing with sleep-bleared eyes, she took the stells in hand and counted them. Adding the sum to the running total she kept in her head, she sat up with a start that made her bed creak.

Scarcheek's more than generous tip had put her over the top!

At last I have enough money to buy my way off this skungeball planet!

She laughed and fell back into the pillows, ran her hands over the stiffer portions of the sheets. *Thank you, Sweetbabe.*

No time like the present, she thought, grabbing her mauve go-bag and shoveling her few possessions into it. All her compressible clothing went in, as did a can of SprayOn and four color heads. She decided to abandon her hustkit, since she whored only to get off Sekhar and soon would no longer need the creams, appliques, drugs, and devices. She did, however, take her ampules of eroflux.

An adulterated form of eroflore, cut several times, eroflux functioned as a mild sexual hallucinogen. Verley had seen the ravages of eroflore addiction and steered clear of it. Still, in her profession she sometimes needed a distraction while her customers enjoyed themselves. Not stopping to wonder why she threw it into her bag, she swept the contents of the nightstand in to follow the ampules.

She picked up the perspak and examined it. It still held

a slight aroma of Jarp. Holding it closer, she smelled other scents. Panishi jazmink, perhaps, and a touch of Ghanji sandlewood. It flopped open in her hands. She unsealed the inside flaps and riffled through the ID papers. Denverdarian Eks.

So that's how Tleewhee' Leeu came into so much money. Up to its old tricks.

She looked at the cassettes and wondered how much she could get for them if she needed extra cash. Well, she'd take anything she could get. Musla only knew she had taken what she could get for most of her life. *Now*, she thought, *things will be different*.

Throwing on a robe, she hoisted the go-bag over her shoulder and stepped into the hallway. As she had done every day since the afternoon her room had been burglarized, she walked down the hallway to the shower, taking her valuables with her. She believed in playing it safe with her personal property.

The practice saved her life.

Disrobing, she sealed the shower door and switched the ultrasonic field to *surface detritus*. The inaudible vibrations gently atomized the night's collection of oil, perspiration, and . . . other fluids. The wall vents gently whisked it all away. She let the vibrations tingle her skin and languidly thought about leaving the planet of her birth tonight. *Today!*

(Down the hallway only a few dozen meters, a young man silently edged an electronic Pikit into the connecting bolt of Verley's apt door. With a low cracking sound, the door unsealed.)

She switched the shower from its first setting to *prickler* and squirmed delightedly, the lower frequency ultrasound almost down to hearing level. The field massaged every square sem of her flesh, sending waves of pleasure through her body. She often wondered whether some wicked genius had made showers slightly addictive, here in repressed Refuge where most considered even sex to be something indulged in only when necessary. She took longer than she usually did, saying a mental goodbye to her apt building.

She sighed. For most of her twenty-four years-Sek, she

had not been a taker of risks. She had done as she was told, married to get away from home—at the insistence of her husband-to-be—and bore a child when told to. In six years of marriage, she had matured nil. Then she had gotten a divorce, thinking it a solution to her problems. As it turned out, it was. Suddenly, she had to think for herself, work for her sustenance, struggle for her goals. She had thought, worked, and struggled.

Thank you, Sweetface.

Now, switching off the shower, she stepped out clean and free. Dressing in an outfit of maroon skinTites, a rust-colored sleeveless blouse that draped loosely over her large and still firm breasts, and a belt with an ornamental dagger, she threw a pale tan Sektent over her and drew on matching heat-resistant boots. With a smile, she stepped into the hallway.

And nearly collided with the manager.

"What's going on?" the diminutive thin-haired woman demanded. She looked as if she had just been awakened. She stared up at Verley, waiting for a reply.

"I was taking a shower," she said. "Why? Did my singing wake you up?"

"Number forty-three complained about a fight in your room. He said it sounded as if you were tearing the place to shreds."

Verley stared in disbelief for only an instant, then felt a sick realization.

"I think they've broken in again."

"*Musla,*" the manager said, following Verley down the hall, "not burglars again. And in daylight!"

"If you'd fix the hall Looker and then watch it sometime, this wouldn't happen."

Verley strode angrily down the hallway, the spike heels of her boots clacking against the plastile like the gavels of judgment.

The door hung all the way aside, its deadbolt lying half a meter inside the room. Verley looked inside, followed by the manager. They saw open drawers, torn furniture, emptied cabinets. What little she had abandoned had been ripped open and searched. The contents of her hustkit lay strewn about the floor in lewd mockery.

"A little messy for burglars," the old woman said. "Good thing you keep your stuff with you."

Verley nodded. Most apt-robbers took only what they could grab on first sight. They never took the time to ransack a room. No one living in this hole could have anything valuable enough to justify the effort. Unless . . .

She turned, the sick feeling growing inside her. Whoever did it left the apt only because it thought that she had already departed for good. She ran down the hall, this time truly departing for good.

"Hoi!" shouted the manager. "Who's going to pay for this?"

She received no answer. Shaking her head, the old woman bent to pick up the deadbolt, debating whether to have it replaced or to let the next tenant worry about it.

Verley peered out from behind the cooltrap doors, checking up and down the street for anyone who might be watching. Seeing no one, she pulled her kaffey bill way down. It cast a long shadow that enveloped her darkeyes and the lower half of her face. Then she wrapped part of the kaffey around her mouth and neck. No one would notice. Many Seks went about fully covered, even indoors. Sekhari fashion reflected the culture's degree of sexual conservatism.

Stepping out into the hot afternoon air, she saw the usual handful of people who, for whatever reason, refused to come in out of the blazing daylight even when its heat reached its peak. She had her own reason. As she walked east, toward the port, her initial alarm wore off.

She wondered—had Tleewhee'Leeu been so desperate for the perspak it had left behind? Sometimes Jarps acted strangely, she mused. If it *had*, she thought, it was going to get a piece of her mind. If it hadn't, maybe it should be warned.

Why? Why not just jump a freighter and jet this place?

Moving through the dust and the heat of the city, she struggled with her scruples. She had not known many kind people in her life. What few friends she had, had been made in bed. Only there could she truly discover whether they were kind or cruel, caring or hurting. Sweetbabe had been kind. As kind as Sweetface before it. Good deserved good back, she mused, remembering her Quran.

She turned down an alley and cut across to Scarcheek's apt. It would only take a few minutes, she assured herself. She entered the building and walked up the ramp to its floor.

From the end of the corridor, she could see Scarcheek's door, open and spilling light.

Open doors served as either invitations or warnings. Verley, raised in a rough city on a cruel planet, seldom considered an unlocked door inviting. Slowly she walked across the metal corridor, remembering the times she had done so before to entertain the Jarp at its own apt.

Her eyes remained riveted to the trapezoid of light wedging into the hall from the doorway. She stepped as quietly as she could, balls of feet first, heels hardly touching. Reaching the door, she looked in.

Scarcheek sat in the remains of its torn shape chair.

It sat upside down, its feet up over the back, its head down. In the bottom of the valley created by its facial scar, a new cut had been made. Deep and red, it followed the scar precisely, from temple to chin. Then it continued, under the Jarp's chin and straight down its throat to the top of its sternum. Scarcheek stared at the doorway, its arms lying outward from the sides of the chair. The blood was nearly dry in the puddle beneath its slit throat. Somewhere in the room an insect buzzed, tapping against a windowpane, seeking light.

Something knotted in Verley's stomach, choked at her throat. She turned, the image of Scarcheek following in her mind. She ran. Her footsteps rang wildly through the hall. Doors opened and tenants stared. She heard other footsteps behind her, then a scream.

The doors burst open before her arms and the momentum carried her into the street. Nearly colliding with Sekhar's main form of transportation, a pedal operated tricycle, she swerved and ran headlong down the side of the street. Only one thought held her mind in its grip.

The spaceport.

Blind with panic, she headed toward the black traffic tower, three and a half kloms away. After fewer than a hundred meters of furious sprinting the heat and terror threatened to whelm her in a faint.

Breathing in gasps, still trembling without control, she leaned against the sandstone wall of a shop and tried to think.

The whole world had gone crazy. Crazier. Someone had killed Tleewhee'Leeu and had missed her only because it had thought she was gone.

Someone wanted something, and Verley feared that she had it.

With a deep breath of hot, dry Sek air, she stood away from the wall and looked about her. (Still trembling.) Nearly every fourth person wore a pale tan Sektent with kaffey and darkeyes. She moved into the crowd under the awnings that thrust from some of the buildings and walked with even, purposeful steps. Over her head whined the airbrakes of a descending spaceboat, its owner doubtless possessed of a purpose of its own.

Refuge spaceport received a small amount of traffic compared to most planets. Sekhar had little to offer except for glassmakers and a silicon superconductor industry based primarily on Sekhar's (over)abundant supply of sand. The reigning bureaucrats on the world strictly controlled the sale and distribution of the TDP anti-glitch device, which meant that the bribe necessary to obtain one from the same bureaucrats was rather steep. So, though Sekhar received few visitors, those visitors usually included a class of wealthy traders and spacefarers.

Verley entered the main terminal, the dry spray of air in the cooltrap blowing the dust from her clothes. Inside, the late afternoon shuttle announced boarding time. She stopped to read the screenlist of flights out of Sekharstation, two thousand kloms up in orbit. No liner until next week. She certainly did not want to take a shuttle up to the station only to be stranded for that long!

She glanced about.

At a loading platform three men stood idly, waiting for a customs official to paw over the contents of a large plasteel case. They wore light gray jumpsuits taken in at the waist with broad necessary belts holding insy bags, the sort that contained incidentals—everything a spacefarer thought it might need planetside. Including a week's hard rations. Each belt bore a holstered stopper, too, the dark tubes sinister against the light beige belts. One of them also carried two throwing knives, simulated antiques.

She removed her Sektent and shoved it into her go-bag. The darkeyes and kaffey followed it. She felt incomplete without her makeup, not having had time to apply it before fleeing her room. Yet the terror lent a new sort of self-assurance. It was called desperation. Striding up to the counter, she looked into the eyes of the man with the knives.

"I want to speak to your captain," she said, in a dead level voice.

The Galactic regarded her for less than an instant before saying, "Jet it, stash, we're busy." The other two men glowered without comment. No one liked being on Sekhar, least of all spacefarers.

Verley let go a suppressed breath and turned away.

Two stations down, a woman leaned against the counter. Her white SpraYon body stocking ran from neck to boots, interrupted only by a sheer white halter and snug, bone-white shorts. Even with the reflective outfit, she found it necessary to fan herself with a folded sheet of printout. Her hair, dyed a flat shade of cloud-white, swirled in magnificent cumulous billows down her back. Only at the roots did perspiration flatten and clump the white mass.

Bet she pops pherinotal so she doesn't have to wear anything else outside, either, Verley thought, walking up to her.

"Shipping out today?" she asked, looking at the only part of the woman left dark—her smooth, yellow-brown face and deep hazel eyes.

The hand stopped fanning and the eyes looked in her direction. The woman's russet lips formed a smile, then parted to speak. "Move on, little one. Tura .ak Saiping travels alone."

Her smile had less cruelty than sadness in it. Her head turned back to its fixation on some far-off vista. Her hand resumed its slow fanning motion. The woman sighed, once again lost in some reverie, lightyears from the dry heat of Sekhar.

Verley stepped away from the Saipese and looked about her. The terminal lacked any other obvious spacefarers. She felt the knot of panic tighten in her chest.

The port served as the only exit from the planet. How long before the killer trailed her here? She headed for the bar, a plan forming.

The bar had the clean but rundown look of a previous decade's architecture. Dark and overly warm, the enclosure smelled of ethanol and smoke. Somewhere to the left, a musicube played raucous skinmusic with holoproj accompaniment.

Heads turned to watch her enter. She stood almost 178 sems without her high heels. Her 96-sem bustline, shamelessly outlined under her blouse, drew the stares of spacefarers and locals alike. Trying to avoid seeming as if she were heading to the first table she saw, she headed for the first table she saw.

The spacefarers, two women and three men, looked up at her as she sat down.

"I want to leave Sekhar today," she said without prologue, "and I've got enough to pay my way. Deal?"

One of the women snickered. "How much?" asked a man who looked as if he had seen too many radiation leaks.

"Twenty-three hundred stells."

"Forget it."

"It's enough to buy a ticket from here to Samanna!" Verley's shock sounded almost childlike.

"On what liner?"

She fumbled with her go-bag, pulling out the SIPACUM cassettes. "I'll throw these in, too." The cassettes clattered on the table.

The same woman laughed again. "They're not worth a thing unless we can tell what's in 'em," she said, reaching across with a black-gloved hand and sliding them back to Verley. "They could be damaged, they could be blank. I've heard tell of some with music recorded on them. The PlotShop's closed for the day. Bring 'em to us tomorrow and we can check them there. If they're any good, maybe we can arrange something.''

Holding back her anxiety, Verley steadied her trembling voice enough to say, ''I can't wait that long. Sorry.''

Verley understood the attitude of a rodent in a corner. She rose and tried another table. She received roughly the same response, plus an inappropriate proposition.

The invitation spurred her thoughts.

''Need a ship's hust?'' she asked at an all-male table, not believing she had actually offered herself so tactlessly.

''Booda blow the ship,'' said the oldest, drunkest one there. ''Where's your hanger, longcake? I could go for a shlice right–'' His friends cut him short, shaking their heads at her.

''Captain's rules, my lady,'' a young man said in a wistful, apologetic tone. ''No animals, no Jarps, no women.''

She shifted in the booth, looked out into the dim barroom. *Nothing*, she thought. *No way out*. Then her gaze fixed on the woman.

She sat in a dark corner, watching Verley. She looked to be taller than Verley, but the 25-sem coil of blue-black hair gave her an illusion of stunning height. Her dress, almost a gown of Prussian blue, wrapped her body nearly as tightly as SpraYon, and tantalized more by revealing less. She was petite nowhere. More than ample breasts threatened to escape from the low décolletage. Her eyes held the promise of infinite delight founded on insatiable desire. Her SpraYon gloves delineated every flowing line in her arms in streams of black and reflected light. Her shadowy outfit blended almost invisibly with her skin, subcutaned a deep walnut hue.

From this dark disguise, in the low-lit corner, Kenowa watched Verley . . . and invited her over with a slight tilt of her head.

4

Attempting to be circumspect, Verley wandered to the bar, ordered a double Welldigger, and drifted around the periphery of the dancefloor. The dancefloor was a formality. No one danced in this heat. After a few moments, she moved toward Kenowa's table.

"Is this seat available?"

Kenowa nodded and Verley sat. Kenowa looked at the other woman, at her attractive, though rather hard-edged face. She seemed familiar. Something about her nervous attitude reminded her of the last time she and Jonuta had been to Sekhar, months before his death at the hands of . . . someone (that trebly-damned bitch Janja?) and his resurrection by the genius of Fumiko Kita-daktari.*

She was about to say something when the younger woman said, "I remember you. You were part of Sweet-face's crew, weren't you?"

The name startled Kenowa, brought back memories. Sweetface, the Jarp crewmember of *Coronet* whose loyalty to that stupid other Jarp Tweedle*dumb* caused a permanent rift between it and Jonuta. This girl before her . . . This girl . . .

"You were with Sweetface, that hust it–" She bit her lip.

Verley didn't notice, her head nodding with desperate eagerness.

"I've got to get off Sekhar. I have money. I'll do anything. Is Sweetface onplanet?" Tears almost crested over her eyelids.

Shaking her head slightly, Kenowa said, "It left us long ago, months ago, uh . . ."

*Spaceways #12: *Star Slaver*.

42

"Verley."

Kenowa nodded, reaching out to pat Verley's hand. *Coronet* had returned to Sekhar with a load of walking cargo for one of the wealthier members of Sekhari society. Jonuta ran a great risk to do this, since his departure previously had caused no small consternation on the part of Sekhar Security.*

Kenowa considered Verley. There were many planets on which this attractive woman might be of some value. Too, a willing passenger would more easily get past a policer scan than a captured slave. And Jonuta, his fortune wiped out by The Gray Organization, could not afford to be choosy. His name, already mud on too many planets, had reached its nadir.

(But then, Jonuta was dead, vaporized in space—or so thought all but one daktari, her aide, and the crew of *Coronet*.)

Kenowa, thinking fast, said, "Sweetface is gone and Captain Jonuta is dead. I and the crew of *Coronet* are trying to keep ourselves solvent by running freight. We'd gladly take you onboard, for a reasonable sum." She paused, as though considering. "In fact, there may be a way for us both to benefit."

Verley listened.

"Well," the bigger woman said, leaning forward across the table, her voice low and conspiratorial, "what you do is pay us for a flight to Panish. There's a rich industrialist there who requires a wife. You fit his physical archetype, more or less, and all you really have to do is keep him pleased on his planet-hopping yacht. He likes some pretty varied and amusing sexual adventures."

Verley frowned.

"Oh, don't worry," Kenowa added, "he's harmless. And not at all unattractive. *And* we would refund your fare from what we receive from the transaction." She took a sip of her drink and leaned back, sure that the antintoxicant she had taken earlier still had some effect.

Verley listened without comment. Even if half of it

*Spaceways #2: *Corundum's Woman*

contained no small amount of hyperbole, at least she would be off the planet.

And it was the best offer she'd had all day.

"Half now," she said, reaching into her go-bag, "and half when we leave Sekhar."

She pulled out Denverdarian Eks's perspak and set it on the table, digging deep into her bag for the money.

(From across the barroom, a pair of eyes watched with care. A hand quietly stroked at a cleft chin.)

"It's in here somewhere," she said, "just give me–"

"It's all right," Kenowa said, flipping her fingers lightly. "We trust you."

She handed Verley the various contents of her go-bag that had been disgorged onto the table. Taking the opportunity to sip at her drink, she scanned the bar once more.

The usual complement of hungry male eyes watched her, plus a few pair of female eyes, curious and envious. Then she noticed a set watching Verley from across the room. Kenowa sat up straight in her chair, pulling her shoulders back to thrust her breasts forward in a smooth, sensual motion. The gaze remained fixed intensely on Verley. Something was wrong with that pair of eyes.

Kenowa—great looking and damned well knowing it— had spent a lifetime dealing with men of many worlds. Her years with Jonuta had given her an intuitive knowledge of what attracted the gaze of human—and non-human—males. Something was definitely wrong.

"Tell me, Verley," she said, "are you in a hurry to leave because of man trouble?"

Verley's hands unconsciously gripped more tightly on her go-bag. Her pupils constricted and the nervous terror running as an undercurrent in her suddenly crested. Her body trembled. And her heart took up racing again.

"I'm sorry," Kenowa said, sliding out of the booth. "We are not in the rescue business. I'm afraid the deal is off." She turned to go.

And faced a gray-haired man.

"Excuse me," he said in a voice like grinding rock, "but the girl and I have to be going now." He elbowed past Kenowa, making sure to brush his upper arm across her cleavage. "She and I have to talk about her friend Scarcheek."

Verley sat frozen for an instant, looking up into the man's narrow gaze. Slowly, she slung her go-bag over her shoulder and slid from her seat. On its edge, she hesitated. Not having a spacefarer's skill at bluff, she looked up at the large man and shouted loudly enough for the entire bar to hear.

"*I'm not that kind of woman!*"

The high heel of her boot shot forward to connect with the man's groin. He regretted the disturbance. Huffing out an uncontrolled gasp, he fell like a knotted towel.

"Shiva's shit!" Kenowa muttered, and unholstered her stopper. She leveled it at the fallen man. She squeezed the grip. Big *myrzha* dimple-chin collapsed, unconscious from a number Two beam.

Verley tried to run and caught her heel on the man's outflung wrist. She fell forward.

Their table exploded into blinding light amid shattering noise. Verley screamed and hit the floor, grabbing at her left arm. From across the room, a young man took a second aim with his pulsar beamer.

Kenowa whipped about in quest of the source of the blast. On the floor, Verley whimpered and tried to stop the searing pain in her arm. Blood leaked through the cracks forming in the cauterized flesh.

A scream shrilled from the other side of the room. A whispery sort of cry, as if from a strangling man. Kenowa watched the man with the plasmer flare into ash. Somewhere, a stopper on setting Three turned him first into dust, then broke the dust into ions and free radicals, dissipating the gunman into the hot atmosphere of the bar. Kenowa glanced frantically about.

"Perhaps you ladies need an escort?" The question came from a handsome man with light coffee-colored skin and deep brown hair. He smiled.

"Kimball!" Kenowa shouted.

Holstering his stopper on his gray equhyde belt, the tall man stooped to pick up Verley, go-bag and all. She leaned against his jacket of deep gray equhyde, staining it with her blood. He carried part of her weight against his gray-clad hip and thigh, dragging her toward the door. Kenowa followed, stopper ready.

Somewhere in the city of Refuge, a telemetry device monitoring vital signs in a body kilometers away suddenly registered the instantaneous cessation of those vital signs. An alarm *pingg*ed softly, flashing a pale amber light.

The man in gray half-supported, half-dragged a shocked Verley into the main terminal. Through the photoptic glass of the terminal's windows shone the harsh light of Al-jebr, Sekhar's sun. Almost touching the horizon and filtered through kloms of dust in the atmosphere, it shone a deep, blinding red. Red as blood. None of the three noticed it. Yet even in the reduced glare, the man's irises—subcutaned a pale blue—constricted almost to points. So did Kenowa's.

A claxon wailed inside the building. Kenowa turned and stoppered the advancing pair of customs guards. They collapsed and slid along the polished sandstone like dolls thrown on tile.

Verley, taking deeper breaths, struggled away from the grasp of the man in dark gray. "I can walk by myself," she said, valiantly trying to run and hold her wound simultaneously.

"Then walk somewhere else, slut!" Kenowa shouted. "You got us into this."

A guard squeezed off a stopper beam at the man in gray, who commenced to jerk spasmodically and pitched to the floor. Kenowa turned and dropped that assailant with a Two-setting zap.

"What have you two gotten into?" the man called Kimball asked, regaining his stance. "I finish up our business here and I find you two gunning it out with the flainin' locals—*duck!*"

His hand shot out to shove Kenowa sideways. The sizzling bolt of a plasma blast blazed over her head, vaporizing half of her Terasaki coil. The bolt impacted a counter. Sparks and flaming debris danced across the atrium. The stench of moldering hair was lost in the smoke from burning plast.

"This way!" he shouted, running down an access tunnel.

Shouts and footsteps followed. Outside, a siren rose in pitch.

"Which berth, Kim?" asked Kenowa, turning to play her stopper beam back and forth along the tunnel. (A beam of white heat exploded a long meter away.)

"Four-eighteen. There!"

Kinball turned hard, skidding the heel of his gray boot against the sandstone walkway. Fingers punched a lock code and the door slid up. "In," he said, aiding Kenowa with an ungentle pat on her backside. Verley he helped with a shove in the small of her back.

"Leave her, Kimball. She's trouble."

"Right," he said, sealing the door and heading down the extension tube to its far end, "and since she's dragged us into it, I want to get my trouble's worth out of her." The door exploded inward. "Even if I have to get it out of her hide!"

5

Coronet's lander lay berthed at the end of the extension tunnel. The man called Kimball pressed his left breast pocket and the hatch slid open. Through the smoke and confusion behind them, he saw figures racing toward the lander. Stopper beams dropped two more men and persuaded the others to reconsider their actions. Kenowa stumbled inside, followed by the man in gray. His arm shot out and grabbed Verley, who stood outside, dully watching the approaching policers.

"Inside, darling," he said, dragging her onboard and sealing the airlock.

Blood loss, shock, and her relief at escaping combined to drain her of all consciousness. Slumping forward into Kimball's arms, she dropped the go-bag from her good shoulder and thumped her head against his chest.

"Great," he said. "Kenny! Get her strapped in."

Without making sure that Kenowa caught her, he dropped Verley and climbed into the pilot couch, flipping switches and powering up the engines.

"This is Sekhar Security," came a tinny voice from the comm, "calling berth Four-One-Eight. You are not yet cleared for launch. Why are you powering?"

He ignored the question. He also ran a high voltage current through the boat's hull to drive back the men trying to deactivate its engines externally. He hit the launch alarm, hearing the satisfying sounds of panicked feet running away.

"This is Sekhar Security to berth Four-One-Eight. You are guidelined to unpower and open your–" The rest of the message was lost in the electromagnetic roar of the lander's main thrusters.

Blasting straight away from a berth was rude in the extreme, since it demolished the berth and put the workers and guards in extreme hazard. But Kimball was in a hurry.

Kenowa, having strapped in next to him an instant before he unleashed the engines, let the acceleration press her into the couch while speaking in an almost conversational tone.

"We didn't have time for intros, but the silly little fobber there is Verley. She was the one Sweetface trysted with while we were here last."

"Think she knows?"

Kenowa shook her head, glancing down at her breasts. Though the 2G acceleration pressed them against her chest, they still swelled impressively beneath her dark blue dress. She tried not to think what her thighs looked like under this pressure.

"I think she believes Jonuta's dead and I'm in mourning and we're all trying to survive financially without the brains of the operation. By the way—how'd the transaction go?"

With little effort, even under acceleration, a muscular hand reached under a gray equhyde pocket and withdrew a small white tablet. Popping it in his mouth, Kimball said, "Arsane er-Jorvistor's successor had heard the news about Jonuta." (Meanwhile, the pill worked its effect. Dissolving the subcutaneous dyes, the chemical returned his color to its previous shade. His skin tone darkened to its glossy, cupric hue.) "He was more willing to deal with Kimball Fordyce."

He looked over at Kenowa, the pale blue eyes darkening to black, or nearly. He looked back to the console, punching a code sequence into SIPACUM. With a sidewise lurch, the in-grav boat shifted attitude.

"I'm heading over to the antipode of Sekharstation," he replied to Kenowa's inquiring glance. "Shig's got my signal to ease *Coronet* out of the station and orbit about to meet us there. Whoever it is that our unconscious friend has following her may not be aware who's responsible for the entertainment groundside."

"They will be, if they saw me." Kenowa reached up to touch the charred remnant of her Terasaki coil. She pulled it off sadly, turning her eyes away from the man beside her. He turned his own gaze away, knowing that she wished no one to see her head, bald and unadorned.

"I'll get you a new one, Kenny," he said.

"Thank you, Jone."

Pulling a long silver scarf out of the compartment by her couch, she fought the acceleration enough to wrap the cloth into a turban. It rode high enough and covered enough that she could have had a full head of hair beneath. Her hands almost unraveled the scarf when the engines suddenly throttled back to less than .5G thrust.

"We're out of the atmosphere." Kislar Jonuta of Qalara unstrapped himself and rolled out of the couch. "Now let's check on our passenger."

Under acceleration, the rear of the boat was "down." Jonuta eased himself over the arm of the couch and floated under .5G to the rear of the boat. His gray boots landed against the padded bulkhead, now a floor, and looked at Verley.

Strapped in by Kenowa, she hardly looked comfortable. One strap lay across her left breast rather than between it and the right. Had she been awake, surely the pain would have been extreme. Jonuta undid the straps and belts, stooping to examine her wound. The plasma bolt had seared through the skin and muscle tissue of her upper left arm. A portion of her deltoid and some triceps brachii, he noted, damning the brainboost that sometimes gave him more information than he needed. The blob of ionized matter had partially cauterized the flesh in its passage through her arm. Here and there cracks and tears had almost immediately appeared, resulting in the blood flow. Red fluid still leaked from the raw mass.

Jonuta sighed. No shipdoc until they got to *Coronet*.

Methodically, he tore away Verley's rust-colored blouse, stained with a hue redder than rust. Smooth brown breasts jiggled lightly in the low-weight condition, the nipples soft and flattened against their dark areolae. He noted (with interest) and went on about his business. Tearing the shirt into strips, he used a piece to wipe away some of the blood that had smeared about her arm and chest. With another strip, he bandaged the wound, wadding the last piece beneath.

Looking at the raven-haired woman under his hands, he realized that the shirt made an ineffective dressing, considering the size of the wound. His hands reached to her maroon skinTites, fingers edging under the waistband, gathering up enough to rip them in one motion.

"Is this what you're looking for?" Kenowa asked, dangling a first-aidpak from a finger. She let it drift down to him. It landed a few sems from his feet and bobbed once in the abbreviated gravity.

"Right," he said, not releasing his grip on Verley's waistband. "Thanks."

"There's a roll of BandiFast inside."

"Umm, thanks." He tore the fabric with one surge of his hands.

"Uh . . . seems hardly the time to act horny, Jone."

"You forget, I was once encephaloboosted to Initial Daktari level."

Kenowa snorted and shifted back around to watch the sky. "Hippokrates would have been proud," she said just loud enough to be heard.

"Who?"

"Mind your brainboosts and I'll mind my holos."

"She's wounded and in shock," he said, gazing at the dark patch of surprisingly straight pubic hair between Verley's legs. "Besides," he added, peeling the skinTites from her thighs and calves, "who could possibly be interested in another woman when you're around?"

"You, m'love."

With a grin that was definitely not denial, he added a few twists of BandiFast to Verley's arm. Her eyelids fluttered weakly, then opened. Pupils of unequal size peered dreamily about. Grimacing, she reached up to touch her wound. She took a deep breath and looked about her.

"I fainted," she said, then looked up at Jonuta. "You're different," she observed, and fell back on the couch. An alarm chittered angrily. She looked up toward the console, seeing Jonuta spring upward and grab the command couch. He clambered into it with a spacefarer's ease.

"Second ship," Kenowa said simply, pointing at the computer simulation before them.

Jonuta nodded and tapped a quick code into SIPACUM. "Looks as if someone can actually run a sum on two plus two and get four. That's a light cruiser trying to block the intercept point between us and *Coronet*. They're—"

An explosion, silent but blindingly bright, flared a few kilometers ahead of them. "Pyrocket," he muttered. Ships sometimes used them to fire warning shots across the bows of other spacers, since most weapons left no visible trail in the vacuum. "Hang on," he yelled behind him.

Releasing a load of foil chaff to confuse the cruiser's sensors, he ordered the boat into evasive maneuvering, inclining its attitude slightly planetward. The cruiser was not able to pull about. It drifted past them, thousands of meters over their heads. He flipped open the comm.

"What flaining idiot's testing its DS on *my lander*? This is Captain Kimball Fordyce of *Worsel's Worry* and I demand to know on whose authority that shot was fired!"

No reply.

Making contact with *Coronet*'s SIPACUM, he ordered an intercept and docking, combat alert modified. The boat drifted and dodged, all the while moving closer to the port docking bays.

"*Coronet*'s DS is up," Kenowa noted, while she adjusted her screen to include simulations of all three craft. "And still no message from the cruiser. No ID impulses, no official markings." She turned her turbaned head to look at Jonuta. "I guess they like surprise parties."

He made no effort at an answer, watching the approach to the docking bay. Only a few kloms away, the freighter filled the simulation screen. Braking rockets fired, shoving them forward against the restraining straps. Verley groaned in alarm. The first-aidpak fell forward and clattered against the viewing port. Their inner ears told them they were now looking "down" at *Coronet*, instead of "up."

"I repeat," he shouted into the comm, "identify yourself, cruiser, or I shall call Sekhar Sec—" An explosion rumbled through the boat's hull, followed by the sound of escaping fuel.

"Booda's balls! That was the dorsal stabilizer. Kenny—

rotate port and starboard to compensate. They're trying to cripple us.''

He tapped furiously into SIPACUM, not hearing the coughing sounds from Verley "above" him. Switching on the direct laser ship-to-ship comm, Jonuta spoke while trying to ease the boat into a correct docking attitude.

"Shig—inslot sixty-three bee when I dock and stand by for tachyon conversion.''

Spaceship *Coronet*'s SIPACUM cassette 63B ordered the ship's computer and ancillary systems to prepare the ship for subspace transition as soon as safe, with only a single *ping* for twenty second's warning.

"*Firm*," came the terse reply.

The boat slowed to a docking velocity faster than normal. Nudging the boat on manual, Jonuta watched the open bay loom only a few hundred meters away.

"They don't want us dead," he muttered, "or we'd be slag right now. But they don't want to talk. Playful lot.''

Kenowa nodded and turned to look at Verley. Jonuta had neglected to strap her all the way in after his medical attention. She hung from her waist with arms, head, and torso stretched in the direction of deceleration. Her hair drifted slowly about, suddenly snapping into fluid waves when the braking rockets cut off.

The docking bay enveloped them. The boat thumped firmly into the shock pads at the far end. Verley released a huff of air and hung motionless in the zero-gravity.

"*Sixty-three bee inslotted and–*"

A *ping* resounded through the ship's intercom, followed by Shiganu's cry of "Shit!" Jonuta, unbuckling himself, frowned. 63B had never found a safe entry to subspace so fast. He turned to Kenowa.

"No time even to bargain with the natives," he said, smiling.

In those twenty seconds after the alarm sounded, SIPACUM seized control of all ship's systems and power in preparing *Coronet* for tachyon conversion, the form of travel that opened up the stars to the Galactics. For eight of those twenty seconds SIPACUM left the ship without any attitude control, external communication, hull sensors, or full Defense Systemry. It was in those eight seconds that the attacking cruiser chanced to launch a missile.

Impacting on a ventral strut, the small payload deformed and gripped the hull in the shape of a thick metallic pancake. It fused with the hull's metal and rode with it when, sneering at Einstein, the entire spacecraft vanished from orbit around Sekhar and hit the Tachyon Trail.

Tachyon conversion—the subatomic transposition of "normal" matter, which had an upper velocity limit of the speed of light, into Tachyons, to which the speed of light was its *slowest* velocity—usually involved some discomfort. Supposedly that discomfort arose from spontaneous gapping of neurons across the synapses in the brain at the instant of conversion. Most spacefarers could handle the physical consequences. The inexperienced often suffered severe headaches, momentary disorientation, and occasionally severe nausea.

A first timer, Verley experienced all three.

Marekallian Eks enjoyed being a sky god. The pay was terrible, but the benefits more than compensated. He sat beneath a *kunda*, one of the tall, leafless trees that sent long, shocking blue tendrils from the bough to the ground. Lazily, he sat braiding five dried lengths of tendril into a long, very strong rope.

On the plain beneath him, a hundred meters away, dozens of Arepienese dug in the mud. Now and again one would shout and hold up a clump of mud or a piece of stone. Eks would dutifully point his laser spectrometer at it and take a reading. If he detected iron, copper, or bauxite, he used a portable loudspeaker to inform all of them, taking the opportunity to tell them what to look for.

"Wash it off," he said over the loudspeaker. "You'll see the telltale green of copper oxide. That's copper that has reacted with the air. You'll learn how to reverse that with heat." He turned to Rakhin Oualama Q'yaba, who sat next to him. The Elder balanced an EverComp high-density memory screen on his lap, working with Marekallian's stylus to create a written language for the clan T'yaba.

"It would be easier," Marekallian Eks said, "if you all learned Erts, of course."

"Yes. But our language and oral history has so much beauty. Our songs, our poetry. These must be preserved." He started a new page on the screen and continued designing a phonetic alphabet with the expertise of his brainboosted memories.

"Tell me more about Arep astronomy, Oualama. Do your people celebrate the various conjunctions and oppositions of your stars?" His hands continued working the *kunda* vines into rope, almost idly.

The Elder paused, letting memories come to him, integrating them into his new knowledge.

"Our astronomy is something more than what you call astrology, but less than a true science. We have a Watcher who knows when the Mother and Her Lover are at angles to each other. I now understand that we live on a *planet* revolving around these *stars*."

He paused to look up at the dimmer star of the binary, a yellowish dwarf. Just past the zenith, it warmed without scorching. Clouds on the horizon obscured the rising of the second sun, a yellow-white.

"Are they both so incredibly huge and distant, Mayekalliah? Are we so puny?"

"The mightiest star cannot blaze with the intensity of a living soul." Eks put down the rope and turned over on his side.

"All races worship their suns, Oualama. Their rituals and legends form the basis of all myth and art. Tell me about your traditions. How you worship the Mother and Her Lover. When, where. Your stories, your art."

Rakhin Oualama Q'yaba shut the EverComp with a loud snap. "It is no longer worthy of discussion! You have shown me that our goddess is nothing more than burning gases. This shames me. It shames my people. Chants and dances must cease, shrine towers must be abandoned. You have thrown my people forward hundreds of lifetimes. You have shown us how to progress a thousand times faster than we would have. And now you ask me to tell you of the past?" He stood up, throwing the pad and stylus to the sapphire-hued grass. "You have cut me off from my history. You will do the same to others. I still think this is good. Yet it is also very sad.''

"Early death in primitive conditions is incomparably sadder, Elder.''

The Elder said nothing, but strode down the hill toward the excavation site. He watched them toiling for a moment, before turning to walk back to the village unescorted.

Examining a few more samples with the spectrometer, Marekallian sighed with mild exasperation. He switched on the loudspeaker.

"*Iron* ore," he said in a mixture of T'yabish and Erts. "Dig up more iron ore. When we have enough iron, we can make picks. Then you won't have to use your hands. Then you can get more iron faster. With more iron we can build machinery so you won't have to strain yourselves. It's worth the effort.''

He leaned back against the tree and resumed braiding the rope. *I wonder what a shrine tower looks like.*

Arepien's second sun rose above the clouds. Marekallian Eks squinted at it for a moment, then looked up into the aquamarine sky.

Where in Theba's name is Denverdarian?

A simple task such as the illegal purchase of a TDP should not have taken him so long. A mindrunner needed state-of-the-art equipment to evade TGW and TAI observation. While he remained onplanet, Marekallian usually dispatched his older brother and the other two crewmembers to acquire components. What spare time he had he spent designing new devices to cloak *Eris* with ever-greater effectiveness.

The weak link in the chain was Denverdarian. Eks wondered if his brother's nervous habit of carrying his SIPACUM cassettes with him might have resulted in their loss. He hoped not. If they were lost, Denverdarian would have to replot a course to Arepien by himself.

And Denvo couldn't plot his slicer into a stash without a manual.

Marekallian stood up and stretched. The air had the fresh scent of sea breeze from the nearby shore. Behind him came the sound of bare feet on grass.

"Biah'Rakhin Mayekalliah," a young woman's voice said, timid and tremulous.

Turning around, he saw a slender cinnamon-hued figure standing before him, eyes downcast. Flowers of green and orange, ruby and pearl adorned her long curly hair. She must have been about sixteen or so, yet stood a dozen sems taller than he.

"Yarala," he said, smiling. "How go your studies?"

"I have learned many new things."

She spoke without looking up. One of a dozen or so young people that Marekallian had brainboosted, Yarala had proven the most eager to learn. She spoke in a subdued tone with her hands hanging, tightly clasped together. Her hair constituted most of her clothing, except for her *t'laan*—the length of crude fabric that wrapped around her waist several times and draped before her. The dark blue cloth hung to mid-thigh. It also hid practically nothing, thanks to the gusts of sea breeze flipping it about.

Oblivious to the wind's teasing, she said, "I sit up at night, now, remembering. I visit places I have never before seen. I feel objects I have never touched. I hear voices that have never spoken to me. The memories say you are not a god, but everything you do makes me think you are."

"There are no gods but us, Yarala. You and me and everyone else. Some of us just have an edge. An edge that I'm trying to give you."

He coiled up the *kunda* rope and slung it over his shoulder. Placing the laser spectrometer and the loudspeaker in a leather go-bag, he burdened his other shoulder with it and walked down the hill. Yarala followed.

"Soon we'll be spacefarers just as you?"

"Well, not *soon*. Maybe within a century or so, if you really put yourselves to it. Brainboosts are the simple part. *Using* that increased intelligence to build the hardware necessary to get offplanet—that's the trick, Yarala. It'll take you just a few months to be ready psychologically for joining the civilization of the spaceways. Industrial lag is the problem. Not to mention that the threat of outside repression always exists because of your Protected status."

"They would stop us if we tried to get offplanet?"

"*Pos!*" he said, the grass beneath him squeaking in protest under the force of his turn. "There are those who would keep you under their heel, their invisible heel! You'll remember their names. TransGalactic Watch. Terra Alta Imperata. *They* are your enemies. And mine."

Yarala unconsciously stepped back from the vehemence of Marekallian's words. One hand reached down to touch the fabric of her *t'laan*. She imagined him, tall and so brown of skin, fighting a holy battle with the faceless monsters. She quaked in fear and rage.

Eks watched her for a moment, noting her reactions. *Good*, he thought. *The metaprogramming works on them. That makes everything a lot easier.*

"I must return to the forest now," he said. "Don't fear your enemies. They're the ones who fear. Why else would they try to keep you in your primitive state? Someday you'll be as mighty as they are."

He reached out and raised her chin so that she looked at him with eyes as dark as the night sky. He saw a stubborn pride mixed in with her awe. He could almost see the new thoughts racing through her mind.

If there were *a god*, he thought, *She would feel the joy I feel watching her right now.*

He stroked her cheek lightly. Smiling, he walked down the hill.

Yarala watched him depart. The warm afternoon air mixed with the cool breeze to send a shiver through her. She pulled an azure blossom from her hair and studied it with moody eyes.

Passing the novice miners, Marekallian paused long enough to organize a team to haul the ore back into the village. That done, he headed into the forest and followed his own path back to the in-grav boat; his lander.

The chirruping of dankflies and the howl of mating greenwings provided background music to Marekallian's evening study. Sitting oncon, he adjusted the horizontal elevation on a computer simulation of Arepien's surface. The screen displayed the planet's three small continents in false colors of crimson, yellow, and varying shades of turquoise. The turquoise shading indicated elevation. He narrowed the scan from the entire planet to one continent. Then from the whole continent to squares a thousand kloms on the side. Then a hundred kloms.

The vegetation of Arepien varied in height from grass of a few sems to the *tabakunda*—thick trees hundreds of meters tall. Each trunk sprouted an individual jungle of mossy vines. After examining several dozen squares—some as small as a klom—Eks leaned back in the acceleration couch and rubbed between his eyes.

And they call it eye-eez, he thought. *I could do this for the next year and still not be sure that I'll see what I want.*

He input a few commands to SIPACUM and lowered his hands to the armrests. The result brought a frown to his face.

Great—over ten thousand discontinuities in elevation on this square megaklom alone. And I don't even know if a shrine tower rises above the surrounding forest to begin with.

He fingerflipped. *A few more questions and I'll have it.* While he lost himself in his thoughts, his hands picked up the *kunda* vines and absently continued braiding them.

6

Verley 2197223SK, formerly of Sekhar, awoke in a coffin.

A white coffin of plasteel, lined with tubes, wires, waldoes, and telepresences. The upper part of her left arm itched madly, but she couldn't reach it in the cramped confines of the shipdoc. Vague, distant sounds filtered in through the lid of the automated medical center. A dreamy bluish light meandered through the mist swirling about inside, illuminating the atomized droplets. Had Verley ever seen fog on a spring morning, she'd have been reminded of it.

Something hissed at her feet. The lid of the coffin eased open, admitting more of the blue light. A head hung over hers.

Its owner's black hair lay vehemently straight over his head. His deep brown eyes tilted slightly, a fold of skin covering their inner corners. His arms reached in for her. A bit darker than his face, they had the color of excellent bronze.

"Sit up," he said in a voice neither harsh nor encouraging.

Verley sat up. From the new vantage, she saw more of him. He wore a yellow tunic with the look of silk. On it, twisting about in fluid swirls, was emblazoned a beautiful dragon. Black tights tucked into black boots completed his attire.

"Sak—Sakyo?" she asked. She hoped she had remembered his name. Sweetface had introduced her to its shipmate on that day a year past.

"Very good, Verley," he said smiling. The smile quickly turned to a frown. "I'm afraid you've got to meet the captain. And he's not pleased with the activities groundside. *Coronet*'s getting a bad reputation on Sekhar."

The smile reappeared for an instant, then vanished.

With Sakyo's help, Verley climbed out of shipdoc and stood on the cool plasteel deck. Oblivious to the gaze of the Terasak examining every sem of her naked body with scarcely hidden approval, she flexed her left arm, then looked it over.

The deep burn wound had healed without a scar.

The automatic daktari had also given her a general physical overhaul. She stretched and took a deep breath of the ship's artifreshed air. Her skin tingled. She felt invigorating energy surge through her muscles and her blood. She felt alive and refreshed and free.

"The captain is waiting."

She turned, reminded of Sakyo's presence. He offered her a simple tan jumpsuit.

"Don't hurry for my sake," he said, watching her don the coverall.

The austere garment fitted snugly everywhere but at the bustline. *Kenowa's*, she mused, gathering in the bodice and strapping the belt tightly. The front opened practically from shoulder to shoulder, descending in a sharp V to the waist. Her breasts, though not the size of the original owner's, were barely contained by the suit's fabric.

"How long have I been in there?"

"Two ship-days. A shade over two days-ess. Now let's go."

"Don't I get shoes?"

This time he grinned. "I don't think you'll be needing them."

Jonuta stood at the con. A man who exercised two hours a day, he refused himself the luxury of sitting except when battle conditions demanded it.

He wore grass-green equhyde tights and a double-breasted longtailed coat. Two gleaming rows of prass buttons ran down the front of the dazzling scarlet fabric; buttons with the sheen and color of real brass. Under the coat he wore a white, buttonless shirt of almost severe simplicity. The open neck plunged to the solar plexus, revealing the dark twists of hair covering his chest as if they'd been drawn there with the blackest of inks.

He rocked back and forth in small, unconscious motions to the music playing on the inship comm. His black equhyde boots reflected the con-cabin's light in random flashes. The muscles under the skin of his hands stretched like taut steel cables as his deft fingers roamed over the con controls.

After their nearly instantaneous escape from orbit around Sekhar, Jonuta had taken the ship in and out of tachyon conversion a half dozen times. Only a few hours ago, he had dropped *Coronet* out of "subspace" into deep interstellar space to tinker with the converters. In this way, he hoped to foil anyone's attempt to follow his ship's "signature"—its trail of ions, analyzable waste, and polarized radiation unique in its sequence and distribution in the ship's wake.

He stood now, wondering what to do with this Sek woman. He watched Sakyo lead her to the con-cabin. Every tunnel they passed through was watched by a TP camera linked with the intership comm network. Jonuta watched in silent speculation.

I doubt that she's trouble all on her own. Sekhar is trouble, and she just happened to be in the vicinity both times I've had trouble there.

And that's too coincidental.

He switched to another TP, continuing his surveillance. He zoomed in on Verley. Her dusky skin had attained a sheen of perspiration from the walk. Her long waves of hair, cleansed of Sekhar's clinging dust while in the cybernetic daktari, flowed breezily behind her. She looked unconcerned about her imminent meeting with the captain.

Or maybe Seks are good at repressing emotions, too. Maybe we can break down some of those walls.

Warm flesh pressed against Jonuta's back. Arms the color of burnished bronze wrapped around his waist, squeezing against his broad cordovan belt. Perfume laced with pheromones filled his nostrils.

"Nice closeup," Kenowa said, looking at the TP screen. "Good warheads."

"Nothing to equal yours, Kenny." He reached behind him to grasp one of Kenowa's, gripping the soft flesh and eliciting a low humming moan of satisfaction from its owner.

A hand touched his tights. "Enough to keep your interest up, though, hmm?"

"Purely physiological," he said, pulling her hand closer. "My thoughts are always with you."

"Flainin' liar." She smiled with as much feline glee as a HRal. "Have you decided what to do with her?"

Jonuta nodded. "I don't know if she was part of another murder attempt—this time against you, since I'm still 'dead.' I plan to find out. Buying a TDP in the counter-economy is illegal, but it's such a little scam I can't understand why the vug anyone would send a cruiser after us. Even if we *did* leave a minor crater in the middle of the spaceport."

He turned toward his *aide* without releasing his grip. He pulled her to him by her nipples, pinched beneath her deep blue skinTite. Her Terasaki coil had been replaced by a short, dark wig that ended in a straight cut at her neckline. Bangs arced sharply across her forehead, nearly touching her eyes.

"If she's important to someone, that translates into money, if it's worth the risk." One hand sought the warmth between her legs. "I think we can try the Hard Keep/Soft Keep routine on her."

Kenowa's hand gripped his slicer firmly. "I suppose you'll be the Hard Keeper?"

She received a squeeze in response.

"Guess who that makes the Soft Keeper?" he asked.

She smiled. Jonuta of Qalara possessed a keen mind, superb body, and a flair for sexual adventure that equalled or excelled those of other great personalities of Galactic history. There seemed to exist some connection between greatness and (what the envious called) perversity. Perhaps the spirit of adventure encompassed all of a person's life, pervading and guiding its goals and passions.

Kenowa knew only that her man fulfilled every fantasy she had ever devised. As she had fulfilled his. For years.

There had been other women, naturally. They all had pleased him, as all the men Kenowa had known had pleased her. She and Jonuta, however, had maintained—bound together by ties stronger than the joy of simple coupling. They were a team. A *dyad,* in the slang of a forgotten language. A word still existed for what bound them. Jonuta had not spoken that word to her until his first "death" on Franjistation.*

The word was Love. Jonuta and Kenowa loved each other with the passion of sexual adventurers and the strength of comrades-at-arms. Kenowa saw no threat in the way her captain and lover watched the Sek woman. Any enjoyment Verley could give would only remind him of how much more Kenowa gave.

The door signal alerted them to Sakyo's arrival.

Pushing Kenowa gently away, Jonuta faced the door and assumed a posture meant to intimidate—feet slightly apart, fists on hips, a menacing glower on his dark brow. He cleared his throat before signaling the door open.

Verley entered, shoved by Sakyo.

"So," Jonuta accused in the deepest basso he could affect, "you're the one who threatened my ship, my crew, and seriously damaged my reputation on your stinking little dustbowl planet! Why? Do you work for the policers?"

Verley stared. Most of her composure fled. She tried to find some place to put her hands, at last folding them under the shelf of her bosom. She looked at the deck.

"I wanted to get off Sekhar," she told it, "that's all. I asked *her*, and then the fight started."

Jonuta folded his arms. The action looked much more threatening than the meek way in which Verley held hers.

"Are you allied with that throatslicer Vettering? Or envious Captain Zo of *Catenary*, maybe?" He paused for only a heartbeat. "Speak!"

The prisoner took two deliberate breaths. *Few will hear the truth*, she remembered from some schoolbook, *even when they are told it*.

"I went to the port to find an outbound ship. A friend of mine was killed that morning and I thought the killers might be after me. I seem to have been right."

The interrogator nodded. "A fine cover story, since we can't confirm any of it." He stepped forward to within a few sems of her. Apprehension spurred a moistening of her skin. She smelled . . . delightful.

*Spaceways #9: *In Quest of Qalara*

Steering her into bed without resorting to rape will take some skillful maneuvering, he thought.

"The spaceways are vast, groundling. No one will miss you if we dump your body out the airlock, and I see no reason to waste any more life-support on an agent of TGW!"

Watching her for a reaction, he was surprised—and impressed—to see almost none.

After a moment of quiet thought, Verley looked up to say, "I knew that when I left Sekhar I would be at the mercy of whatever spacefarer took me on. I would rather risk death out here than spend the rest of my days back on Hell. If you choose to kill me, I can hardly give defense, for the strong may always devour the weak. Only the heart can restrain the fist."

You glib little bitch! he thought. He tried to hold back a smile. Instead, he spoke through it.

"Heart? A slaver has no heart!" He rocked back and laughed his best heartless laugh. "I surrendered my heart gladly for a fistful of stells years ago." He turned to Kenowa, who lay back in her chair watching the exchange.

"Drag this miserable slut out of here and throw her into the brig. Feed her nothing but gray waste until her little grat face speaks something other than lies! Now!"

Kenowa jumped up, took the woman's hands, let her feel the trembling in her own grasp. Verley, timidly, stood her ground. Her eyes never broke their gaze at her captor until the door sealed between them.

Jonuta chuckled. *Your turn, Kenny.*

Kenowa escorted Verley along the tunnel, speaking softly and patting the prisoner's wrist. She'd drawn her method of consolation straight from the holomellers she watched so often.

"He's a man, Verley dear. Just a beast driven by his lusts. It forces him into those rages. But I have my ways with him. I won't let him be as hard on you as he might."

Verley nodded, glancing sadly at the plasteel walls of her new prison. They entered a smallish cabin.

"Is this the brig?" she asked, looking at the bed with

aquamarine sheets and lapis lazuli covers. The overhead
light bathed the room in a soft golden glow.

"I won't put you anywhere near the brig. This is
Sweetface's old cabin. The new crewmember has a bunk
near the engine room."

Verley started slightly, then looked about a second time.
She wanted to feel his presence in the room, but couldn't.
She sat on the bed, her head hanging.

Good, Kenowa thought. *Hit her right where it hurts.
Now we can be sisters.*

She had guessed at Verley's soft spot. Now she applied
firm pressure.

"You really liked him, didn't you?"

Verley nodded. She knew whom Kenowa meant. Even
though Sweetface was both a "he" and a "she," the
masculine pronoun seemed more fitting to its disposition.

"He taught me how to love someone. And he taught me
how to love *me*."

"So you thought you'd find him somewhere along the
spaceways."

Tears dropped from the younger woman's eyelashes to
land on her breasts, darkening the suit cloth. The anguish
that gripped her throat and choked her breath shocked even
Verley. Kenowa's simple question suddenly made coher-
ent the urges that had tugged at Verley for the past year.
The Jarps she husted were all Sweetface. The overpower-
ing need to leave Sekhar was her need to find Sweetface.
Her actions to get to *Coronet* stemmed from the thought
that maybe—somehow—the ship would provide a link to
Sweetface. To *him*.

Kenowa put her arms around her shoulders and pulled
her close. Verley's tears now stained the other woman's
breasts. They could hold many tears. Kenowa ran a ringed
and braceleted hand over the Sek's smooth, dark hair.

"Poor, dear thing. I'm sorry I can't help you find him.
As long as Jonuta thinks you're some sort of spy, I won't
be able to–"

"But I'm *not*!" she cried, her words running together.
"I was running from whoever killed my friend Sweetbabe!
It left me in the morning with enough money to buy a
ticket out and when I got back from the shower they'd

ransacked my apt so I went to find Sweetbabe to give it the perspak it'd left and when I got there it was dead. They'd killed it. Upside down.''

Her head rubbed back and forth, wet eyes sliding against soft fabric and softer skin. She sniffed back a choking sound.

"I went to the port. No one wanted to take me. I thought I might have been followed. Then I saw you. I thought you could help. I didn't think they'd find me. I'm sorry.''

Her words became sobs and then quiet whimpers. Kenowa stroked and patted her head, rocking gently. Occasional pacifying sounds escaped her, while her mind raced.

Sweetbabe. The kid's totally locked on Sweetface. Calls other Jarps by almost the same name. Someone killed the Jarp and ripped her place. Probably those two bastards in the bar. But what did they–

"Verley?" She pulled away a little and bent to look into liquid eyes. "Verley, dear—what did you say the Jarp left at your apt?''

Verley blinked wet lashes. "Just a perspak. ID papers and some cassettes that nobody would buy. I tried to sell them for–''

"You brought them with you to the port?''

"Well, when I found S-Sweet–''

"That's fine, dear. Just lie down and sleep awhile. I know you won't feel like it after two days in shipdoc, but try. I'll be back with some food. Would you like some wine? Or marijane?''

"Actually, I'd just like some everchil pop, please,'' Verley said in a small, tired voice.

Kenowa smiled tenderly. "Lanatian Cherry? Firemint? Raspberry?''

"Blackapple?'' the small voice asked, even smaller.

"I'll see, darling. Now lie back. Good.'' *I should've been a dam' wetnurse.* "Sleep a while.''

Kenowa sealed the door and let out a pent breath. *A perspak, is it? And her go-bag is . . . where?* Walking quickly down the tunnel, she remembered.

•   •   •

The air in the portside lander bay smelled of grease and ozone. A short, thick body sprawled on top of the in-grav boat, surrounded by sparks.

"Sisterslicin' gratsuckin' bastardballer dungfuckers!" it shouted to no one in particular.

Nothing seemed to be wrorg. The low, wide body with its round, masked head moved with deliberate, slow motions.

Kenowa left the access hatch open and stepped across the plasteel ramp. Leaning forward on the railing purposefully so that her chest hung suspended in space, hidden only by the millimetric thickness of her skinTite, she watched the crewmember.

"Vark, dearest," she shouted over the hiss of the molecuwelder.

The sparks stopped instantly. A white glow on the boat's hull dimmed through orange to cherry red. The small, squat figure turned its head toward the source of the interruption. Gloved hands set the welder aside. Thick arms pushed the body up into a kneeling position.

"What the vug is it?"

The protective helmet came off and hit the plating with a clang. A face the color of soggy toast looked up at Kenowa. An eye as cheerful as the bottom of a dirty plass stared at her astonishing décolletage with stern approval. Where the left eye should have been, a TP glinted like a dark jewel.

"Well?" he demanded, pulling ths gloves from his thick fingers, "It may be eternal flainin' night outside, but that doesn't frinkin' mean I don't got to put in a dam' day's work!"

Kenowa only smiled and leaned over farther. The Bleaker's pattern of speech amused her. She shook her hair—the wig design was straight out of a Cleopatra holomeller—and drew a long fingernail along the line of her jaw.

"I've got to get inside the boat. Can you stop welding for a moment to let me get inside? We wouldn't want me to go up in flames, would we?"

Vark only grunted in answer to the second question.

"Welding? Who's welding? I'm just playing doorbot." He stood up to his full 154 sems and bowed. "Ent-er puh-lees," he said in a mechanical tone. "A-void the shi-it und-er-foot."

Kenowa laughed and climbed down to the airlock, ignoring the clanking of tools and muttered curses of the Bleaker. They had hired him after Jonuta's death, picked from a list of employable spacefarers they'd received at Employment Central on Bleak (*Yuk*, she thought, summing up her opinion of that planet).

She moved to the airlock, bits of slag crunching under her feet. Looking inside, she saw what she wanted—Verley's go-bag. In the corner where the wounded woman had dropped it. Kenowa hefted it onto her shoulder. *Blasted thing weighs a ton if it's a kilo.*

"Thanks, Vark!" she said, waving as she climbed the stairs to the exit.

The muscular little man flipped his fingers in exaggerated anger. "Doesn't Jo Tuna have better things for you to do than play streepin' baggage handler?"

Without waiting for her reply, he put on his helmet and turned to pick up his gloves.

Kenowa smiled and walked to the access hatch, rolling her hips in sensuous undulations. She looked over her shoulder to see Vark standing, gazing after her. He lightly touched his forehead, then his chest, then his groin, muttering something that she could not hear.

She knew what he'd said, though.

His damned litany! Tossing her head about in a mockery of fierce annoyance, she strode out of the lander bay. Only when the hatch sealed did she allow herself a small outburst of laughter. The go-bag slapped against her thigh with every step.

She glided into the con-cabin and saw Shiganu oncon. He turned, saw her, smiled.

"First Mate Kenowa," he said formally. His appreciative grin was less than formal. "Please to sit down, Boss Lady. We're about to drop into normal space."

SIPACUM pinged a warning. Kenowa remained where she stood. *Appearance is everything*, she reminded herself.

Shig flipped his fingers. "SIPACUM's come across a nice fat collapstar this time—"

The universe seemed to pull inside out. Shiganu took a

deep breath and tried to meditate on the Tao. Kenowa leaned against the bulkhead with stoic silence, trying to find some way in which the experience of tachyon deconversion could be sexually stimulating. In twelve years she had still not convinced herself that the general discomfort and disorientation involved could be made arousing even to the most confirmed masochist. She swallowed and heard her ears pop.

Shig took a deep breath and let it out slowly. "Any idea when the captain will decide on a course for us? I'm still not sure why he's so worried about those Sek trafficnippers."

"Captain Cautious, remember? Local policers usually identify themselves. They don't get their jingles much otherwise. When a spacer tries to stop us without conversation, Jonuta worries."

SIPACUM pinged a second time. Shig checked the readout.

"On our way again. This time in the general direction of . . . Samanna, for Boodassake!"

Reaching into Verley's go-bag, Kenowa felt around and peered into its stuffed depths. *The things some people carry*, she thought, moving over to third chair.

Everything converted to tachyons in mid-step.

She clutched the bag close to her stomach and wished all bad tidings to whoever invented the flaining device. In an instant the subatomic malaise passed and she dumped the contents of the bag onto the seat.

"What's that?" Shig asked.

"Our guest's luggage. I'm playing customs inspector."

"Damn' strange custom, if you ask me."

She pulled a bulky gray perspak out of the clutter of clothes, mementos, loose change and knickknacks anyone who'd been offplanet *once* would never bother to bring. She opened the perspak and frowned. Just some papers. . . .

And three unmarked SIPACUM cassettes. *Hardly anything to kill people over*, she thought, but her frown didn't go away.

Shig turned back to his instruments, whistling along with a tune by a BrutaLith band called Stash Fraggers. He whistled the soothingly melodic chorus while trying not to think about the song's lyrics, which in standard BrutaLithic style contained the most invidiously sadistic overtones.

The papers indicated that one Denverdarian Eks, born on Resh but a naturalized citizen of Outreach, had clear passage to Sekhar from Sekharstation in his own landing-boat. She recognized the usual docking forms, noted that spacer *Eris* had a skeleton crew of three, all onplanet. That was it. Maybe.

She had seen enough Akima Mars holodramas (all of them, in fact—again and again), and she knew what sort of messages could be coded or micro-engraved onto anything. She turned the perspak over and over, lost in thought.

"Where's Jonuta?" she asked, pivoting suddenly about.

Shig hesitated. Keeping his stare fixed on the console, he said, "He's interrogating the prisoner."

Silence filled the cabin, broken only by the whisper of ventilators and the electronic tones of Stash Fraggers.

"I see."

Kenowa tapped her nails against the three cassettes in her hand. She smiled. *That little hust's getting more than she deserves. And he'll be getting less.* She thought about what Change she would put him through for an after-dessert-cake dessert. *Something that'll smooth out his disappointment and remind him of what he's got.*

"Tell the good captain that I will be in his quarters. Out of her hearing, tell him that I have what he wanted from the woman." She slapped shut the perspak and walked toward the hatch.

"You'll have what he wants," Shig repeated. "Firm."

In more ways than one, she mused, sealing the hatch on her way out.

7

Verley heard the hatch unseal. She shifted around on the bed, smelling the musty oldness of sheets undisturbed for a year. She had managed to drift into light dozing after only a few minutes. She wondered how long she had been so.

"Kenowa?" She hoped the big woman had brought the blackapple everchil.

The hatch sealed shut. The lights dimmed.

Verley realized that she wouldn't be getting anything to eat just yet.

Jonuta faced the woman in bed. He had left his scarlet coat somewhere and wore only his tights, boots, and the soft white shirt of Panishi cotton. He was a handsome devil, she realized with a thrill of terror. Far more handsome than any man on Sekhar. His skin, dark and smooth, lacked the wrinkles and dessicated roughness of desert men. His powerful build showed no trace of weakness, either physical or mental.

And he was pulling the shirt from his chest, his gaze never leaving her.

Oh, she thought. *Time for the captive to get raped.*

Verley had made love to men before—strangers, soft men, hard men, fools. This would be just like all the others. If she pleased him, though, she would not receive money. *I'll get to keep my life.*

Silently repeating a prayer from the Quran, she slid aside the covers.

Jonuta looked at her, starting with her strong brown legs. His gaze worked up to her thighs and her round yet slim hips, then paused at the dark patch of hair masking her pubis. He stepped forward with a hand at his belt buckle, undoing its molecular binding.

The gentle curve of her belly flowed perfectly in with the narrowing of her slender waist. *Her navel*, he mused, *should have a ruby in it*. She arched her back slightly, thrusting her chest forward. Her twin lobes rested in dusky repose on the softly indicated ripples of her ribcage.

The belt dropped to the floor. One booted toe nudged the heel of the other boot away from Jonuta's foot.

Her long dark hair spread about the sheets like a black starblaze. She looked up at him with cool eyes. Her arms lay above her, thrown up past her head in a gesture of surrender. She looked away and closed her eyes.

The boots hit the floor. She heard the wisping sound of tights sliding away down over powerful thighs. She turned back slowly to look.

He stood over her now. His coppery skin glistened in the low light. He smiled. The smile held neither threat nor guile. It could have been the smile of a friend.

Verley thought it was the cruelest smile she'd ever seen.

Putting a knee on the bed, he reached out a powerful hand and slid it gently under her head. He bent towards her, at the same time pulling her mouth up to his. The scent of sweat and passion flooded into her nostrils, flaring them as their lips touched. His tongue sought hers.

She raised a hand weakly, felt his other hand grasp it, push it aside. Then he grasped one of her breasts, feeling its smooth, round shapeliness. The nipple swelled under the urgings of his thumb and index finger.

Without thought, she moved her hand to touch his slicer. Hot and firm. It felt powerful, insistent. She guided it to the valley of her legs. If this devil fancied rape, she'd just thwart him by being a willing rapee! He did not, after all, know her occupation. Her former occupation. She thought.

He found the way on his own.

She gasped when he entered her, and her legs twitched. She had been used to the smaller penile size of Jarps, or of the usually pitifully endowed Sek men she had . . . serviced. She tingled in an admixture of pleasure and some pain. He pushed in and in until he was against her cervix, an invader seeking entrance even there.

He supported himself on his hands, not crushing her beneath his leonine body. He waited, poised there . . . and watched her begin to move, responding to his persuasive presence within her.

Remarkably tight for a hust, the walls of her stash rubbed with grasping heat against his penis. She reached down and touched his scrotum, gently scratching her nails along the rib of skin separating the twin eggs.

A shudder of pleasure rippled through him. He responded with small bites at her nipples. Her areolae were small to begin with, and their diameter crinkled to even lesser size under his tongue.

They shifted about till they lay on their sides. A dark hand reached down to knead her pliant buttocks. Occasional scratches and jabs elicited squeals of shock and delight from her mouth, which had come open.

She rolled over and straddled him, thrusting downward, riding to an inner rhythm. Her clitoris tingled to every movement as it was pressed and released between their pubic mounds.

Her mouth formed a circle and she moaned, thrusting down harder on him, feeling him deep inside her. Suddenly she quivered and cried out as she flashed. Sliding forward, she buried him in her hair, covered him with her body.

For a moment she lay still, feeling warm and liquid and ethereal. He let her. For a little while. Then he began to move.

His strong, persistent plunging brought the tingling back to her again. She reached down and felt his slicer moving in and out in slow, long motions.

She had to be near it. Closer still.

Moving off him, she grasped his pump in her hand and stroked its slick flesh. Sprawling luxuriantly across his chest, she lowered her lips to the length of his member and kissed it passionately. It grew even firmer against her tongue. She traced the shape of his glans, then—unable to forestall the moment—she lowered her head and took him in.

Praise to Musla, she thought, trying to swallow his slicer all the way to its root. His thrusts became emphatic, unstoppable. His hand moved to her hair. *Praise to Musla*.

An instant later, Musla showered her with praise.

•   •   •

Space is vast, and the distances between stars—even deep in toward Galactic center—are great. The massive ships that pierced through the darkness were as dust motes in a silent night.

One of those specks in the parsec abyss bore the name *Coronet*. Another was called *Paraida*.

Major Haatan Zahrad listened patiently to the voice on the commbox.

"–shot up the port bar, killing an operative, blasted straight off from their *berth*, doing massive damage. My gunner managed to launch a lamprey tailer which impacted just before they converted."

The voice paused, awaiting a reply. Zahrad drew the pause out, then spoke slowly.

"You used a tailer lamprey, not a computer traumatizer?"

"We received orders from the surface not to endanger the crew of the target. We were to intercept if possible— without identifying ourselves—or trace if not."

Zahrad, a small, lean man of walnut complexion and thinning hair of a darker brown, stroked at his graying goatee. A touch at his arm interrupted his musings. He switched off the comm.

"We've just received a tight-beam message, sir," the lieutenant said, her voice low, "from the surface. It requests that TGW involve itself in tailing the spacer and recovering ship and crew intact."

"Source?" he asked.

"The message came in under clear code suffix R-P-A, sir."

Major Zahrad stiffened slightly. "Anything else, Lieutenant?"

"We're to await a passenger from Sekharstation who will oversee analysis of the target ship's cargo."

Zahrad took a slow, deep breath. He was getting too old for intrigues. Well over eighty but looking under fifty years-ess, he more frequently considered taking his pension with every passing month. He did not think about that at the moment. He punched on the commbox.

"Captain Verbistor of Sekhar Security ship number Thirty—" (he smiled at the high number for the third ship in the planet's "fleet" of four) "—TGW destrier *Paraida* will investigate this target spacer and its crew's cavalier treatment of Sekhar's public property. We await computer-link feed of recognition code and will depart with all due haste."

"*Thank you, Major Zahrad Sir!*" The voice on the commbox practically sparked with military crispness.

TGW majors seldom deigned to track down rude spacefarers, and the captain of policecraft 30 prided himself in his ability to persuade Major Zahrad of the importance of the mission. TransGalactic Watch—*now* things were under control.

Captain Verbistor had no knowledge of the beamed message from planetside, nor of the addition to *Paraida*'s crew shuttling over from Sekhar's only orbital facility. He proudly ordered his communications officer to beam the recognition code to *Paraida*.

The lieutenant checked her readings on SIPACUM before turning back to the major. "Recognition code for ion tailer merged with guidance and nav, sir. SIPACUM ready. Docking reports approach of shuttle to starboard."

Zahrad's face contorted into a sour smirk. "They had it planned out rather handily, Lieutenant, no?"

"Firm, sir, they always do. The shuttle must have been fifteen minutes out from the station when we received the beam."

She watched her major nod slowly. His smirk faded, leaving only the sour curl of his thin lips. He straightened out his moustache and looked up at the lieutenant. She stood twenty sems taller than he, her hair cropped shorter than his and hidden under her duty cap.

"So we serve once again as errand runners. I wonder what they want out of this ship . . . what is it called?"

"No name included, sir. Just the code for tracking the ion flux." A readout in eye-eez turquoise blinked rapidly, accompanied by a low-volume beeping. She glanced at it. "Shuttle has docked, sir. Passenger onboard."

Major Haatan Zahrad sighed and rose from his chair. Checking his gray uniform for wrinkles or specks of dust, he said, "Have the passenger escorted to the con and inslot SIPACUM with cassette programmed to tail the target spacer *at maximum distance*. Firmed?''

"Firm, Major."

And if our guest is at all friendly, maybe it will let us in on what the mission is. The major glanced at his status screen. SIPACUM indicated that it had plotted a course through subspace based on the lamprey's coded ion trail. Tachyon conversion in two minutes.

"I'll be in my cabin, Lieutenant, if anyone needs me."

TGW Major Zahrad always retired to his cabin to be alone during tachyon conversion. Forty-five years in the Watch had not altered his specific reaction to conversion. Now that he had his own spacer, he could at least remove himself from sight.

It would damage his authority if he allowed his crew to see their commander lose control of his stomach and bladder at the instant of conversion.

Ashtaru and Geb had waited two days-Sek for Denver-darian to return to the hotel before risking inquiries. Discreetly, the two other members of *Eris*'s crew checked out Refuge's jails, hospitals, and morgues.

They found him in the morgue.

Ashtaru ran a hand through her short, green-dyed hair. Her ebon hand continued back to rub the base of her neck, now tight with anxiety.

Geb nodded to the attendant. "That's him, all right. How'd he get it?''

The attendant checked his portable telit. "This one? Strangled.'' He lowered the telit. He was short and ordinary looking for a Sek. His fingers constantly flicked at his white Sektent, as if picking off bits of lint or dust. "Crushed trachea. Old-fashioned, but effective.''

"Did he have anything on him?" Geb peered over the edge of the body tray. He was more than short—Geb was a midget.

Such genetic defects—sports, they were called—were rare in the Galaxy. Most parents chose to correct such problems *in utero*. Geb's parents were poor and ignorant. They sold him into slavery on his twelfth birthday. He escaped shortly after his eighteenth, killing his Reshan owner and stowing away onboard a freighter from Outreach. The freighter *Eris*.

The morgue attendant referred to his telit. "Nothing but his clothes and pocket change. I can arrange for them to be—"

"Never mind." Ashtaru slid the tray back into the wall with an angry shove.

"Do you want to claim the body?"

"What for?" She stared at the attendant with eyes as black and cool as unburning coal. "Cremate him. Or distill him, or whatever you do here." She slapped the back of her hand lightly against Geb's shoulder. "Let's go."

They redshifted. Neither of them looked back.

The searing heat of noon hit them full force when they stepped out into the street. Ashtaru wore a pale green Sektent, the same hue as her light Panishi cotton shirt and shorts. Both matched the dye job on her hair.

Geb wore a white jumpsuit and white Sekcap. He did not bother with a Sektent, claiming that heat didn't bother him as much as it did large Galactics. He had less volume per square sem of surface area, he pointed out more often than Ashtaru cared to hear.

They walked side by side, the 155-sem-tall Ashtaru taking one stride for every two of Geb's. Passersby would give no notice to the pair until they observed that the "child" next to the woman carried an adult-sized pulsar beamer in his holster.

Geb spent a good portion of his time staring down the curious. His darkeyes made that difficult, on Sekhar.

"No navcassettes." Geb tossed a rude gesture to a gawking matron passing them. "That means no way back to base."

"Unless we can get back to Arepien." Ashtaru's gaze continuously scanned the street. She kept her right hand near her stopper, thumb tucked into her marijane-green equhyde belt.

"That's no real problem. Take me about a day to program in all the niceties." (Geb did not bother keeping his hand anywhere near his pulsar beamer. His draw, as several laughing Galactics had discovered to their next-of-kin's chagrin, was startlingly quick. He eschewed stoppers anywhere except onboard a spacer, where a plasma weapon could cause a devastating blowout. As much as he liked the flash and noise of a pulsar beamer, he hoped not to have to use one while out of reach of easy escape.)

"The real problem is that someone has the cassettes." He patted Ashtaru's thigh and pointed to their rented vehicle—an enclosed tricycle built for two. He held the door open for her.

The only beasts of burden on Sekhar were too large to ride except in howdahs and were too big to be allowed in Refuge. The city, Geb noted, was too filthy already to permit large animals to roam about. Water was scarce on Sekhar. So were petrochemicals. And who needed an internal combustion engine's waste heat anyway? Hell was hot enough.

Even electricity was at a premium. Sekhar's only orbital solar collector already operated at capacity to keep the main city powered. Electrical vehicles belonged only to the very rich who could charge them from expensive home units—or from government sources.

Enclosed, human powered vehicles suited both the environment of Sekhar and the abnegative temperaments of the Sekhari.

Geb hated Sekhar. His feet couldn't reach the pedals.

Ashtaru cursed, pedaling powerfully to get up to speed. She tried to speed through a traffic light and failed. Brakes skidded on the sand covered pavement.

"Flaining lights! A hundred eight thousand people and they need traffic lights for trikes!" She resumed her pedaling when the light turned blue. "Back to the lander?"

"Might as well," Geb replied. "We're checked out of the hotel. Make a left here."

It took them half an hour to reach the spaceport. Ashtaru climbed out of the trike unsteadily, her legs cramped from the uncommon exercise.

Geb took their go-bags and offered his shoulder for support. She reached down and straightened her arm, using him almost like a cane.

The spacefarers and natives who saw them enter the terminal did not stare too long. His darkeyes removed, Geb returned every look with a fierce glower.

After a few minutes of stretching, Ashtaru took her own bag and walked steadily. She shed her Sektent and Sekcap. "Got a pherinotal?"

Geb handed her two halves of a broken tablet and took a half dose himself. "Looks as if someone's had quite a party here." He pointed at a couple of maintenance women repairing plasma burn holes down the length of the terminal's counters. A lanky male janitor slowly electro-scrubbed stains out of the sandstone floor.

Ashtaru hefted her emerald-green go-bag higher on her shoulder. "This place is more exciting than the travel brochures indicated." She glanced up at the signs. "Berth ninety-three's this way." Her boot heels clacked in single-time to the tap-tap of Geb's double-time.

"Hold it." Geb peered down the corridor.

A plain-looking man of ordinary height and weight leaned against a stanchion a few doors down from the berth. He read a news screen held casually in his hand.

"Am I being a nervous-nevvie or does that face say 'nipper' all over it?"

Ashtaru glanced at the man and nodded. "Let's keep walking." She slid her thumb into her belt, close enough to the stopper that her green, glittering fingernails tapped against the black tube with each stride.

They passed the man. He idly glanced up at them, then back at his screen. Geb felt very conspicuous. At times like this, he wished he were small enough to avoid scrutiny completely. He didn't return the man's stare.

They turned a corner and stopped at a water fountain.

"Half a stell for a flaining gulp of water!" Geb said, slipping a token in the slot and standing on his toes to reach the spout. He spoke loud enough for others to hear. Spacefarers smiled sourly at the comment. Seks smirked; another offworlder shucked!

Wiping his mouth on the back of his hand, he whispered, "I say we leave the lander and take a shuttle up."

Ashtaru scanned the corridor unobtrusively before

answering. "We can set off the charges from *Eris*. They should ruin anything interesting onboard the boat without harming the berth much."

"Marek'll be mad."

"He'll be more than that if we don't get back with *Eris*."

Geb glanced around and nodded. "I don't look forward to what we'll have to deal with up at Sekharstation."

"We'll improvise."

"I was afraid you'd say that."

Jonuta walked back to his cabin, alone with his thoughts.

Verley had pleased him. A mighty enthusiastic "rape victim"! She'd brought him to release. He felt drained and not yet filled. Other women instilled in him the same feeling. All others, except for Kenowa. And Janja. *Janja*. No man had ever bested Captain Cautious in a fight. Not even the resourceful pirate Corundum had been able to harm Jonuta, either by ambush or open battle.

Janja—a primitive slave—had killed him.

Twice, he believed. Once she had Poofed his holographic projection, thinking it to be the slaver in the flesh. And then surely it was she who had murdered his true flesh, blasting his landing-boat as it descended to her native planet Aglaya. *Protected* Aglaya.

Alive again, his memories intact in this cloned body, he still could not hate the smallish blond. She had done what no other had. She had beaten him. Who else could be more worthy of his respect than his destroyer?

Someday we may meet again, Janjaheriohir.

He occasionally imagined how the meeting might proceed. It usually ended in a heat of sexual passion. No other woman could provide that feeling of conquest.

And only one other could provide the feeling of ecstasy. Only Kenowa could both drain him and leave him filled with energy, with power.

He punched the code to his cabin hatch. It unsealed.

From inside drifted the scent of burning woods and resins. A languid melody played softly, as if distant and muted. Stepping inside, he sealed the hatch and stood silently listening.

The cabin was dark but for a faint, indistinct glow between him and the bed. The incense filled the room with a haze that blurred vision even more. Slowly the music grew in intensity. With it, the ruddy glow in the middle of the cabin increased in brilliance.

Holoproj, Jonuta thought. *Of what this time?*

With eerie swirls and wisps of color and light, the glow before him took form and substance. Its color brightened to yellow, then to white. The brilliant light bathed the entire room in shimmering beams. The music rose to a crescendo. In the middle of the almost blinding light a figure took form.

She stood at just about Kenowa's height. Her skin, however, was not the brass-bronze color of Jonuta's aide. This woman's skin glowed with the color of copper-alloyed gold. Her long, scintillating hair shone like silvered gold. The diaphanous gown that draped about her high, firm breasts hid nothing of her dark areolae and small, erect nipples. The golden triangle of curls at the apex of her long thighs showed through just as visibly.

She gazed at him, her arms outstretched in supination. Her rowan lips parted and she spoke.

" 'I am the flame that burns in every heart of man, and in the core of every star. I am Life, and the giver of Life, yet therefore is the knowledge of me the knowledge of death.' "

"Who—who are you?" Jonuta asked, forcing a slight quiver of awe into his voice.

"I am that which is found at the end of desire. I am the Goddess of the Spaceways."

He bowed deeply. "How have I come to be so blessed?" he asked in a worshipful tone.

The ethereal light blazed and vanished. Before him stood the Goddess of the Spaceways, as solid as a convincing holoprojection aurasuit could be.

She moved toward him with slow, sensual footsteps. "I bring to you the answer to your troubles. I bring you what your enemies seek. I hold the solution to the enigma of the hust Verley."

"And what, O Goddess, is this answer?"

"Only the truly worthy may know. Prove yourself!"

Her golden hair whipped about as she threw her head back, The transparent gown vanished in a flare of orange light. She stood before him—naked, waiting.

He advanced, seized upon her, and proved his worth.

8

Sakyo pushed a finger at the cassettes. They slid over to Shiganu, who pushed them back.

"Do you know," Shig asked, "how long it takes to run a comparison through SIPACUM?"

They sat oncon, side by side. The cassettes slid back to Shig.

"The good captain brought these to us to analyze, not to quibble about." Sak straightened his dragon coat and leaned back in the chair, gazing out the viewing port. Computer simulations could tell him more about the conditions outside the ship, but the psychological effect of looking out into the darkness of Space rather than at the light of a computer screen soothed him.

"If you don't want to quibble," Shig said, "run your own dam' simulation."

He smoothed down the molecular binding on his deep-ruby hued shirt with one hand, running his fingers across the circular design on the front. With the other hand, he edged the cassettes back.

Sakyo thought for a moment. He enjoyed working with SIPACUM—so much so that he disliked tying it up with time-consuming simulations. He liked even less the idea of tying up his own time. He put his hand on the cassettes.

Something clattered in the tunnel outside. A muffled voice cursed.

"Sisterslicin' whitebitin' buggerhumpin' bastard sonof-abitch!"

Metal crashed and the hatch unsealed. Sak and Shig spun their chairs about and stared.

Outside the hatch, a squat, stocky man stooped to pick up the contents of a drill set.

"You're hell on tools, Vark," Shig said turning back to the con with a laugh.

"Damn' pumpsuckin' dungthumbers are *too damned light!*"

Sakyo snorted. If Vark had ever spoken a sentence without imputing sexual deviance to its subject or object, Sak hadn't heard it. He watched the short man pick up the drills.

"Do all Bleakers have the same attitude?"

Vark looked at Sakyo. Shoving the drills into their case, he said, "We don't have a flainin' attitude about anything. The universe just sucks, is all. And a Bleaker knows that from personal experience, not just from Boodaballin' philosophy." He thrust the drillcase into his grimy coveralls and stepped into the con cabin.

"You can tell Jonuta I got the flainin' lander repaired. And tell him not to get the locals so gratslicin' worked up next time."

"It's a tradition," Shig said. "Every time we go to Sekhar, we leave them something to talk about."

Vark unsealed the upper part of his coverall and scratched his chest. It always itched beneath the ornate dagger mounted on his tunic. He scratched with his left hand, which bore an armored glove. The glove he seldom wore on the job, but donned at every other opportunity. The chest dagger never left its resting place above his sternum, unless it was drawn from its sheath. In his three months on *Coronet*, that had yet to happen.

Sak watched the Bleaker for a moment, then glanced at Shig. Their eyes met and a smile flashed between them. Sak picked up the unmarked cassettes and tapped them against his fingertips.

"Say, Vark," he said, "you've never put your fist through a computer screen, have you?"

"Who wants to know?"

"We've got a project for you. Captain's orders." He put the cassettes on the ancillary con to his right. "These three cassettes have to be run through SIPACUM. We need to know where they're programmed to take the ship."

Vark snorted. Almost without thinking, he touched two

fingers to his forehead, heart, and groin. He said, "Who knows? Who cares? Why bother?"

"I knew you'd agree," Sak said, rising to go. "Comm us when you've got the answers."

The most junior crewmember of *Coronet* grunted and approached the con. His meaty hands reached for the first cassette. He inslotted it.

"Know the originary points for the dam' buggerin' programs?" he asked.

"Try Sekhar first," Shig said, joining Sak at the hatch. "If that doesn't work, you'll just have to have SIPACUM run a searchback."

Vark grunted again. "How many hours till destination?"

"We haven't got one yet," Sak said, grinning.

"Maybe we'll have one when you're done," Shig added, stepping out. Sakyo followed.

The hatch sealed shut and Vark turned to the console. "Piece of slok to be lowcrew," he muttered. *Almost makes me long for the dungfarm back home*. He tapped coordinates into the computer with fingers wider than the keys. *Almost*, he added mentally, *but not quite*.

"They seem to be following a random course, sir." The lieutenant looked up, the light from the screen limning her features in gold and turquoise. Major Zahrad stepped over to face her. He glanced at the screen with military crispness, then looked up at the lieutenant.

"They suspect they're being followed," he said, "but by a signature trace, not a tailer. We'd have been thrown off by now by such evasive maneuvers. Expect them to pick a destination sometime today."

"Yes sir," she said, and bent back to the screen.

The major watched her dark eyes scan the computer simulation. The slightest trace of non-regulation perfume touched his nostrils. He breathed it in. Why, he wondered, had he ever left the art institute for the military? The ancient statues and paintings that glorified war? TransGalactic Order prevented war and any of its supposed glories. And minor skirmishes with smugglers and thieves hardly constituted adventure.

He'd had lovers at the institute. He realized that was the

adventure he'd blindly surrendered. He'd ascetically re-fused involvement with his crew as a military man.

Maybe when I retire I'll head to Ghanj and sketch temples–

Angry footsteps interrupted his reverie. He turned to see their passenger from Sekharstation. He entered the con-cabin.

"Well?" The voice had all the charm of sand thrown in machine gears.

Major Zahrad stared at the man who was younger than he but looked years older. His loose go-suit of Peatmoss Nebula gray nearly matched his hair. Hands on hips, he stared back at Zahrad from a face of deeply etched lines. His chin thrust slightly forward, its deep cleft like the dented prow of a battered old warship.

Zahrad spoke slowly.

"We are still on trail, Myrzha Gheraka. That is our current–"

Gheraka cut him off with a savage motion of his hand.

"Why haven't we engaged the target yet?"

"The target," the major said with admirable patience, "happens to be—as we are—tachyons. Battle under such condition is, to say the least, difficult." He refrained from adding a condescending smile as punctuation.

"We don't want to engage them in battle," Gheraka said. "We want to board them and recover some items of great value and delicate nature. *Delicate*, Major."

"Then I suggest, sir, that we engage them by stealth and total surprise *when they've reached a destination*. There are procedures for this sort of operation. And I try to follow the book, in the interests of my ship and crew." He stared up at the man who topped him by several sems.

Prick, Gheraka thought, then said, "Very well, Major. Notify me when you *surmise* that they've reached a destination."

He strode from the con unaccompanied.

The lieutenant peered intently at the screen, hearing the silence left in the passenger's wake. *Bullying prick!* She tried to ignore the tapping of the major's fingers against the console. Only when she heard him walk slowly away from the con did she allow the breath held tightly in her chest to escape. She searched her insy-bag for an Enkephax tablet and found none. Deciding that tension would keep her alert, she continued tracking the tenuous flow of coded ions from the target spacer billions of kloms ahead of them.

Thousands of parsecs away from either *Paraida* or *Coronet*, Marekallian Eks faced a group of young and old Arepienese. All had been brainboosted to an awareness level sufficient that anything he said in his lecture would seem self-evident to them. He lectured only to trigger associational paths in their memory matrices so that recall and utilization would be easier after his departure.

"Disease," he said, walking slowly back and forth in front of the ruddy faces, "is caused by several outside factors. Germs, bacteria, and viruses are three forms of microscopic life that can attack the body and cause weakness, illness, or death. Various chemicals in the soil or in foods can trigger toxic reactions–" He paused, watching their eyes. Satisfied that most of them were "remembering" and listening with interest, he continued.

"Such toxic reactions have almost identical effects. The healing power of certain other compounds can be discovered by experimentation." He paused and addressed Rakhin Oualama Q'yaba.

"Are you making lists of your people's folk remedies?"

The Elder folded his arms, a look of displeasure crossing his face.

Still annoyed at showing up your gods, hmm? Fine. "You know that medical companies will pay well for any indigenous plants or animals that possess new hormones or protein complexes for research. Some planets have become quite wealthy members of the galactic community by that method. Of course—" (he slowed his speech to somber, direful tones), "repressive military segments such as TAI or TGW—even TGO—may not find it in their interest to allow a Protected planet to amass any real wealth."

Eks watched their puzzled reactions as their special encephaloboosts transferred his own political philosophy to their conscious minds.

"These agents of suppression can blast you right back into your current condition. They have no morality, no scruples, no goal but the maintenance of their positions of power.

"However . . . they have very little power over individuals. They may hold whole planets in their merciless grip, but once you have reached the spaceways, you will be free. It is imperative, then, to build your ships and send as many of you away from here as soon as you can. Only then will they be forced to recognize you as a spacefaring race, free to roam at will and return in peace."

Eks paused. "I seem to have diverged a bit from my subject." *Like hell.* He looked at the faces before him, seeing rage, fear, revulsion. *And every time they think about TAI or TGW, the imprinting will reinforce itself.*

"I might use this unplanned digression to ask some questions of all of you." He chose his words carefully. "Now that you realize that people as ungodlike as I can drop out of the skies, how will this alter your rituals and worship?" He looked at the woman in the front row. "Yarala?"

"Flying boats will make it much easier to reach the shrine towers. Why, we could even re-enact the Desce–"

"*Silence!*"

All eyes turned toward Rakhin Oualama Q'yaba, then turned away in shock. He stood, pointing at Yarala. His hand made a fist, his thumb pointing at her from between index and middle finger.

"Biah'Rakhin Mayekalliah admits that he is no sky god. He has brought us much, but he is still *ba T'yaba*—Outsider. I am truly sorry, Mayekalliah," he said, lowering his arm and turning toward the Galactic. "The clan T'yaba still has its pride."

The Elder turned back to Yarala. He stared coolly at her trembling body. Slapping his thigh twice, he snapped a name: "N'gyah Oualama M'yaba!"

A muscular young man arose from the middle of the group and stepped forward over the legs and shoulders of the others. He looked sad, knowing what the Elder desired.

"Follow her from the village," the old man said. "She is to remain in the forest or on the southern shore until the Mother has passed angles with Her Lover. That will be four days."

He paused to glare at Yarala with as much malice as he could muster against one who had erred in enthusiasm. "In that time, may she learn the virtue of measured thought and silent reflection."

Yarala's downcast eyes raised for a moment, glanced to Eks, then lowered again. Silently, she walked to the edge of the clearing, followed by her older brother; N'gyah Oualama M'yaba.

At the edge of the forest, he gave her a light slap on the backside—as much punishment as he seemed to allow himself after the brainboosts—and watched her walk sullenly into the darkness.

"Hmm, yes," said Marekallian, watching N'gyah Oualama return. "Now, I was discussing disease and its control. Infant mortality can be drastically reduced by the following steps—"

Marek old boy, it's a day well spent when a clue comes as easily as that one did.

Eks walked through the moonless night to his lander. Around him, creatures of the night rustled, scampered, howled, and hissed. Many of the animals and insects ran or flew from the beam of his handflash. Treading carefully through the jungle of vines and roots, he pondered Yarala's outburst.

Shrine towers are hard to get to, then. Separated by forest? Water? And then she almost said "descent." Same as most sun religions. Comets and meteors turn into gods coming down from the sky. He smiled, nodding. *A few spacecraft could be an impressive sight for such a ritual. Fireworks.*

Breaking through into the small clearing, he shone his torch on the lander, admiring the way its black exterior absorbed the light, reflecting nothing. Alloys in the hull also absorbed or refracted nearly every frequency of electromagnetic radiation, making the boat invisible to standard scanning techniques. *Eris* utilized the same technology, though her degree of detectability could be altered to accommodate traffic control on legitimate planetary flights.

Thinking of *Eris* reminded him of Denverdarian. He tried to squelch the thought that there might be trouble brewing. *If any spooks are on to us . . .* He tensed at the thought of having to fight his way off a planet again. The last scrape had resulted in the loss of two crewmembers and the destruction of a Tri-System Accord orbital cruiser.

If there was any trouble on Sekhar, I hope Ashtaru and Geb had the good sense to dump Denvo and save Eris!

Something rustled near the boat. Flicking his handflash toward the noise, he saw a dark, lithe body leaning against the hull. Eerily, she appeared to be leaning against nothing, since only her flesh reflected the light ruddily.

"I thought you'd been exiled," he said, signaling open the boat's hatch.

"This is part of the forest. He did not forbid me to speak to you." She stepped aside from the dilating hatch and watched him through half-closed eyes.

Eks noted that she had abandoned her *t'laan* somewhere between the village and the lander. Her long black hair curled over her breasts. Deep rust-red nipples peeked through the swirls.

Something . . . *pheromonal* about her made him pause on his way into the craft. He nodded toward the interior.

"Come on in."

She followed him inside, where she stared in wonder at the plasteel surfaces and cyprium bulwarks.

"I should give you a mild memory wipe as punishment for approaching the lander. I'd warned all of you—"

"I want to be the first of my people to leave this planet. Take me with you when you go."

Marekallian Eks threw his head back and laughed.

Yarala lowered her own head slightly. Still she looked down on him from her height. Even so, she had created the illusion that she was looking up at him, imploring.

"Biah'Rakhin Mayekalliah—I look at the sky tonight and I see the stars and I know they are as full of life as the forest. I want to see it! New worlds, new people—"

"All a spacefarer usually sees is grimy spaceports and fragged-up crew from other spacers. They drink, they fight, they fuck." He suddenly reached out and grabbed her arms. "You—you're so lovely and gentle. Sometimes I feel like Shaitan himself for bringing you and your people into this. The spaceways are not for kind people.

You'll become hard and bitter—gray—when your dreams face reality. Stay here and send your children to the stars. They won't know a life any different."

She stared at him with tears forming in her eyes.

Damn. I've frightened her. Pulling her close, he lowered her head to his chest and held it there, stroking her hair, feeling her flesh against his clothes. He fought the fear that surfaced whenever he faced a truly adventurous person. Those willing to jump happily into the unknown shocked him, saddened him with their naivete.

"Every dream you have could be destroyed out there, Yarala."

"Is it not better," she asked through small tears, "to have a dream and see it die than to have no dream at all?"

"Once you leave your world, you might never return. You must think long and hard." His hand unconsciously rubbed her strong shoulders, her smooth, warm back. She pulled closer to him.

He found himself thinking not of his mission, or of shrine towers, or of his missing ship and brother. He thought only of her burning body against his, and his loneliness.

When she offered her lips, he accepted greedily.

"It's an indignity I refuse to suffer!"

Geb stared up at Ashtaru's face, a look of cold anger in his hard brown eyes.

Ashtaru ran a comb back through her green, straight hair and fingerflipped when she'd finished. "Doesn't mean a jinkle to me. How else will we fool any nippers that may be hanging around?"

Geb sat up in his seat. The shuttle steward had asked him to stow his beamer in the weapons locker near the con. That always made him nervous. He wore his stopper instead, as did most of the spacefarers taking the shuttle up to the orbiting docking facility. The weapon (which he always kept on setting Three) did little to soothe his anger. It was the principle of the thing. He took offense at any bureaucratic effort to disarm him, no matter how sensible.

"I don't know how we'll deal with them. I just think

we're conspicuous enough that my pretending to be your brat wouldn't fool anyone tipped off about us.''

"You're assuming a rare efficiency on the part of the Sekhari civil service. Odds are they don't even communicate with each other.''

Ashtaru stopped combing her hair and looked out the side window. The planet spread out overhead in a vast curve of reds, browns, rusts, and yellows. Only one small patch of pale, sickly blue was visible on this portion of the planet—the Great Northern Sea. She had seen lakes larger than that on other worlds.

The pair spoke quietly. They had picked seats to the rear, away from others. The flight had passed uneventfully and they spent the hour discussing strategies. Ashtaru had made the last suggestion out of desperation. She gave up.

"If it wounds your sensibilities to use your Gri-given talents—'' she ignored the acrobatic suggestion he interjected, ''—we'll just have to act on the inspiration of the moment. And you know how Marek frowns on that.''

"Looks as if the time's arrived.''

An orange light glowed over their seats. One minute until docking. Geb looked across the aisle to see the bulky wheel of Sekharstation out of the opposite window.

No one stood outside the docking berth.

Without incident, Ashtaru and Geb walked cautiously down the connecting tunnel to the hatch of their spacer. The cheap phosphor lights of the tunnel, Geb noted, colored Ashtaru's hair and clothes an even more unappetizing green than their actual (artificial) hue. He listened at the hatch.

The flexible connecting tunnel had a significant bend in it from snaking to reach *Eris*'s hatch. This prevented anyone in the station's corridor from casually peering in and having a straight line-of-sight to the hatch. Geb was thankful for small favors.

They both drew their stoppers. Ashtaru signaled the hatch to unlock and cycle open. The hull had a grayish tinge to it—an overcoating that would be shed soon after departure. The spacer would then be almost completely non-reflective to light, microwaves, and most other portions of the electromagnetic spectrum.

Geb crouched down and ducked silently inside the airlock. Ashtaru followed, walking tall and loudly.

The outer hatch sealed. The ship's lights colored her clothing more favorably than those in the tunnel. She sniffed at the air.

"Smell that?" she whispered.

Geb nodded. "Seks are born sweating." He reached up, set the inner hatch cycling, and jumped noiselessly aside. His fingers tightened around the stopper grip.

Ashtaru unsealed the molecular binding of her blouse in one swift motion. Her small, high breasts lay exposed. Excitement hardened her dark brown nipples. She held her stopper behind her go-bag.

The inner hatch unsealed. The green-haired woman stood nearly nose-to-nose with the uniformed Sekhar Security man inside. He was young, with weathered desert skin and a leer that took in all of Ashtaru's body in one long glance. His stopper pointed straight at her.

"Welcome aboard, Licorice-cake. Do you always strip before–" The guard's voice caught on his next word. A vague, imperceptible hum replaced his words.

Ashtaru stepped back.

The security man seemed to crystalize. For an instant he looked like a grainy hologram. Then he flared into ash.

Geb held the stopper beam steady. The ashes twinkled away into scintillating motes that sparkled temporarily and vanished. He had been *Poofed*. Fried. The stopper beam had reduced him to particles and then cleaned up after itself. Geb switched off the beam.

Hearing the click, Ashtaru jumped forward into the ship's tunnel. She held her stopper out, ready for use.

Geb slapped the cycle switch and followed her. "Let's zip up and redshift!" he said in a low hiss. The hatch sealed behind them.

"If there's no one else to deal with. And must you keep that thing on Three? What if he was wearing a lifelink?"

"Those cheap Seks? Small chance, Ash. They probably won't notice he's gone till he misses a caf-break."

"Keep dreaming."

Geb stopped at one of the computer terminals posted at strategic points throughout *Eris*. He tapped in a series of commands. "You're the one that's so sure they're incompetents." He looked up at her dusky face. "They sure found it easy to get someone onboard."

"All the compartments are sealed from the main tunnel."

"That's what I'm checking now. Life scan shows us alone. All the compartments read sealed since we left. Except for the airlock. And your tunic. Seal up—you're making me feel like a Jarp."

"Just because you're hung like one–"

"You'll never know, Ash my stash. I'm small but fun. There." He jumped away from the terminal and pulled his go-bag farther up on his shoulder. "The con's open—let's go."

They ran through the main tunnel to the con-cabin. Ashtaru had to sprint to keep up with the little man. He ran in such a way that he barely touched the deck long enough for the balls of his feet to make contact and propel him forward. His daily exercise and ingestion of muscle enhancers made him a match for people twice his size.

That most Galactics were more than two and a half times his size hardly fazed him. He carried the Great Equalizer in his holster.

They arrived at the con-cabin full speed. Ashtaru sealed the hatch while Geb stashed their bags and strapped in. He mentally cursed Denverdarian for leaving the seat out of adjustment, then regretted thinking ill of the dead. *Gri's grick*, he thought, *Denvo got us into this mess. Why should I gnash for him?*

He switched on the commsender. "Spacer *Eris* to Sekharstation. Request clearance to depart." He could guess what the answer would be.

"Ship *Eris*, this is Sekhar Security. We show you as having a detain request. Please do not power until we've checked this out."

Geb bit his lip and ordered SIPACUM to power up the ship. He released the connecting tunnel by firing off explosive bolts around the airlock's outer hatch.

"Uhh—*Eris*," the voice on the commbox said nervously. "We show you powering. The connecting tunnel has disengaged, activating the pressure seals. Please unpower and await reconnection.''

"Tractor field," Ashtaru said. She strapped in while consulting the array of telits glowing before her like a tray of bright gems.

"I sure wish we had that TDP now. Denvo's never made such a big bungle."

"He won't anymore," Ashtaru noted. "You're not planning on using the slipfield, are you?"

"Can you think of another way out? They've got us grappled."

She flipped her fingers. "I hear threats work well."

Geb looked up over the side of his chair. "That would be all Marek wants—a whole planet complaining that *Eris* tried to shoot up their only station."

"Just a thought."

"I think it would be preferable to have them think their tractor field failed. Besides—Marek's been itching to have the thing tested since we built it." He started tapping at the keyboard with his small fingers. Codes and initialization sequences flashed across the screens before him.

"Without the anti-glitch device, it may be a short experiment. You could frag every circuit on the ship."

He smiled at her, his fingers working the keys by touch. "That's what circuit breakers are for."

She threw her hands up and turned back to her telits. "They've got cyber-searchers on the hull." A thin film of perspiration broke out over her skin.

"This is Sekhar Security. You have not unpowered nor acknowledged our transmissions." The voice sounded alarmed. They must have tried to contact the guard posted onboard *Eris* and received no reply. The game had suddenly taken a quantum leap in seriousness. "You are hereby ordered to—"

Geb switched off the comm. "Frag this slok," he muttered, sending the last of his commands to SIPACUM.

He pulled a cassette from the rack on his left and inslotted it. The program it contained ordered SIPACUM to find any safe entry in subspace and take the ship in to defeat infinity with two loud buzzes as thirty seconds' warning.

"Watch this, flainers."

He actuated the program he'd given SIPACUM. The ship's attitude thrusters edged it a few dozen meters from the side of the station. The tractor field prevented any further motion.

"Here's where we find out how good an engineer Marek is." Geb threw a switch.

The lights dimmed. Ship's power routed into a field generator that emitted a circularly polarized field of synchrotron radiation. The frequency of the field matched that of the tractor field but was directly out of phase. The full power of the ship fought at resisting the field generated by the much more powerful space station.

Ashtaru felt a wave of nausea overcome her. Every cubic sem of her body seemed to be turning to jelly. *Musla—could it be taking energy straight from my body?* She looked over at Geb.

In the faint light, he looked seriously ill. Telits glowing. A weak red illuminating his face. He frowned.

As swiftly as a Narjeelan roobaball. the countervailing forces batted *Eris* away from Sekharstation and into open space. Geb actuated the SIPACUM cassette and blasted away from the station under full proton-proton reaction engines. The p-p engines took them up to full acceleration in a few seconds.

"Don't you want to hear what they're saying about you?"

Geb glanced at the commbox. "No—too busy with the ship. It needs too much power to run safely without a TDP. If only Denvo—"

SIPACUM buzzed twice.

"Damned alarm sounds like teeth being sawed off. Hang on." He checked his straps and gripped the armrests.

Ashtaru scanned the computer simulation of the ship's aft view. "There's a policer closing in on us."

"Let 'em eat tach—" Geb swallowed hard as he felt invisible hands try to squeeze him smaller than he already was and stretch him out like Lanatian gumtaffy. The disorientation filled him with a queasy disquiet bordering on nausea. He withstood it with Stoic silence.

Ashtaru moaned once or twice, her eyes tightly shut and

tearing. She always experienced a rushing, spinning sensation, as if she were being sucked down a whirlpool.

Their sensations lasted only a few seconds. By the time they had recovered, *Eris* and all inside it had become an organized cloud of tachyon particles moving faster than lightspeed.

"Congratulations, *Myrzha* Geb Mardurki. You've managed to test a device that makes me just as ill as subspace entry." Ashtaru unstrapped and stretched.

Geb started the ship spinning for some artificial G-force. Inslotting a blank cassette into the programmer, he called up star chart simulations and began the tedious process of plotting a course for Arepien.

He felt no sympathy for Denverdarian Eks.

9

Vark looked at the readout again and glowered. He cursed under his breath. It didn't make any sense. Stiff-lipped, he told SIPACUM to verify the findings. And he waited. Flexing the fingers of his left hand, he listened to the grind of metal against metal made by his armored glove. The panel directly before him flashed a blue light and displayed a message. Vark frowned and gritted his teeth.

"Same slicin' answer!" He scratched around the black optic implanted in his left eye socket. "Ballbreakin' bitchslicers."

"Anything, Vark?"

The deep rumble of that voice was followed by its owner as Jonuta entered the con-cabin. He was followed by Kenowa in a wig (deep indigo), a few spots of SpraYon (varicolored but mostly black and indigo), and precious little else.

"If these're someone's navigation cassettes, Captain, I'd take a flight back to Bleak rather than be on the poor bug's ship!" The Bleaker pulled the last one out of the slot and held it up as if it might be a carrier of Meccan tongue-rot.

"This one here, f'rinstance. It's got an open origin on it. You can use it from any point in space—just input your coordinates and it has SIPACUM plot everything for you and shoot you to your destination." He set the cassette to one side, with distaste. "Very elegant. Trouble is it takes you to a part of the Carnadyne Void that's never been explored. Not officially, anyhow."

Jonuta nodded, standing before the con and looking out into the parsec abyss. "Sounds as if we can consider it explored, now."

"Uh. And this one"—Vark held up another cassette, this one newly marked and numbered—"leads to another uncharted . . . place. On the *far* side of the galaxy!" He set it on top of the first with a little clicking sound. "A long trip, considering that it apparently drops you into deep space once you get there."

Kenowa sighed with quiet boredom and eased her voluptuous curves into the third chair. Idly she flipped on the holoproj and selected a holomelodrama she hadn't seen for some time. *The River Nihil* portrayed the adventures of a slavegirl in a legendary land called Egypt.

(Kenowa's collection of mellers—holovisual mellerdrammers—constituted an impressive assemblage of what was once called truconfessions and bodice rippers—a sexistly female form of pornography. She enjoyed the subjectified sexual parts, the domination. They relaxed her, titillated her everready appetite for arousal unto consummation, and provided her with raw material for little surprises for her man. Her Changes, they called them. Jonuta delighted in each new Change Kenowa came up with. So did she.)

"This one," Vark was saying while he watched that extravagantly formed body snuggle into the chair, "at least takes you somewhere that's charted. It leads to a planet called Arepien. A Protected planet."

Jonuta's eyes widened a bit. He continued to stare out at the stars drifting lazily from the blurred field of bluish light dead ahead. Thinking, he hardly saw any of it.

Arepien, he mused, and a smile traced the edge of his mouth. *So whoever owned these cassettes must've been a slaver. Or* someone *with an interest in sticking its nose where policers forbid it.*

"Know anything about that planet, Vark?"

The Bleaker rubbed at his jaw, then reached down to scratch idly under the dagger sheathed at his chest. "I've been on one planet in my life—Bleak. That was enough to send me into space and keep me here. I don't touch down on planets and I don't know much about 'em."

"You've always remained onboard when the rest of the crew went onplanet?"

"Same as I do on *Coronet*, Captain," Vark nodded. "On the ship, or no farther than the space station." He put

the third cassette atop the other two and leaned back in the
mate's chair, watching Kenowa glance longingly at the
inactivated holo. Then she returned her gaze to her man.
"If you ask me, Captain, I'd say Galactics should get into
space and stay there. Here. Leave the dirt behind."

He's absolutely fobby, Kenowa thought, while Jonuta
nodded, hardly listening. His thoughts strayed to his finan-
cial situation.

His resurrection had cost him nearly everything except
his ship. Now he was in debt to Miko Kita, who had
presided over his . . . resurrection. He'd had little left after
the destruction of his interplanetary caches of wealth by—
presumably—TGO. The load of walking cargo he'd taken
to Sekhar had paid for the trip and gotten him current.
They were common stuff, four men and two women.
Young. Attractive. Drifters that happened to get caught in
Jonuta's net. Hardly worth the effort of him who had so
recently rivaled Ramesh Jageshwar, so-called King of the
Slavers, in wealth and influence.

Jonuta forced a calm over himself and picked up the top
cassette. Turning it over in his hands, he watched the
reflection of con-lights from its black surface.

Arepien. He had no idea what the inhabitants looked
like. Certainly he knew that primitives off Protected planets fetched superb prices. They were novelties especially
dear to the decadent and bored. Curiosities, trinkets,
playthings.

Jonuta decided with an abrupt nod.

He inslotted the cassette and issued a string of commands to his First Mate, which was what he called
SIPACUM. His pride in the quality of *Coronet*'s led to his
repeated remark that he'd had nine First Mates, none of
which had ever died or been fired. And none ever backtalked
the captain.

Vark watched his captain program a course change. An
off-white light glowed briefly in indication that SIPACUM
understood the commands input and the information on the
cassette. Immediately after the light winked off, a turquoise one flashed. *Initiated*. After a few seconds, all the
lighted panels flashed three times. First Mate had made the
course change.

Jonuta switched on the inship commlink. "Changing course for planet Arepien. Object: check out the pickings. Prepare all necessary equipment for onplanet recon and recovery."

Next he programmed the spacer to detect other ships at maximum possible distance and issue immediate alerts if any appeared suspect. Meaning dangerous to *Coronet* and Captain Jonuta of Qalara.

"Vark: prepare both landers, just in case. And there are packets of colorful junk in bay seven—put those in the lander. Sometimes it helps to bargain."

Vark nodded and moved out of his chair to head for the hatch. The Bleaker paced with quick, sure strides when he chose to.

Glancing back at a readout, Jonuta added, "Arrival in fourteen hours, so get some sleep between now and then."

"Firm, Captain."

"Oh—and make copies of those cassettes and give me the originals." Jonuta accompanied his little smile with a wink.

"Firm," Vark said, and redshifted the con-cabin.

Maybe now we'll have a chance to start all over again. He smiled at Kenowa. *New Jonuta, new fortune!*

"Target changing course, sir."

Zahrad twitched a dial, switching to a view of the other screen. The computer simulation displayed a snaking ruby curve that represented the path of their quarry in non-spatial perspective. The curve altered sharply at a point and headed off in nearly the opposite direction.

Major Zahrad switched to a holoproj view and interlaid a galactic scale-map on the simulation.

"Any ideas, Lieutenant?"

"Lots of planets in that direction, sir. They could stop at any one. Or they may plan another course change." She turned to look at her superior, awaiting his order.

"Take the con and stay on the trail. I'm going aft. Keep the crew on standby alert."

"Firm, Major."

I can feel it. Something's about to congeal. Zahrad sighed quietly, then rose from the command chair and left the con-cabin. *More action. I suppose that will please* Myrzha *Gheraka.*

Moving slowly, Major Zahrad felt his age.

They had spent the short Arepienese night wrapped in lovemaking. Well into the morning of the planet's first sun, Marekallian Eks lay on the acceleration couch he had converted to a makeshift bed. One arm lay across the smooth red shoulders of the woman beside him. The lander, sealed, admitted no sound from outside. Only the gentle buzz of machinery provided a background of soothing white noise. He shifted a little and his fingers moved down to the slope of Yarala's breast.

The *pinnngg* of the alarm sounded twice as loud as usual and made him jerk as if in guilt.

He needed only an instant to orient himself. Sitting up on the couch, he turned from the naked girl-woman without a thought of her, and punched at the keyboard on his side of the bed.

Yarala stirred, made a little sound, turned over. Muzzily she watched him work. Her lips slowly formed a smile at the memory of the night just past. *With him, with him.* Then she was fully awake, and the smile vanished as she took in the nervous speed with which Eks tapped out commands. She sat up quickly, with hardly a jiggle of girlishly taut breasts.

"Is something happening?" she asked—just as the lights dimmed and the buzzing sounds died.

"There's a ship up there, orbiting. And it's not *Eris.* Could be a spook. I'm powering down to broadcast as little energy flux as possible. I'm hoping they haven't already scanned me."

The hatch whined open.

"Head back to the village, Yarala. I've got work to do." He turned to plant a swift kiss on her mouth. It opened softly, but he pulled his head back. "And don't worry. Just . . . if you see any hint of bright light, fall to the ground and cover your eyes."

With a slap to the tight curve of her backside, he reached back for the con. Forgotten on the instant, Yarala departed. Eks considered what he knew.

Big ship, moderate mass. Could be an empty freighter. He scanned the craft in passive mode. That way he picked up what information he could from its orbit, thermal index, neutrino flux, and other radiation without sending his own scanning beam. That would have revealed his position.

Slavers? Maybe—just what I need! A kidnapping incident to make offworlders unwelcome here. Damn! Thank Theba primitive societies have no mass-comm. I might still have some time.

A sonic boom demolished that hope.

While Marekallian Eks wondered who/what/how, Kislar Jonuta piloted his in-grav boat—working hard not to think about what had happened last time he had headed down onto a Protected planet in *Coronet*'s lander. (Not this one. It replaced the one that had been destroyed . . . along with Jonuta.) Sakyo sat beside him, overdressed in his freshly-cleaned dragon-shirt. Jonuta wore his dramatic scarlet coat and gray-green tights. In his broad belt he carried both stopper and plasma beamer, holstered cross-draw style.

"There it is," he muttered. "A small lander in that little clearing."

He pulled up and circled out over the shoreline, heading inland again toward the forest. Its indigo blue met the sapphire tint of the ocean along a double border of off-white sand and brown soil.

Sak watched his computer simulation. The neutrino flux from the lander showed as an occasional blue dot. "And you think that boat belongs to the same person as these cassettes?"

Jonuta grunted. "There's no spacer in orbit except ours, Sak. The cassette leads here. There's a ship called *Eris* docked at Sekharstation, according to the papers Kenny found." He banked over the village and sought a clearing deeper in the forest.

"Over there?" Sakyo pointed at a rocky patch surrounded by low trees and bluish scrub brush. "It's a couple hours' run from the village in case they decide to investigate, but it's close to the, uh, target."

Jonuta nodded and brought the little flier to a vertical landing.

•   •   •

Marek old friend, the Mindrunner thought, *it's a good thing you like excitement.* He took a deep breath and considered his courses of action. A glance at the heap of clothing on the deck reminded him that first he'd better dress.

Pulling on tan baggies, he checked that all the flaps were sealed on the dozen pockets covering the pants. Custom made for him of heavy-duty Panishi khaki, they matched the pocketed jacket he pulled on over a light blue shirt of Panishi cotton. He slipped into his boots and sealed the molecular bindings. The boots were of leather, the real thing, dark brown. Crafted for him on a Protected planet by a grateful villager, their only concession to technology was the binding.

Marekallian Eks gave no thought to the origin of his clothing while he threw them on hurriedly. His mind was dancing over his options.

Without Eris, *I couldn't fight even a lightly armed merchanter. I could win a lander-to-lander fight.* He considered the controls to the burrowing laser custom-fitted into the nose of the spaceboat. A turquoise light flashed, indicating that it could be brought online instantaneously.

I could win a fight—but where would I escape to?

He picked up some hardcopies and threw them into the trash scintillator.

Damn Denvo! Where is *he?* His blood began to race. He felt a tingling in his fingers and groin. He loved the excitement, he knew. At the same time, he preferred the kind over which he could exercise more control. He swallowed and took a deeper breath. *You've talked your way out of this sort of thing before, Marek. Bluff first, then fight if you gotta.*

He smiled. Leaning back in the chair, he put his feet up and started to weave his story. His hand idly patted the pocket that held a small stopper.

The sound of another in-grav boat coming to ground hastened his preparations. He straightened his jacket and retied the black queue of hair at his nape. Resting one hand idly on the controls to the boat's Defense Systemry, he closed his eyes partially and feigned sleep.

• • •

"Close to the other clearing, right?"

Sakyo stared at the wall of vegetation before them, then at Jonuta. He flipped his fingers. "Close as the birds go, Cap'n."

Jonuta boosted his stopper's setting to Three—Fry. He beamed the blue web of vines and branches before him. The organic matter vibrated for an instant before disintegrating into a little swirl of dust. He had cut just deep enough to make a passage through the immediate tangle. Squeezing through the opening and between two trees beyond, he motioned to Sak.

Sticky vines and barbed branches caught at their clothing. Overhead chittered and warbled birds of yellow and blue, red and pink. The interior of the forest trapped the heat of the double suns and mixed it with a wilting humidity. Sakyo's hair lay even straighter to his head and looked greased. Jonuta's black waves grew wet with sweat and humidity.

Something growled, to their right. Whipping his hand about, the Terasak aimed for the source of the noise. A strong hand stayed him.

"Calm," Jonuta muttered. "We probably don't smell like food to—that. And we don't know whether someone's watching. Just use it to clear a path."

"I just hope they don't use their teeth to clear a path to my insides," Sakyo said low, pulling vines out of his way.

The ground was seldom visible under its covering of twisting roots, vines living and dead, and patches of algae-covered water. Jonuta swatted at an insect the size of his finger because it showed too great an interest in his longcoat's prass buttons. More than once his boots slipped to throw him against a tree trunk or into a curtain of mossy vines. Sak fared less well.

"Whoever it is certainly won't be expecting us to sneak up on him this way." Sak broke a branch out of his way with an angry crack.

"*Sh!*" His captain had stopped.

Two smooth-boled trees ahead, the forest ended. In a small circle of sickly turf rested a sleek black boat. Its surface revealed no detail because of its light-absorbent paint job. Any shadows cast on it were lost in the craft's perfect blackness.

Jonuta smiled, one brow up. *Cautious bastard!*

Signaling Sakyo to head around to the far side of the clearing—keeping to the trees—Jonuta paused a few moments and picked the last bits of jungly forest from his clothing.

"In position," a tiny voice said in his ear.

Raising the wristcom to his lips, he whispered, "Firm. Stay hidden, Sak."

Jonuta stretched and casually strolled out of the jungle. Thumbs in belt, eyes taking in the view. He could have been wandering by for a morning chat. At the lander, he cordially rapped on the open hatch, three times. He heard no reply. Shoving a hand into his coat pocket, he walked in.

A tall, slim man sat back in his acceleration chair, apparently asleep. Jonuta pulled his hand from his pocket as he approached.

"Here," he said, tossing three black objects onto the man's stomach. "I was just passing through and thought you might want these back."

Eks didn't bother pretending to awake. He looked down at the three unmarked guidance cassettes, his forehead knotted in puzzlement. Slowly his brow unwrinkled and his eyes widened. His hand moved away from the DS control to pick up the modules. He gave Jonuta a bland, brows-up look. Guileless, wide open. He covered well; Jonuta was an impressive figure.

"I'm afraid I don't know what you're talking about."

The newcomer flipped his fingers. "Pity. There's a ship called *Eris* over on Sekharstation. Sitting there running up a devil of a docking fee."

Eks swallowed. His finger tapped slowly against the cassettes.

"By the way, I couldn't help noticing that you're here without a ship in orbit. Shall we talk about that?"

Eks drew a deep breath while he turned the cassettes over in his hands. At last he set them on the console. "I don't see that there's much to talk about, though I do thank you for this gift. Might I ask how they came into your possession, *Myrzha* . . .?''

''Haruna. Alydar Haruna, captain of *Boskone*.'' Jonuta inclined his head amiably and leaned against a bulkhead, watching the other man with more care that he showed. ''I bought those on Sekhar from a drunken Outie–''

·''That son of–'' Eks almost jumped out of his chair. A push from Jonuta's left foot sent him back.

''Oh,'' Jonuta said, ''you know him. A jacko named Denverdarian Eks.''

The other man sighed. ''My brother.'' Shaking his head, he looked up to the overhead and asked the world, ''What will the Institute do to me now?''

''The . . . Institute?''

''My name is Marekallian Eks. I'm an anthropologist and sentenologist for the Institute of Hominid Studies on Qalara–''

''You picked the wrong planet. There's no such institute on Qalara.''

Marekallian paused, staring at this fancily-coated spacefarer. ''I suggest that you check again,'' he said as calmly as he could before he added the lie: ''There most certainly was one two years-ess ago!''

Jonuta smiled. ''Unfirm. No institute would finance an illegal study of a Protected world.''

Eks let a thin smile lift his lips. ''The IHS doesn't question my methods as long as my results are acceptable.'' He put his hands behind him and leaned back in the chair again. ''Besides, I've made no contact with the natives here, so there's no taint of–''

''*Mayekalliah*!'' Behind that shout Yarala ran into the boat, ducking under through the low hatch. ''Another boat fell from the sky–'' She stopped when she saw Jonuta. Wearing only an *oh-oh* look, she stared, her breath labored.

Thanks, Marekallian Eks thought.

Jonuta smiled. ''Nice looking crew, Professor Eks.'' His gaze moved up Yarala's long, slender *red* form in swift assessment. Hominid all right, *and* mammalian, and sparsely haired. He glanced around the cabin.

''For your personal use?'' he asked, nodding at dozens of liters of encephaloboosting compounds.

Marekallian's eyes widened. His hand edged closer to his jacket.

"I like to keep up on things," he said. *Move out of the way, you dam' fool girl,* he thought, *or I'll have to zap you both.*

"Sounds like too much of a good thing. Especially when she speaks Erts." Jonuta looked again at Yarala, and smiled. "You know, I've never met a Mindrunner before." And he turned back to Eks–

In time to see the Mindrunner level a ministopper at Jonuta's face.

"I hope you think the honor's worth it, whatever your name is, because I've met agents of TGO before."

Jonuta laughed. This was too much! He hoped Sak was hearing it all via his captain's wristcomm.

"You deranged little thoughtlegger! What interest would The Gray Organization have in your meddling? Their only concern is in preventing war." *And maybe just ruining the fortunes of those they think do 'em dirt.*

Marekallian's jaw tightened. He was silent for a long moment. Then:

"Of course. But since you introduced yourself without the usual fanfare of TransGalactic Watch or TAI, I take it that you have as little legitimate purpose here as I have." He smiled back at the crimson-coated man. He did not lower the barrel of his little stopper.

Yarala watched in shock, her gaze darting back and forth between the two men. The one in scarlet, black and gray-green puzzled her. *I'd thought his enemies would be ugly. Monsters. This one—this one is handsome. And strong.*

The blood in her head threatened to pound its way out. She leaned against the bulkhead. Meanwhile, Jonuta held his smile and said nothing.

"Ahh," Eks said to fill the silence. "Who besides a Mindrunner would be interested in a Protected planet? Scout for the pharmaceutical companies? Prospector for TMS Mining?" His fingers flexed on the ministopper. "Or maybe you're a slaver, come to steal living flesh." His voice dripped loathing.

"That makes two of us," a voice said.

Eks turned swiftly to see Sakyo in the hatchway. The

stopper he held was full sized and looked huge to the Mindrunner. When he looked back at Jonuta, Eks was staring down the barrel of another stopper.

Marekellian Eks lowered his own weapon.

"Of course, I'm not one to judge my fellow man." He grinned, slowly pocketing the stopper. He put his hands in plain view on the arms of the chair.

"I don't believe I caught your real name, Captain *Haruna.*"

"I am Jonuta, a Qalaran."

The Mindrunner ran up an eyebrow like a flag. "Sometimes I can barely get the Onboard News Service out here. Last I heard was that you had, uh, been permanently stopped." He looked at his fingernails. "Not that I follow crime reportage, naturally."

Jonuta holstered his stopper. "I'll avoid using the cliché about rumors of my demise. The evil slaver still covering you is Sakyo. May we converse civilly?"

Eks flipped five. "Let Yarala outside. She's been exiled. Can't go back to her village."

"Keep an eye on her, Sak."

"Hard not to, Captain." The smallish man from Terasaki inclined his head toward the exit. Yarala looked from him to Marekallian.

"It's all right, Yarala. Just some sky-god business that has to be cleared up. Wait outside." He smiled gently.

She hesitated a moment, biting the corner of her lower lip in thought. With a frustrated sigh, she turned and departed leggily, looking down at Sak even as she lowered her head to pass through the hatchway. A puff of morning breeze caught her hair as she stepped out, swirling it about her back and waist.

Sak followed, happily watching the undulating sway of her ruddy backside.

"Business," Eks said at once. "You somehow got those cassettes from Denvo. I know only that my ship isn't here. I'm stranded without *Eris*. Take me and my lander onboard your spacer when you leave and I'll provide you with as many pieces of . . . cargo as you please."

The slaver folded his arms and laughed. His black eyes sparkled with delight.

"I can take all I want whenever I want! Why would I need your help?"

Marekallian Eks spoke slowly, choosing his words with great care. He had not overlooked the pulsar beamed in the holster opposite Jonuta's stopper. He didn't know that the slaver would hardly ever resort to using it, or to using the Fry setting on his stopper.

"I can convince the natives to go with you willingly, Captain Jonuta. I can provide those that are already brainboosted. It's in my interest to get as many of them onto the spaceways as possible. Even as slaves, they have a chance to escape or be freed. Maybe a few will return here and ruin Arepien's Protected status. They–"

"Nice altruistic motive you've given yourself! What's in it for you?"

Eks stood up slowly, looking eye-to-eye with the other man.

"I've chosen to fight for freedom. The freedom of any race to join the Galactic community."

"Even for races not yet ready for it?" Jonuta waved a hand. "They're free."

"Especially for such—and no they aren't. They are prisoners of disease and aging and primitive tools along with their beliefs."

"You're a fanatic."

"Conveniently for you! Shall we agree to it?"

Jonuta eyed him carefully, thoughtfully. *If the rest of these Areps are as lovely as that one outside, they could be valuable. That reddish skin is as rare as an Aglayan's paleness, and nearly as exotic.*

Eks stared back, awaiting an answer with concealed apprehension. This fabled slaver held the upper hand. Right now.

Always better to be friendly. Jonuta smiled and clapped the Mindrunner on the shoulder.

"Done. Understand—I can't offer you passage back to Sekhar to reclaim *Eris*. My ship is headed elsewhere."

"Perfectly understandable, Captain." Marekallian glanced at Jonuta's hand, back at Jonuta. He cleared his throat politely. The hand remained on his shoulder. Sighing, he raised his own to Jonuta's shoulder.

"Firm. Deal."

Eyes met; two arms dropped. Marekallian picked up a tan Wayne from atop a pile of brainboost ampules. He adjusted the orange-and-black headband—which Jonuta observed was *real* Saipese lichen-lizard hide—and placed the big hat on his head with studied precision.

"Now that the distasteful economics have been worked out, would the good captain care to bring his crew down for shore leave in our jungle paradise?"

10

It was another world. *Another world!*

Verley almost stumbled, not watching where she stepped. She tried to look everywhere at once. From the blue and purple trees towering hundreds of meters over her to the billowing white clouds blanketing the horizon. From the incredible expanse of blue-green water majestically sweeping to the edge of vision, to the twin stars that hung above her nearly at right angles. She stared, trying to absorb every photon of image. Her mouth was open and she neither knew nor cared.

The air that blew through her hair was heavy with moisture. It smelled of salt and soil and life. Her heart pounded with excitement. *I'm a spacefarer,* she thought.

And: *There* are *wet worlds!*

Kenowa waited patiently for the woman in front of her to descend the short ramp from the lander. *Tourists!*

Yet she admired the childlike enthusiasm of the younger woman she thought of as a girl. After a while, planets began to look the same. Especially the ones without civilized facilities. The only real adventure a seasoned spacefarer experienced was ultimately in the mental-emotional realm. She soared with Jonuta to domains far more exotic than the planets of the spaceways.

Eventually Verley moved on, ambling out onto the soft loam and turning around.

"Isn't it beautiful?"

Kenowa nodded. Her smile was pure kindness to the novice. They joined Sakyo and Jonuta before a throng of curious Areps. Marekallian Eks removed his Wayne and bowed elegantly.

"Captain—you didn't tell me that your crew included the

loveliest ladies in this arm of the Galaxy!'' His smile was warm and genuine.

Kenowa smiled graciously. Warned by Jonuta of the local flora's affinity for fabric, she wore a close-fitting concoction consisting mostly of SpraYon. The design she had chosen captured the color of a Jarp's skin—bright orange. It contrasted stunningly with the overabundance of blue on this planet.

Noting the Arep's lack of clothing taboos, she'd covered her legs with an orange zebratige design. Her own bronze flesh provided the alternate pattern. The gold braidwork about her waist supported a black breechcloth of ridiculously small proportions. Nothing covered her torso but a thin film of moisture from the humidity.

Kenowa understood the necessity of mystery. She could have worn no clothing at all without offending the local population. Instead, she had elected to use the orange SpraYon to create an intricate pattern around her breathtaking décolletage that seemed to reveal everything while actually exposing nothing.

The native males watched her with extreme interest. They hardly noticed Verley, who wore the beige flight suit and a pair of brown boots that rose to midcalf. She hardly noticed them either, except as portions of the scene. She seemed trying to commit every detail to memory.

Then she saw Marekallian. Automatically she responded to his bow with a nervous bow of her own. She smiled awkwardly, regained her composure, and nodded.

''Marekallian Eks at your service, ladies.'' The gentle sea breeze flipped his longish hair around as if striving to undo the thong tying up his queue. Positioning his Wayne at a raffish tilt, he turned to Jonuta.

''I return the compliment, sir. A nice looking crew. Just four of you, then?''

Jonuta fingered some controls in his coat pocket. The lander hatch whirred into life and sealed shut. ''No. Someone's still onboard.''

Two someones, actually. Shig had drawn duty oncon, and Vark hated planets. Jonuta still considered the Bleaker a newcomer not to be entrusted with *Coronet*'s care until his worthiness had been proven to an extent beyond that of high-quality mechanic and technician.

Captain Cautious—or Captain Chicken as his shorter-lived contemporaries called him—thought it best to be vague on several points with his new . . . partner, Eks. The Outie did not press him for details.

"Hail, people of the clan T'yaba!" The Mindrunner threw his arms back and shouted loud enough for the entire village to hear. He spoke in a bastardized mixture of Erts and T'yabish, punctuated with grand gestures.

"Greet these visitors! They are spacefarers just as I am! Their desire is as great as mine to see the clan T'yaba become the first clan of Arepien to travel to the stars. I personally–"

"Feast! Feast!" some children shouted. Older members of the crowd took up the cheer.

"They like excuses to live it up," Eks muttered to the man at his side. "We may be in for a treat."

From the large hut at the southern point of the village circle, Rakhin Oualama Q'yaba strode with long, regal steps. His skin glowed as if oiled. He held his arm high in greeting, a friendly smile on his face.

"May your gods have sexual congress with you!" he exhorted, walking up to Eks and facing the crowd. (The Elder's qualifications for Elderhood extended far beyond his age. He knew what his people enjoyed. And he usually let them have their way.)

"The Mother and Her Lover are almost at angles. Soon will begin the Dance of the Mother and Her Lover. A feast of welcome to inspire us on! Yes." He offered his arms to Jonuta, hands bent and pointing upward, thumbs pointing outward.

"Touch the backs of his hands firmly and repeat the line about sex with your gods," Eks whispered. "That is, if you want a feast."

Noting with appreciation the many attractive women in the crowd around him, Jonuta firmly touched his palms against the back of the Elder's upturned hands and said, "May your own gods have sexual congress with you."

He looked toward Kenowa. She winked.

"If a god trysts with Its creations," Marekallian asked

in a distinct East Qalaran accent, "does It commit bestiality or incest?"

Jonuta shot a piercing glance at the Outreacher. *How does he know that accent? And know that I know?*

Eks smiled and turned to the Elder.

"Rakhin Oualama Q'yaba—I am honored that you welcome my fellow Galactics to your village. We await your pleasure." He bowed magnificently, touched the offered hands and said quietly, "They'll have far more interesting stories to tell than I, Oualama."

"And fewer questions."

Eks cleared his throat and nodded cordially. *Ahh, the sound of an Arep early warning alarm. Careful, Marek. Wear soft gloves and smile a lot.*

He smiled at the Elder. And at Jonuta.

Marekellian maintained his smile with greater ease as the evening approached. The villagers brewed a drink of singular potency—*hahabi*. The cup he sipped from was about the size of a child's head. To his left sat Jonuta, nursing his own drink. Rakhin Oualama Q'yaba sat to his right, guzzling and talking in voluble spurts.

The Mindrunner knew better than to get too drunk. He watched the assembled tribe perform an adoration to the second setting star of their binary. The boys and girls of the clan performed simple dances and carried out the chores of pouring the *hahabi* and serving the food.

Wood conies seemed to be the delicacy. Eks had already discovered the lack of large animals in the vicinity when he was trying to find beasts of burden to pull the carts he'd designed. The vegetable portion of the meal consisted of highly spiced *gliitu* bulbs. Eks had had difficulty thinking that anything colored such an intense electric blue could be edible, but had gotten over it long ago.

"Rather . . . uh—bright, isn't it?" Kenowa said, turning to address Eks across Jonuta, to her right.

"Their binary has a peak radiation output in the blue part of the spectrum, even though what we see is almost yellow. The plants filter the excess light accordingly."

Kenowa nodded and bit into one of the bulbs. It tasted startlingly hot and altogether delicious. At her feet sat a large, muscular man whose long black hair flowed over his shoulders and chest like a waterfall of jet. He offered her a drink from his goblet.

I hope the antintoxicants can handle this, she thought, lifting the cup to her lips.

Jonuta ignored the lithe, lean woman at his feet and leaned toward Eks. He hoped that the *hahabi* would loosen the Mindrunner's tongue.

"Don't you think you're wasting your time brainboosting people so primitive? Won't they just forget in a few generations and revert to their present state?"

"You can't forget evolution." Eks wiped his mouth on his sleeve and set the wooden goblet down by the log they sat on. "You can't show a people how to do something right and then think they'll forget it and go back to the harder way. No." He took a mouthful of cony and continued speaking. "The changes a Mindrunner makes are for good. And I mean for *good*. If you found an infant in the wilderness, you wouldn't just leave it to fend for itself—"

"I might."

"—you'd give it the means to survive and grow." His speech accelerated in pace and volume. "Now, TGO is committing a crime agaisnt humanity—no, against *sentiency*—by backing up the post-Imperium Accords and denying the benefits of civilization to untold worlds. They—"

"Why do you keep mentioning TGO? Their only concern is preventing war."

Eks paused, looking at Jonuta for a long moment. The smile faded. His eyes glimmered for an instant with the look of a trapped animal.

The smile returned. "Of course. TransGalactic Watch is the real culprit. It's just that TGO's clandestine method of operation makes it a convenient whipping girl." He raised his cup. "I apologize for the factual error." Taking a long draught, he smiled and said, "While I was living on Outreach, I had a chance to think about these things. It was there, among men and women who view life as an adventure to be dared to the fullest, that I decided to risk certain death at the hands of TGO—I mean, TGW—to battle what is nothing less than technological oppression! To bring the wonders of science and progress to developing people everywhere.''

Jonuta was less impressed with Marekellian Eks than Marekallian Eks obviously was. The Mindrunner hardly risked "certain death" at the hands of anyone he didn't openly provoke. The slaver knew from bitter experience how the peacekeepers of the spaceways operated. He took a long swig of *hahabi*.

"Surely you don't expect to live long enough to see the effects of all your efforts?" Kenowa asked, pulling at a strand of hair that had fallen across her jawline. Her fingernails glinted in the orange light from the bonfire being ignited in the center of the village.

"I've been a Mindrunner for six years on nearly a dozen Protected planets. My contributions"—he took another large bite of meat and washed it down with drink—"while modest, will have repercussions throughout history."

Young women and men, most already taller than Eks or Jonuta, began to dance slowly around the fire. Jonuta's gaze drifted now and then toward them. Marekallian's gaze remain fixed on those he addressed.

"No one can tell how much sooner these seemingly backward people will advance to the stars. When they do, though, it will be because I and others have committed these defiant acts here and now. And yes—I may just live to see it. Not this planet, maybe, but one or two others further along."

He smiled and finished the contents of his goblet. A short-haired girl with firm, high breasts and a look of pleasant inebriation refilled it instantly. He was obviously having difficulty focusing on Jonuta.

"Oh—" The Mindrunner swung an arm grandly about, nearly bullseyeing the Elder on his right. "I get the satisfaction of striking a blow for the downtrodden. You called it—I'm a fanatic, remember? Too, I get to see worlds few ever see—"

"And how do you pay for all this?"

Eks tipped back his big hat and leaned into the body of the willowy woman standing behind him. He tugged at his queue before stretching his arms out. "I'm the son of a wealthy Reshi priest in Menre, thanks be to Gri of Might."

He began to laugh uncontrollably. His fingers reached back to entwine the hair of the woman against whose belly he rested. "And of course," he added after a moment, "whatever tokens of appreciation the natives sometimes give me are converted right back into helping the next planet."

This drink is starting to get to him, Jonuta thought—*and me!* He set down his cup and stood, stretching.

The dancers began to chant. They were accompanied by drums patted with long fingers and instruments that sounded like low-scale flutes. The light from the fire glinted off the naked, rubicund flesh of long, long bodies. Verley, seated between Kenowa and Sak, watched in total fascination.

Jonuta moved past them and headed for the bushes that bordered the village. Areps with even more urgent calls rushed past him. They returned less frantically and looking happier. Jonuta's call, however, was not that of nature. Seeking out a secluded piece of vegetation, he spoke softly into the little commlink set into a BOOPFAITU bracelet worn by Boodists both devout and otherwise.

"Sak."

In the village, the Terasak heard his captain's voice. Shifting his body, he set his chin in his left hand. That moved his head within speaking and listening distance of his own wristcomm, which was not a Boodist bracelet.

"How're the reds working?"

Sak blinked, considering. He had taken one of the antintoxicants, but . . . "I think I'm losing it," he muttered.

"Then slack off on that booz and fake it for a while. I want you to keep an eye on Dogooderian Eks and let me know anything he does unusual."

"Uh. You know me, boss." Sakyo stared at the undulating body of a mighty young woman in the sweat of a maddened dance. Looked mighty close to 200 sems long, that one, and two meters was a lot of woman—or girl—of about sixteen. Sak seemed to be muttering boozily to himself: "I'm ever willing to engage in your inscrutable intrigues."

"Uh-huh. What's he doing now?"

"Talking to Old Baldy."

"Firm. Try to listen in. I'm coming back."

Sak lifted his head slowly, scratching his sideburn before dropping his wrist. He was farthest from Eks. Over the crackle and roar of the fire, the thut-rumble of the drums and drone of the music along with the hum of the chanting Areps, he could hardly hear Verley, right beside him. Or the native woman on his other side, who was murmuring sweet nothings in his direction. Unfortunately she had a face like a used teabag and her breasts bracketed her navel.

"It's the most beautiful thing I've ever seen!" Verley gushed, and glanced behind her. Beyond the circle of huts she could just make out the reflection of part of the lander's hull. "Spacecraft," she murmured, as much to herself as anything else. "And tribal rites. Together!"

(*I'd like to climb that,* Sak was thinking, staring at the dancer he'd singled out. *Just because it's there!*)

Verley focused her attention on Marekallian Eks. Through the warm, blurry haze of her vision, she watched him move. The crimson, black, and pale olive figure of Jonuta briefly crossed her view, unnoticed.

Seeing that Kenowa had begun to run her hands over the smooth shoulders of the entranced man at her feet, Jonuta sat closer to the dancing so that he appeared to ignore Eks and the others. Now and then his gaze took in the Mindrunner, merely seeming to drift his way.

"Biah'Rakhin Chonuda," a voice said beside him.

A woman several sems taller than he knelt at his side. Her hair had been plaited into three long tresses that reached to the gentle curve of her buttocks. Her eyebrows, dark and arched slightly upward at the ends, combined with her dark eyes to intensify the power of her gaze. And her waist was unbelievable.

"I can make the ground soft for you," she said softly. She stretched her body out and looked up to him. Her bare calf rubbed his legging.

Jonuta glanced about. Here and there, the dancers and other celebrants had commenced to recline in pairs and even larger groupings. They caressed, kissed, fondled. Still, he noticed no actual sexual activity. Satisfied that he understood the guidelines-meaning-rules, he unsealed his coat and laid it aside. The frontmeld of his tights he left alone. His hand slid onto the calf moving against him, and up her long, sleek form.

Her body was hot from impassioned dancing. Almost as hot, he realized rather wistfully, as that of HReenee, the felinoprimate he had rescued from Menekris the pirate—former pirate. Along with her step-sib HRadem. Jonuta regretted HReenee's precipitate decision to ship out—precipitately—from Qalara after his . . . death. At the time he had hardly been in a position to stop her. (HRadem's departure he regretted not at all.)

The woman in his arms reminded him of HReenee only in her warmth and by her small-breasted, slender litheness. She had other traits all her own. He enjoyed them all, if not quite fully. (Including legs and arms like a pair of sentient vines seeking to entwine him.) Almost he wished he had time to teach her a bit about kissing. She kept her mouth too widely open, too much. On the other hand. . . .

Kenowa enjoyed the Arep male who was trying to wrap himself around her plentitude in the manner of an erotically predatory vine. He let her know wordlessly how intrigued he was with her SpraYon "clothing." The rangy young rascal's long, long fingers kept tracing out the tiny "seams" where SpraYon met skin. Though long and narrow, his ruddy hands were strong. He smiled up at her, his teeth brilliant in the firelight, and began nuzzling between her breasts. A glance around informed Kenowa that it would be perfectly acceptable to clasp his head to her. She did. It was perfectly acceptable to both of them, too.

She ran her nails lightly over his muscles, long wiry muscles, and felt a tremblor and little writhe of pleasure go all through him. He nuzzled, blew hot breath on the inner surfaces of her breasts, slid a hand over her thighs. She sighed and lowered her head. His long hair smelled as fresh as sea air. She smiled into it.

His hand and mouth grew a lot fresher, too. Kenowa felt her antintoxicant losing its battle against the native booz. With long lean fingers seeking a path into her—and finding it—she didn't feel like getting out another of the red pills. Instead, she began fondling small tight buttocks while the young Arep's hands and lips played her body in a warm serenade of tactile sensation.

His head moved between the great balls of her breasts, freeing his mouth.

"My body calls me into the woods," he said in his language, reciting the Arep euphemism for the need to eliminate. "Come and hold my hand?"

Kenowa, of course, did not understand a word. That did not mean she did not understand. She accompanied him away from the firelight and its encirclement of writhing red-bronze bodies. Well into the forest, she even held his hand. Nor did she need a lot of explanation to discover that he wished her on her hands and knees, with him kneeling behind her.

Quaint, she thought, then *"uh!"* she gasped softly, when he came into her. He was not long and thin everywhere, and the hands on her hips were indeed both long and strong.

Verley took Jonuta's place beside Marekallian Eks for the purpose of seducing him. She was too far along the road to drunkenness to be good at it—though she had no way of knowing that he was dissembling his own inebriation and had no intention of being distracted. Verley had to content herself with sitting close, leaning against his arm and side. He ignored her as if she were an article of clothing.

"More *hahabi* for Rahkin Oualama Q'yaba!" he shouted suddenly, holding up the Elder's goblet, and Verley slipped.

The Outreacher handed the swiftly filled goblet to the old man, who happily lifted it to his lips while Verley lay full length and blinked in muzzy surprise at the sky. A very young Arep appeared, smiled in a flash of good teeth, and squatted. Each of his hands was immediately planted on each of Verley's breasts, while she inebriatedly wondered if she should do something about the pendant of his loins, dangling a few sems above her face.

"Now, Oualama," Eks was saying, "can't you still appreciate the rituals of the clan even though you're brainboosted so far beyond the need for such worship?"

The Elder nodded and looked down at the alien to his world. "Pos . . . pos. When it involves *hahabi*, pos. When it is here in the village, pos. But to have to sail all the way to Round Island every time the Mother and Her Lover are at angles seems so—wasteful, now. We could be constructing better huts—*homes*—building hydroponic troughs, taking better care of new mothers, making—''

''It can't take that long, surely, sailing to get to the shrine tower!'' Marekallian's hand had tensed around the base of his goblet. He wished that he had not interrupted, in his eagerness, but at last at last—he felt very close to his goal.

(Unnoticed by the two men, Verley was bereft of her attentive young swain by his mother, no less, who guided him firmly away with several stern glances back at the sprawled foreigner. A wave of soberness washed over Verley, and she began to consider the best way to re-achieve the sitting position.)

Rahkin Oualama Q'yaba shook an arm drunkenly about and had to touch the other man's shoulder to keep from toppling sidewise. ''Neg . . . no. But even three days seems so long when I think that you can travel from one entire world to another in the same time!''

Three . . . days, Marekallian Eks thought, and did his best not to show his excitement.

Verley, having eased herself back and sat up, triggered a warning from her bladder. At the same time she noted without cheer how intently Eks was listening to the Elder. With a sigh, she stood. She looked to where the Areps headed to relieve themselves and did her un-level best to betake herself there without staggering. More than one male offered support. She turned them down with something approaching couth coolth.

Once she was well into the forest and thought she was alone, she began opening the lower meld of her flight suit—the top had been open to the waist for the past half hour. That was when she heard the voice behind her.

11

"What the–"

Shiganu stared at the computer simulation of *Coronet*'s hull. He tried not to panic. Slowly, methodically, he reran the hull integrity confirmation program through SIPACUM. The anomaly showed up again in the same place. One of the ventral struts possessed a roughly circular deformity.

Realizing what it must be, Shig punched up a radiation reading.

Ion flux.

"Yark!" he shouted into the commbox. "Get up here fast!" Flipping a switch, he beamed a message down to Arepien's surface.

"Captain!" He waited for a reply. At first, he heard only muffled sounds.

"*Captain*. Emergency. Shig here."

"*What is it?*" Jonuta's voice sounded alert but woozy. Drums throbbed in the background.

"I've found a lamprey on the ship's hull. A tailer. It must've hit us just before we converted."

"*That means we should expect company. Kenny, Sak, nod if you heard all that.*" The voice paused. "*Firm. Now I want us to get back to the lander without attracting any attention. You first, Kenny. Sak, you keep watching Eks and I'll–*"

"He's getting up to go."

"*Follow him. I think he can give us some answers. Shig.*"

"Here."

"*Get to work on removing the lamprey and patching the hull. Is it over any sensitive area?*"

Shig rechecked the location. "It's over food locker

seven. I don't see much of a problem. We just might not have time."

"Work fast." The voice and the sound of drums ceased.

"Shaitan's arse!" Vark sealed the hatch behind him. "What's so Muslasuckin' important that you wake me up?"

"We're going to take a walk." Shig channeled all the ship's alarms through his wristcomm and jumped out of the chair. "Suit up."

Verley turned around to see a tall woman in the darkness.

She faced the Arep without putting her jumpsuit back on. "What do you want?"

"I saw you watching Mayekalliah."

"So what?" Half out of drunkeness, half out of a desire to insult, Verley squatted and relieved herself, avoiding the surprised eyes of the other.

"Are you his mate?"

Verley snorted lightly, sealing her suit and standing. "I haven't even spoken to him yet."

"He is very dedicated to his mission." Yarala stroked her long hair and looked Verley up and down.

"Whatever it is," Verley muttered quietly. "Why aren't you at the feast?"

"I have been cast out until the next angle of our stars. Just a few days."

Verley turned toward the village. Yarala caught her by the arm.

"Do you enjoy being a spacefarer?"

Verley's wry smile was barely visible in the gloomy bushes.

"It's had its moments."

"When did you leave your home world?"

"Last week."

"Oh." Yarala let go Verley's arm. "I want to leave Arepien. I want to see other worlds–"

"Avoid the one called Sekhar." She looked at the woman for a moment. "What's your name?"

"Yarala."

Yarala towered over Verley, yet her ingenuous attitude

made the offworlder want to . . . what? Verley frowned.
Well, that bastard did *ignore me.*

"You say you can't go to the village?"

The tall woman shook her head with a curious slanting
motion.

Verley stepped close to her and smiled. "You must be
lonely."

Yarala shook her head. "It would be nice to feel you
against me. I remember that this is not uncommon in your
cultures?" Her hand reached down to touch Verley's.

Verley smiled and grasped the hand.

"I know a place," the Arepienese woman said, "where
we will not be interrupted." She pulled her toward the
forest. Verley followed, drunk and pleased.

They walked through a darkness scarcely relieved by the
small amount of light that filtered through the *kunda* vines
from the night sky. Yarala led the way with easy familiarity.
Verley stumbled several times, but the strong arm of the
native woman caught her before she fell. Eventually they
reached a clearing.

Verley squinted. Something seemed to be blotting the
light out of a portion of the center of the clearing. She
didn't have time to consider it further. Yarala's hands
reached gently into her plunging neck line. She reciprocated,
running her hands over the tall woman's firm, smaller
breasts and over the rest of her warm soft flesh. With a
few tugs, the flight suit lay heaped on the ground to serve
as a blanket for their lovemaking.

About them, the forest was alive with the sounds of the
night so alive to Verley of Sekhar. The scent of their
bodies mingled with the sea air and the smells of the
forest. In the light from the moonless sky, Verley could barely
see her lover as they moved together, lips and tongues and
fingers coaxing each other to sensual heights. She felt
warm and tactile and drunk and happy.

Footsteps crashed through the clearing.

Verley quietly rolled over and listened. Behind her, the
blot of darkness began to whine into life. She looked in its
direction and saw an outline of light appear in the blackness.

The lander's hatch opened, flooding the area before it
with light that narrowly missed the pair of women.

Into the clearing ran Marekallian Eks. He hurried across the sward, his handflash bobbing with each step. He paused to listen. Hearing nothing, he stepped into the lander.

Verley's inebriated, sexually aroused mind formed a quick plan.

"Let's sneak inside," she said, "and rape him."

Remembering her own night with the Mindrunner, Yarala readily agreed.

Quietly they rose and sneaked toward the light-absorbing hull of the in-grav boat. Verley made it up the ramp in barefooted silence, with Yarala right behind. They fought to suppress a mutual urge to giggle. Verley had not felt so girlish for years.

Eks slid into his con chair and issued commands to SIPACUM. Oblivious to the two naked women approaching him, he ordered the hatch shut. An instant later, the engines—under manual control—kicked into life and punched the lander into the night sky.

The shock threw both women against the rear bulkhead with stunning force. The sound of the of their bodies hitting the rear of the ship was lost in the roar of the engines.

The craft's exhaust lit the night sky for kilometers around. A watching Sakyo shielded his eyes and needlessly shouted into his wristcomm.

"There he goes! What now?"

"Get to the lander. We're tracking him."

"What about Verley?"

"Forget her." Jonuta's voice held no anger, just cold efficiency.

Sakyo switched on his handflash and ran back through the jungle. After long minutes of sprinting, he said in gasps, "Go—without—me."

"No," the voice on the wristcomm replied. *"We may have to give up and get back to* Coronet *if a spook appears. We won't be coming back, Sak. Hurry. The locals looked worse than fobbed."*

Sak burst out of the forest and headed toward *Coronet*'s lander at a full run. The hatch yawned open and the engines were powering. The launch alarm wailed, keeping the curious at a worried distance.

With a shout, Sak leaped into the lander and punched the hatch shut. He wasted no time belting down into the first available chair and looked at Jonuta.

"Spacefarer First Sakyo repor–" Acceleration choked his words into a strained huff.

Jonuta concentrated on the simulation screen. The faint blip of Eks's lander was hardly visible, a testimony to its evasion engineering.

"I don't know where he's off to, but it must be someplace more interesting than the feast."

Kenowa looked at Jonuta and smiled. *Maybe,* she thought, *maybe not.*

Jonuta kicked his engines into full power, instructing SIPACUM to follow the other boat and close in to three kloms' distance. At their current velocity, that gave the boat a healthy five seconds to respond to any course changes the target might make.

The first alarm to vie for Marekallian's attention was the load distribution telit.

"Damn!" he shouted, looking around the cabin for a reason. Directly behind him, sprawled in hues of brown and red flesh, he saw the answer.

"Damn," he said again, his skill at cursing no match for a Bleaker or even most Outies. Just then the pursuit alarm sounded.

Captain Jonuta, you're about to get the surprise of your life. He ordered SIPACUM into evasive action.

The engines cut off. The exhaust ports sealed shut to prevent leaving a thermal trail. Looking behind him, Eks saw the unconscious form of Yarala and Verley float away from the bulkhead in free fall.

Sorry if you get knocked around, girls. I haven't got time to tuck you in.

The cabin went dark. SIPACUM shut down all systems except for the altimeter. The lander fell, a black radar-and-sensor-invisible mass falling through the night. Marekallian felt a thrill rush through him, the exciting terror of not knowing whether the systems could come on as they were supposed to. The chance that the lander might fall straight into the ocean at nearly four times the speed of sound raised his pulse to a rate greater than that of an orgastic peak.

The lander vibrated when the wake from Jonuta's craft, kilometers overhead, thundered past. Eks's stomach threatened to knot into itself. He could see the actinic glimmer of the other's engines reflected from the surface of the ocean he was falling toward.

SIPACUM *ping*ged once. Aerofoils eased out of the hull and bit atmosphere. The bodies hit the back of the con chair with loud thuds. A red arm dangled past Marek's head. Air brakes screamed into play, throwing him forward and crushing him against the straps.

Leveling off sharply, the lander switched on its engines and shot forward, parallel to the ocean at less than a klom of altitude.

The bodies flew back against the rear with a sickening sound.

Eks ignored his passengers and cycled through a series of computer simulations after assuring himself that he had ducked under the horizon of Jonuta's line-of-sight and was at least temporarily safe. After a few moments, he found what he wanted.

It's a round island, all right. With a vertical anomaly right in the center. He smiled and punched the coordinates into the computer. *Just about time to worship at the shrine tower of my choice.*

Jonuta watched the orange blip disappear from the computer screen. He ordered a full spectrum scan and received the results five seconds later.

Nothing.

"Just like that?" Kenowa asked, looking at the results repeated on her screen.

He ordered the ship to climb, hoping the wider angle of scan would help. "Very impressive technology he's got. He'd be quite an ally." (The higher scan revealed nothing. He banked the boat around, heading back to where contact had been lost.) *If I don't have to kill him first.*

12

Shig looked at the planet over his head. Mostly blue on both land and sea, it looked like a giant flawed sapphire suspended on black velvet. He adjusted his safety line and sealed the ventral airlock.

"Start evacuating food locker seven, Vark."

"*Firm*," the voice in his helmet replied.

Shig walked with long measured steps across the outside of *Coronet*'s hull. The molecular-bonding grippers on his bootsoles kept him from floating away—the ship's rotation had been stopped to allow him to remove the lamprey. Even in freefall the cutting laser was a cumbersome burden to carry. Shig had strapped it to his chest and reached around it to play out his safety line.

"Flainin' stashrippin' slicersucker!" the voice on the commlink blurted.

"What's wrong?"

"*Nothing*," Vark said. "*Something burst from the shitsnortin' pressure drop*." He breathed heavily with every word. Though the Bleaker disliked planets, his stomach still favored gravity to weightlessness.

"I'm over the lamprey now."

Shig looked down at the two-meter-wide patch of smooth metal attached to the hull. Had it been a computer traumatizer, they probably would have been dead by now, destroyed by some error in judgment on the part of a SIPACUM being lied to by the parasitic device.

Shig considered the tailer just as threatening. The danger lay in the future, a form of deferred deadliness. There was no way to know how soon the ship that followed the homing device would appear out of subspace. The sooner it was off, the sooner they could leave without risk of being followed.

If they weren't caught in the middle of the operation. . . .

"How's the pressure?"

"You can start, fer Boodasake. It'll be down to damnear zero by the time you cut through."

"I'm in a hurry, Vark, but I'm not going to risk a blowout. Ever been through one?"

"I got a suit on."

"Not the point." Shig undid the straps and set the tripood up over the lamprey. He powered up the laser. "If we were on some cheapshit freighter without sealable compartments, we couldn't even try this. Pressure?"

"Zero-point-fuckall."

"Right." The Terasak calibrated the distance to the nearest thousandth of a millimeter at the edge of the deformed metal leech. "Shout if I hit you."

"Thanks."

Shig switched on the cutter. A thin beam of emerald green glowed between the exit optics and the hull. Gasses and vaporized metal expanded away in a spherical cloud.

Slowly he traced the circumference of the lamprey with the green photon scalpel. After a few minutes, the slag-lined incision met its starting point and flared. Shig shut off the power.

"Did it cut through all around?" he asked.

"Nearly."

"Float up there and give it a kick." Shig strapped the laser to his chest and stood back.

"Flainin' shit!" Vark cried. *"Nearly broke my foot!"*

"I didn't see it move."

Shig heard a muffled sound of exertion. The section of hull with the lamprey attached moved outward a few sems.

"Prickstrummin' fartbreathin' stashdiggers!"

The circle of plasteel and cyprium shot away from the hull, followed by a pair of pressuresuited feet. Shig reached out to grab the Bleaker, but the stout body stopped halfway—Vark's powerful arms had grabbed the slag-crusted edges of the hole.

Shig pushed on the soles of Vark's boots, propelling him back inside. "Sorry—you can't come out to play."

"Damn' bitchfucker thing wouldn't move!" Vark grunted—as his helmet hit the bulkhead.

"Well," Shig said, looking out at the receding section of hull and lamprey, "it's moving now. It'll either go into a new orbit or burn up in the atmosphere. Hand me the patch."

A gloved hand proffered a roll of thick white material through the hole. A smear of red stained it.

"What's this?" Shig asked.

"I think it's Lanatian Cherry. Some of the skweez-paks–"

"Forget it," Shig said, grinning his relief. "Get yours ready."

He waited for Vark to position the interior patch and tack it down with low level microwave.

"Go," Vark at last said.

Shig tapped at the interior patch. The Bleaker's work was always flawless. Pulling a cannister of insulfoam from his necessary belt, he filled the void between the interior patch and the surface of the hull. Before it had a chance to set in the vacuum, he unrolled the exterior patch and laid it over the hole. Made of partially monobonded cyprium, the patch was as pliant as thick rubber until bombarded with high frequency microwaves.

Taking the bonder from his belt, he set it to tack the edges, made sure the fit was smooth, and upped the power to sealing strength.

"Got your damn' side ready?" the inside half of the repair crew asked.

"Couple of seconds. Pos."

Shig tapped the patch, now as strong as the fully-bonded monofilamental hydrogen—cyprium—that made up the rest of the hull. Stronger than steel, titanium, or even high tensile graphite fibers.

"All set. Bring it up to pressure and check for leaks. I'm coming in."

"Firm."

Shig took one last look at the planet and the agoraphobia-inspiring vista of stars and space. He unconsciously scanned for spacers, too, though *Coronet* could be vaporized from a distance great enough that no Galactic's eyes could resolve the image of a ship.

*   *   *

Marekallian Eks piloted the lander with nervous efficacy. Alternating between powerless glides and bursts of thrust, he headed for the approaching line of dawn. His gaze darted back to the computer simulation of Round Island and the decreasing distance on the telit.

Looks as if I'll have light to work by, at least.

He cut power a few kloms out from the island and coasted in silently, a huge dark bird against the reddening sky. Banking and turning, he scanned the island once for any evidence of life. He detected nothing, though the shrine tower rose prominently above the center of the island like a shiny black spike 200 meters tall.

Finding a clearing, he glided across the shoreline and fired the braking jets. The boat landed with hardly a bump. Marekallian smiled and unstrapped.

And now to—shit. He slid out of his seat to see the bruised bodies of Verley and Yarala. He unsealed the hatch and picked up Yarala.

Still breathing. Fine.

He dragged her out of the lander and leaned her against the hull. The sandy ground adhered to the blood smeared on her legs. Eks looked at her for a moment, decided that nothing appeared broken, and entered to retrieve Verley.

She had fared better. None of her bruises bled or even seemed extensive, although she remained unconscious. He dragged her out—adding a few new bruises—and set her back-to-back with the other woman—*shit, the girl of sixteen,* he added mentally.

"Sorry to leave two such lovely ladies here all naked and unravished, but business comes first," he muttered. He trotted back into the cabin and picked up the rope he had been making from *kunda* vines. At last he had a use for it!

"Wish I could be doing this under more intimate circumstances, dear cakes," he muttered, wrapping the rope about their waists, across their breasts—and snugging it in there, deliberately, wickedly—and finally around their arms. *A pretty pair. Or pair of pairs!* He admired them only for an instant, availed himself of only the swiftest (and vicious) pinch, and hurried back to the lander.

From a locked compartment he drew a large backpack and cutting laser. Shrugging on the pack and attaching the cutter to its side, he checked the weight distribution with a few practice bounces. Satisfied, he nodded and redshifted the in-grav boat.

He pressed a device in one of his jacket pockets. The lander went dark. All systemry shut down and the hatch locked shut. After one last look at all that bound naked flesh, he turned and trotted toward the sparse forest. His gaze was on the black shrine tower.

Jonuta cursed mildly.

The scan showed no evidence of the Mindrunner's lander. *That's no stock boat. Must've cost that sanctimonious phony more than most people spend on a whole spacer!*

"Hang on," he growled.

He kicked the lander straight up ten kloms and leveled off, advising the onboard computer to spiral out from the last point of contact and scan various portions of the electromagnetic spectrum.

Sak looked up from his own screen. "Want me to comm Shig?"

"No. If we have visitors, we'd only announce ourselves by sending messages up. If he's not under comm-silence, he'll comm us."

"Jone . . ." Kenowa had been watching the computer simulation.

"Uh?"

"I think I just caught a neutrino reading. Very light." Tapping a few keys, she reran the scan. "See? Can't even be lander engines."

"Um. It's something, though. A powerpak–"

"It's coming from the big island in that archipelago. The round one." Sakyo called up an enhanced image.

Jonuta smiled. "Let's drop in. Quietly."

SIPACUM responded to his gentle urgings.

Shiganu was halfway out of his mobile life support system—mlss—when the alarm whined over his wristcomm.

He clambered out in a weightless tumble into the main tunnel and sealed the hatch. He knew he had only a few seconds before SIPACUM's contingency program activated. Pulling the mlss off his legs, he cut the alarm and spoke into the comm.

"Guests, Vark. Prepare for–"

The room went dark as obsidian in a black hole. The aircon wheezed to a halt. All sound faded away until Shig was left with only the sound of his breath and his beating heart.

He felt his way to the stanchions along the tunnel and pulled himself toward the con. SIPACUM had shut down nearly all power on *Coronet*, effectively rendering the ship dead in space. Good. Shig had programmed the ship to do just this. He hoped that *Coronet*, though not as undetectable as Eks's ship *Eris,* would appear to be an orbiting derelict.

With the lamprey tailer in a different orbit and damaged, maybe it'll throw them off long enough to let me think of something.

When he reached the con, Shig sighed in relief to see the hatch partially open. Inside, Vark moved about in the dim light from a handflash.

"What the vug happened?" The Bleaker floated over an access panel, ready to tear at wires. He wiped sweat from around his TP "eye" and rubbed at his real right eye.

"I had it set to system shutdown. Let's see who's here."

Shig picked up the hardprint that SIPACUM had thought-fully spat out before shutting down. It indicated that a *destrier* class spacer had come off the Tachyon Trail at about 100 planetary radii and was now making for Arepien on its normal double-drive.

"TGW," Shig said simply. "Here's where I earn my pay."

Vark flexed his armored glove and said nothing.

13

Coronet's lander sped over the ocean at less than five meters altitude. Jonuta—flying on manual—kept the velocity as low as possible.

Sakyo scanned the beachhead with the forward TP. He frowned.

"Something on the south shore. Looks like a boat. Pos. A nice black one."

"Any readings from it?"

"Neg. The neutrino flux is from the base of that obelisk in the center of the island. The lander's dead." Sak made a sound with his tongue. "Hmm—I like what *Myrzha* Eks left wrapped up for us."

The lander rose to twenty meters height and flitted over the other boat and the pair of bound and naked women beside it. Jonuta smiled at the aerial view of Verley and the red girl. He banked toward the forest.

In the orange light of morning, a green light flashed at the base of the shrine tower. Through his protective goggles, Marekallian could see nothing but the glow of melting rock. The hiss and crack of disintegrating layers of material masked the sound of the lander circling at a distance. The Mindrunner worked feverishly, but with care and precision.

The lander, unnoticed by Eks, grounded out by *Eris*'s boat. Jonuta jumped off the ramp before it had fully extended and ran across the sand to the nude captives.

Verley had regained consciousness. She sat with her head down, struggling to get free. The *kunda* rope resisted her attempts. As a matter of fact, she had managed to get the rope in such a position around Yarala's throat as to begin strangling her.

"Homesick for Sekhar yet?"

"I'll kill that sisterslicer when I get my hands on him!" She looked up at Jonuta, fury burning in her dagger gaze.

"I may let you," he said, pulling a knife from inside his boot. He severed the knots.

Yarala fell into Sak's arms. He immediately began to restore her circulation by enthusiastically massaging every unbruised portion of flesh. After a moment, her eyelids fluttered and opened.

"The tower!" she cried, staring at the structure with unfocusing eyes. Then she collapsed.

"Leave her, Sak. Kenny can revive her. I want to see what Eks is up to."

Sak laid the unconscious Arep carefully down on the sand and glanced at Kenowa.

"I'll be all right with them," she said.

Sakyo ran into the sparse woods after Jonuta, jumping over rocks and vines and broken logs. He realized that he was still drunk from the *hahabi,* even with the antintoxicant he'd taken. He inhaled deeply of the fresh morning air, cleansing his blood and meditating on the Tao.

Verley watched them go, then knelt by Yarala to help Kenowa revive the native woman.

"Get some water from the lander," Kenowa said, checking Yarala's pupils for dilation. She took the skweez-pak from Verley and trickled the cool liquid onto Yarala's battered forehead.

The red woman rolled her head aside, reached up dreamily and dropped her arm to the sand. Her eyelids opened.

"Am I dead yet?"

"Do you feel dead?" Verley asked, smiling and taking her hand.

"Worse, I think." She tried to sit up. "This is more painful than the scourge at coming-of-age."

"Can you move your fingers and toes?" Kenowa applied BandiFasts to the cuts and abrasions on the woman's thighs and arms.

Yarala nodded in her sidewise manner and took a deep breath. She shuddered and looked up at the shrine tower. She turned away with a weak smile.

"Here." Kenowa put a pill in Yarala's mouth and

handed her the skweez-pak of water. "Swallow. It's called Stand-up. Metacerebrinene. Helps us get around without stumbling on planets of various gravities. You'll need it just to get on your feet."

Yarala downed the tablet. Almost immediately she straightened up and stood without assistance. She tossed her head, throwing her hair behind her, and exhaled sharply.

"Is space travel always so painful?"

Verley smiled a tired smile. "Only when you don't strap in." She looked at the tall structure rising from the forest. "What is that?"

"That is the Father of Shrines. It is the birthplace of our race."

Kenowa listened while trying to find something for the naked women to wear. She also took the opportunity to throw a trio of foodpaks into the boat's minuscule warmer.

Verley looked around like a rubbernecking tourist. Her hands never stopped massaging sore muscles.

"It is a gathering place for many of our rituals. I have never been here before."

Kenowa tossed Verley a pair of olive-green equhyde tights and matching boots. "Here."

Verley slid the tights on and sealed them up. She caught the dark blue halter thrown in her direction. Easing it over her tender, abused chest and ribcage, she nodded to Yarala. "What about her?"

"What do you want to wear?" Kenowa asked.

The Arep looked about, spied a blue bush maintaining a tenuous grip on the sandy ground, and plucked its bright violet flower. She tucked it into her hair over her left ear.

"There–?"

Kenowa smiled and stopped rummaging through the lander's stores. "Lovely, dear."

"Usually," Yarala continued—blissful at her chance to be on the island—"no one except the Elder and his family travel to the Tower. The distance for our clan is too great. Also," (her skin blushed even redder), "I have only just come of age. Those unable to perform the Dance of the Mother and Her Lover are forbidden to see this isle." She looked at the tower and blushed again.

Something made a *peep*ing sound inside the lander.

Kenowa retrieved the food skweez-paks and tossed one to Yarala, one to Verley. "Breakfast."

Verley helped Yarala open her pak. The naked woman sniffed at the yellowish paste and made a face. "Is this what spacefarers eat?"

"Not usually, dear," Kenowa replied with a cheerful smile. "Your friend Marekallian has made circumstances quite out of the ordinary."

"They're going to get less ordinary," Verley said, standing up and looking out to sea. "We've got company."

Kenowa followed Verley's gaze. Yarala smiled and stood up, waving.

"It is the clan T'gita come to prepare the shrine. A great ritual is set to occur this next threeday."

Kenowa switched on her wristcomm. "Jone?"

No answer.

She tried two other frequencies before giving up. The wrist commlinks routed their signals through the powerful receivers and transmitters of *Coronet* when the distance separating the units was more than a klom. Something must have happened to *Coronet*.

Kenowa swallowed. "Verley," she said, and motioned the Sek inside the lander. When Verley followed her in, she said, "Head into the woods and find Jonuta. Warn him about this. I'll stay here and work things out through Yarala." She handed Verley a stopper. "Take care."

Arming herself, Kenowa followed the other woman out of the lander.

Verley ran up the shore to the woodline, a blue-green tree nymph vanishing into the foliage.

Kenowa sealed the lander. The morning light and warm breeze blowing toward the sea belied the tension that tightened her movements and sharpened her judgment.

"They don't look too pleased to see us."

"We are not supposed to be here." The realization wiped the happy expression from Yarala's face.

"Can you intercede with them? Stall for time?"

The native woman smiled a sly smile. "I think I can. On the condition that you take me with you when you leave Arepien."

Already thinking like a Galactic, Kenowa thought, shaking her head. She smiled back. "Of course, dear. We'd be happy to have you along." *Though in what capacity remains to be seen*.

Yarala grinned happily and walked to the shoreline.

"I repeat—identify yourself or prepare to be boarded!"

Major Zahrad paused, counting slowly under his breath. Gheraka held the comm-mike lightly in his hand, speaking in that agitating voice, ordering crew around as if it were *his* ship! The major reached a sufficiently high number and spoke.

"*Myrzha* Gheraka. There are set procedures for approaching a ship that gives evidence of being derelict. I will not risk my crew in boarding a craft before we've determined whether—"

"This is more important than a few crew, major."

"Not to me." The little man straightened. "I've served TGW for nearly sixty years-ess in one way or another. I've had to send men and women to their deaths more than—"

"I'm sure this is leading up to a fine speech, Major. Could you deliver it in the tunnel and let me get on with my work?"

The lieutenant kept her stare fixed on a computer screen. She scowled, anger clamping her jaw into hard angles. She wanted to flatten the arrogant fart—and could do nothing more than listen to the humiliation of her commanding officer.

The major leaned one small fist on the edge of the con. "I remind you that all conversation on the bridge is recorded as a matter of course."

"Why do you think I haven't told you anything?" Gheraka raised the mike to his face. "Derelict spacer, prepare to receive a boarding party." He smiled and scratched at his cleft chin. "Major—I'll require a team of four, stoppers set on One only. And no one is to touch *anything* without my—"

"*C Y R! C! Mayday! Red Rover! Mayday!*"

The message crackled out from the comm loud enough to startle Gheraka. Quickly regaining his composure, he looked over the lieutenant's shoulder at her computer display.

"C Y R!" cried the message in a code based on Erts, the Galactic language.

"Need any more proof that it's safe to board?" Gheraka turned a cool gaze on Zahrad.

"If this is the target spacer that tried to escape Sekhar, why would they want our help?"

Gheraka dismissed the implication with an impatient wave. He switched on the comm-mike.

"This is TGW destrier *Paraida*. We read your distress call. ID yourself."

The wavering image of a yellow-bronze skinned man appeared on the screen. Beside him a Bleaker slumped forward in his chair, obviously unconscious.

"This is Captain Hoyuko of Terasaki-registered freighter *Zinja*. Please take us onboard!"

Gheraka frowned. This was not the reception he'd expected.

"We show your ship as being dead in space. What happened?"

"Please!" the Terasak cried. "Take us onboard! The other ship damaged our double-P engines and they might blow at any second. You can't leave us here to die!" His long, sloping eyes almost squinted in pain as he spoke. His longish, straight hair hung in sweaty tangles.

The body of the Bleaker didn't move.

Gheraka switched off the commsender. The lines on his forehead stood out in even deeper relief. For a long moment, the only sound in the con was that of SIPACUM's audio responses.

"Well?" Zahrad asked. "That seems to be an invitation to board."

After a thoughtful pause, Gheraka clicked the comm on again.

"Captain, uh—Hoyuko. What other ship are you talking about? We read our two ships as being the only ones orbiting this *Protected* planet."

The man called Hoyuko shuddered. "We'd come out of subspace to do a quick repair. We detected another ship in orbit. Just like that"—a weak hand tried to snap its fingers and failed—"the ship powered up its DS and attacked. I think it might have been . . ." He broke off long enough to gulp. "J-Jonuta of Qalara."

"Impossible," Gheraka said. "We have verification that Jonuta is dead. Rely on that. All that remains is his ship and crew."

"Then they're just as savage as he was! And as skilled. We maneuvered for hours exchanging and ducking shots. We–" The captain lowered his head and began to weep. "My crew. Most of them died in the exchange. My dee-esser managed to get in a lucky shot just before she was killed. The other ship was destroyed. But my crew . . . my ship. . ."

"Sir." The lieutenant pointedly addressed the major, ignoring Gheraka, who was watching the flickering image from the other ship. "SIPACUM detects the lamprey tailer in a lower orbit. It appears to be partially damaged and attached to a fragment of hull."

Zahrad said nothing. His nod was tiny. He smiled.

Gheraka pulled at the skin under his jaw. "Do you agree to a boarding party?" he asked Captain Hoyuko.

"A rescue party! Please! There isn't much time!" The captain of *Zinja* almost screamed the words.

Gheraka flinched. He had expected resistance, possibly battle. He had expected deception, or maybe an extended chase. He'd never expected a Red Rover plea. He hesitated.

"Well?" Major Zahrad asked, smiling at the undercover operative's deliberation. "Do we pull back to a safe distance and send a lifeboat out with one operator as it says in the book? Or do we sit here practically strut-to-strut and wait for their engines to blow with four of my crew trying to board?"

"We board," a strained voice replied.

14

The stone surrendered to the heat of Marekallian's laser. He traced the beam slowly across the base of the shrine tower, cutting a narrow gap in the rock. The thin channel glowed white where the green beam hit, and faded to red almost instantly after the light moved on. Eks studied his work.

It had taken him less than five minutes to cut a rectangular design in the face of the monument. He brought the end of the burning channel to meet the beginning and shifted about.

Pointing the laser up at an angle, he cut a diagonal groove from the bottom of the block he'd created to where he guessed the top of its inner side would be. This cut took longer, since it was across the hypotenuse of the triangular prism he was fashioning. After a few moments, he shut off the beamer and stood aside.

From his backpack, he pulled a self-fastening piton. Laying it against the rock wedge he'd cut, he set off the charge.

The piton bit deep. Eks threaded a monofilament cord through its eye and wrapped a few lengths around his waist and right arm. He backed up.

The rock protested with a grinding sound. Marekallian felt his joints pop. This was the part of his work he hated most. He pulled harder.

With a scraping sound that irritated his nerves, the wedge of black stone slid down and out of its resting place. Its corner hit the wet dirt and sank several sems. He stared at a square cut in the wall that sloped up and diminished to nothing before reaching the other side.

Try again, he thought, unwrapping the cord and picking

up the beamer. This time he scrunched himself into the narrow triangular indentation and fired downward, to where the bottom of the initial cut would be on the far side.

He added a few strokes at the top of the hole to free the new wedge and provide a place to grip. Now he could smell the dead air of the shrine mixing with the dusty odor of burnt rock.

Fingers wriggling into the slot above him, Eks pulled his legs up and pushed them against the rock. It edged forward a sem. He strained harder—and kicked.

The stone slid suddenly, grating with a hideous noise, and fell inside the tower. An unprepared Marekallian Eks followed, losing his tenuous grip on the overhead stone and landing against the sharp angles of the fallen wedge.

"Theba take it!" he muttered, feeling about in the dark.

He pushed off the rock and removed his goggles. And looked around in great pleasure. Threats could not have removed the smirk from his face.

Marek my boy, not bad for a preacher's son!

He pulled in his cutter and backpack and fished about for his Wayne. Finding the hat, he pulled it on and attached a lightflash hatband. The beam illuminated the dark chamber in which he stood. To his right and left, corridors beckoned. He fingerflipped and took the one to his right, whistling an ancient tune as he went.

Jonuta and Sakyo lay in an outcropping of granite. They had watched the Outreacher's operation from a dozen meters away.

"That's his scam, all right," Sak whispered. "Do we follow?"

Jonuta nodded, turning away from the tower and touching his wristcomm. "Kenny?"

No response.

"Hey!" Sakyo laid a hand on his captain's shoulder and pointed. "It's Verley!"

Jonuta turned toward the tower.

Verley ran from the woods straight to the only apparent entrance to the tower—the freshly excavated rectangle. Stepping over the angular bottom cut, she slid into the chamber.

"Jonuta?" she whispered at a bobbing light receding down a tunnel to her right.

The footsteps halted. The light spun about in her face. "Stop," a familiar voice said.

Verley said, "Oops."

Eks held the cutting laser pointed at a spot between her breasts. "How'd you get free? And what're you doing following me?"

Verley took a deep breath. "Listen," she said, her hands moving in placation. "The Areps are here. A lot of them. They cut us free and questioned Yarala. They're not in a very good mood about this. I barely escaped alive to warn you."

"Escaped? Fully clothed? When I left you naked?"

"She wanted to preserve her modesty," a deep, rumbling voice said.

Jonuta straddled the wedge of rock in the entry chamber, casually pointing his stopper at Eks. "I think she blends in well with the local flora, don't you."

"Redshift, slaver. I'm not getting in your way."

"We're leaving. Now. I can't get through to *Coronet*. That means it's under surveillance and we've got to run. You wanted a ride?"

"You *fools!*" Eks shouted, not lowering his beamer. He pointed down the passageway. "Just a few meters away there's enough wealth to buy your damned ship five times over!"

"Gold?" Jonuta laughed. "You'd have to carry quite a bit out. We don't have time. Not if Verley's right. And not if I'm right about *Coronet*."

"Not just gold. Not just *metal*. I'm talking about *artifacts*. The things collectors will pay ridiculous sums for. Art and pieces of history from planets they're forbidden to explore."

Jonuta slid his other leg around and stood up in the chamber. Sakyo followed him.

"So our friend of the downtrodden is nothing more than a tomb robber," Verley said, almost spitting the words.

Eks flipped his fingers in angry agreement. "What else have primitives got to repay me for my efforts? They won't be needing their gods anymore. Without idols to worship, they'll just progress that much faster."

An incredulous Jonuta stared at the shadow of Eks behind the light. "You can't actually believe your rationalizations."

"They're true enough. These people can't be held back by superstitions that waste their time and resources. Someday they'll have to join with the other Protected planets in revolt–"

"Revolt against what?"

"Against the Galaxy's secret masters—*TGO!*"

Sak threw his arms up in exasperation. "What?"

Eks said nothing, letting his implication sink in.

"But TGO exists solely to guard the spaceways against war." Sakyo recovered from his outburst and aimed his stopper again at the Mindrunner.

"*And who shall guard us from the guardians?* No one. TGO won't permit it. Any form of defiance is considered an act of war by them and summarily dealt with." His speech accelerated, like that of a child rattling on about some special interest. "Sure, they have their euphemisms for crushing their opposition. And the historians go right along with it. You have to dig pretty deep to find out that the supposed 'despot' Fod Rakir of Jahpur had gathered popular opposition to TGO on Panish, Shankar, Resh, and a dozen other worlds before he mysteriously 'vanished' off a spacer in mid-flight."

He's definitely on the edge, Jonuta thought, fingering his stopper lightly. Taking a lackadaisical step to the side, he asked, "I suppose good old Artisune Muzuni the pirate was also the victim of rewritten history?"

"He was a hero on several worlds. What the historians called his 'extorted' protection money was freely given by most. Not only did he charge less than TGO extracted through the planetary governments, he protected the *people* of the planets! From TGO *and* from their own governments." Eks slammed fist into palm. "Oh, he was a great man. Did you know he only seized government cargo vessels? No—they don't mention that in the histories. And he never enslaved a living so–"

"Shut up." Jonuta's voice was cold and insistent.

Eks took in a sharp breath and held it. He still kept his lase-beamer pointed at Verley.

"We're going back to the lander to try to escape," Jonuta said. "Play in here all you want and dream of revolution. If you can make it into orbit before we redshift, I'll let you onboard." He paused. "For half the loot."

Marekallian Eks laughed. It was a deep, hearty laugh that held none of the manic intensity of his recent speech.

"Captain Jonuta, I want you to remember this moment. There'll come a day when you'll gladly pay to ship with *me*." He grinned. "I'll give you a quarter of it."

"You're in danger of being abandoned and you're haggling?"

"I've still got the laser."

Jonuta sighed. "Sixty-forty, my end low."

"Deal. However, I need a hostage as a token of good faith."

Sakyo said, "I'll give a Fry beam as a token."

Eks continued to smile. "I don't need tough talk. Just deals. Captain?"

Jonuta, weary of it all, moved his finger slowly against the switch of his stopper.

"I'll go." Verley walked up to the muzzle of Eks's beamer. He frowned, but did not move.

Jonuta frowned, too. Verley hardly mattered to him. She'd caused him more than enough trouble in the first place and she must know it. *If this is her way of giving us a chance to get away, I'm not about to let her waste her martyrdom.* He fingerflipped.

"Stay if you want. We won't wait long, once we're on *Coronet*." He nodded to Sak. "Go."

Sak ducked through the wall and into the daylight. He pointed his stopper through the hole and covered Eks while Jonuta slid through.

"Get in front," Eks said to Verley. He prodded her around a corner and they descended into the labyrinthine shrine.

With the light behind her, Verley walked into the cool, musty passage of the ancient structure.

As she moved cautiously ahead of him, she did something she had not done in years. She prayed—actually *prayed*—to Musla.

•   •   •

Shig nudged the microswitch, cutting off the comm-link with *Paraida*. A burst of static preceded the cutoff, making it seem that the unit was suffering from battle damage.

"So what do we do when a flainin' gang of TGW gricks board us? Bend over and salute?" Vark lifted his head and stretched his arms.

"They're not going to board us."

"That sure as shittin' isn't the impression you gave them, begging 'em to come onboard."

Shig smiled and leaned back in the captain's chair of *Coronet*. "Strap yourself in. Securely."

He tapped at the con's keyboard, sending orders to Defense Systemry. Without enabling DS, he set up a series of functions to be controlled from the buttons on his right armrest. Then he strapped his arm firmly to it so that he could reach the controls no matter what happened.

Vark watched the procedure with calm curiosity. Now and then he would cover his right eye and squint a bit through his left, focusing the implanted TP to get a closer look.

With his free hand, Shig tapped a few more commands into SIPACUM. He poised a golden-hued finger over the pearl-white *enable* button.

Vark had seen what Shig entered. He strapped himself in. Securely. Looking impressed.

"Who knows. Who cares. Why bother," he murmured, touching the corresponding points on his stout body.

"Hang on and try not to make any noise." Shig eased by the microswitch to the comm.

"*Zinja*," a voice said. "*We lost contact for a few minutes. Is your portside bay ready to receive the board—the rescue party?*"

"Still trying to repair the airlocks by TP. It's not easy. Crew's dead. I'm doing all I can. Please stand by. Don't leave us. I'm sure I can fix—"

The transmission faltered. Shig's index finger brushed against the off-white button. SIPACUM silently took control of *Coronet*.

Shig felt his body press into the chair. Slowly, the ship began to rotate. Slowly, centrifugal force increased his weight.

"Captain Hoyuko! Your ship is rotating. Abate it or our boat won't be able to–"

"Calling *Paraida!"* Shig said in choked tones. "The ship's rotating. The spin thrusters have come on. All the circuits are crossed somewhere. I can't—I can't find where–"

A gravelly voice cut in. *"This is the rescue boat. What the vug's going on in there?"*

"Artificial gravity actuated. The limiter's broken. We're out of control!"

Shig forced as much raw terror into his voice as he could. He had set the upper limit for six Gs, but expected to be rid of *Paraida* long before then.

"We can disable your thrusters with DS." The voice was losing patience.

"Negative, Gheraka." Onboard *Paraida,* Major Zahrad spoke sternly into the comm-mike. "To do that might set off the ship's engines. I won't risk being anywhere near a proton flash."

"Then pull back! I'll handle it from here."

"Not with my crew. Not according to regulations."

Gheraka almost snarled. *"We'll worry about regulations when this is over . . . Major."*

"Indeed we will." Zahrad smiled to his lieutenant, then spoke clearly into the mike.

"Boarding party crew are advised that anyone ordering a DS attack on the derelict is to be arrested and returned to *Paraida* under restraint by order of Major Zahrad, Trans-Galactic Watch."

He covered the mike for a moment and let go a tight breath of air. His mouth tasted of nervous terror. Had he gone too far?

The reply came after a few seconds. *"We shall definitely discuss this, Major. Meanwhile—I am asking for a volunteer to attempt a jump and grapple to the derelict. Objective to be manual disabling of spin thrusters. Do you grant permission? And-you-had-better?"*

"Only," Zahrad said slowly, "if it is totally voluntary." He knew that he had to grant Gheraka that much. It was in the book. Somewhere.

Onboard *Coronet,* Shig checked the readout. Two gravities. *No problem.* He looked over at Vark.

The Bleaker lay quietly in his chair. The weight was not much more than he experienced on the surface of his (never-to-be-sufficiently-cursed) planet of birth. For the benefit of viewers on the other ship, though, he lolled his head to one side and looked nearly dead. Also, Shiganu of Terasaki thought, positively revolting.

Shig felt a heavy weight pressing against his heart. The readout indicated 2.8 G. As centrifugal force threatened to crush him into his chair, he heard a throbbing noise in his head.

Maybe I've miscalculated. . .

15

Kenowa self-consciously straightened her auburn bangs. She stood as tall as she could without the illusion provided by a Terasaki coil. Running her hands over her SpraYon outfit, she tried to relax and face the approaching mob.

"Marekallian never got to this clan, did he? They don't speak Erts?"

Yarala shook her head.

"Can you interpret for me? Will they listen to you?"

"We are about to find out." Yarala performed a deep prostration, then stood.

"May the gods have sexual congress with you and your offspring, Biah'Rakhin Ndyanda Q'gita."

A tall, weathered-looking woman approached the pair. She wore a simple wrap adorned with twin starburst designs and her head was shaven.

"Who are you?" she asked indignantly. Others stood alongside her, creating a wall of flesh between the trespassers and the ocean. "Why have you built these huts"—she pointed at the landers—"on sacred land?"

"I am but a servant of this sky-goddess." Yarala turned to Kenowa and whispered in Erts, "I told her you're a sky-goddess. Do something to impress them."

Smiling and sexy and nervous, Kenowa inclined her head to the Elder and drew a pulsar beamer from her holster. Still smiling as if in patient restraint, she pointed it at an outcropping of gray rock a good twenty meters to her right. "Yama-skiffee!" she intoned—and the plasma bolt flared and exploded the boulder into fragments. Newly exposed surfaces exhibited an odd blue-green color shot through with red and yellow streaks.

A much impressed Elder raised an eyebrow. Nevertheless,

she retained her regal calm: "It honors me and my clan to welcome you to our shrine tower. I beg that you will not perform sacrifices in such a manner." The voice was not begging.

Kenowa looked at Yarala.

"She hopes you don't plan to roast them. And she welcomes you."

"Tell her that I'm honored—no! That I am *pleased*. And have no desire to sacrifice loyal tribespeople." And Kenowa affected a divinely imperious expression. She hoped.

Yarala relayed the message and listened to the reply of Rakhin Ndyanda Q'gita.

"She says they are here to prepare the temple and grounds for the Dance of the Mother and Her Lover." The ruddy-hued girl averted her eyes (and Kenowa wondered if she blushed). "It is to take place tomorrow, when the Mother and Her Lover are at angles."

"Uh. What sort of Dance is it?"

The girl Kenowa thought of as Eks's pet Arep blushed, definitely, red skin or no. "It is a three-night dance of hundreds of clans . . . it is . . ." Yarala broke off shyly and lowered her eyes. "I believe your word for it is 'orgy.' "

Sounds delightful. Maybe we should stay, Kenowa mused, admiring the men and women arrayed before her without benefit of clothing. She noticed more than a few appreciative gazes, and remembered their customary greeting. She felt a thrill flit through her. It emanated from her loins.

"Uh . . . what did she just say?"

"The Elder says that more pilgrims are expected later today."

Great. Reinforcements. "Tell her that the sky-gods have come to outfit the temple as it truly should be arranged. The profane must not be allowed to see the gods at work, for the mere sight would cause madness and death."

There. Maybe I should be writing *holomellers!* She listened to Yarala's voice as she translated.

A brash young woman stepped forward after hearing the warning. She wore the garb of a lonefighter—deep maroon breechcout and a halter of silvery *n'gyabla* fur. Yarala rarely saw lonefighters, who kept to themselves and lived as hermits.

"I will see the sky-gods. I will risk their punishment and become Elder-in-Self." She turned to Ndyanda. "To be Elder-in-Self is the highest honor, to which even Elder-in-Age must defer."

Yarala whispered a translation to Kenowa.

Kenowa sneaked her hand down to her stopper, unobtrusively twisted it to point at the outspoken woman, and squeezed.

The lonefighter jerked suddenly and her muscles twitched in a maddened rictus. The number Two beam of Kenowa's stopper confused and jangled her nervous system, turning the woman into a manic puppet that shook and twisted in a spasmodic dance.

"See?" Kenowa shouted. "They punish even from afar!" She nudged Yarala, who stood gawking. "Translate!"

"The sky gods punish her for her foul words!" She hesitated. "They—Kenowa–"

The crowd surged past her, the Elder at the lead. They rushed toward the tower.

Losing her grip on the stopper, Kenowa dropped it and prepared to fight hand-to-hand. She didn't have to.

"Where are they—Why?"

"You made the lonefighter dance. A stopper, yes?"

Yarala looked worried. A few stragglers ran past them, including the lonefighter who had recovered from the stopper beam.

"Yes. Number Two beam. Why?"

"Kenowa—among our people, dancing is considered a sign of divine possession. Of divinity itself."

"Oh, bungle."

She rushed to the lander, unsealed it, and clambered to the loudspeaker system. Turning to outer speakers to full volume, she patched in the comm-mike.

"Jone! The whole clan's heading for the tower and stoppers don't scare them! They worship dancing!"

The sound of her voice carried and reverberated across the island. She repeated the message a couple of times and switched off. *Time to get ready to go,* she thought, powering up the lander and checking its systems.

"Take me with you?" Yarala asked, fearful that the unfortunate turn of events might have soured Kenowa on their agreement.

"When we go. I'm just making sure we can jump when we need to." *Be safe, Jone my love.*

The sound of the loudspeaker could not penetrate the walls of the tower. Marekallian Eks moved deeper within, unwarned.

"Quiet!" he hissed at Verley, moving ahead of her.

She stopped walking and held her breath angrily while she waited for him to finish scanning a wall with a sonar hand unit.

"I don't have to be quiet for you," she said. "After what you—"

"Look—" He turned around and waggled the sonar unit at her. "You're a hostage. At least give me the courtesy of acting like one." He turned and scanned the opposite wall. "I don't even know why you volunteered."

"Because I don't trust Jonuta any more than I trust you. He'd sell me into slavery the first chance he got. He came here to get slaves."

"That's the kind of people you travel with?" Eks scanned the wall where the passage branched. "Hmm." He tapped it with the butt of his stopper.

"You're choosing to travel with him, once we get out of here."

"Well," Eks said, shining his lamp down the twin corridors, "that's the chances you take in life."

"He'll sell *you* if he gets the opportunity."

Eks smiled. "Hardly."

Verley followed him through the gloomy hall. It expanded into a dead end. She turned, expecting him to run ahead of her. Instead, he stopped at the blank wall and scanned it.

"Ah!" Unbuckling his cutting laser, he powered it up and slipped on his goggles. "Sounds like a main chamber on the other side. Stand back."

She shielded her eyes from the green light and the white flare of vaporizing rock. The musty scent in the air quickly gave way to the stinging odor of heated stone.

"Besides," he said, in a voice loud enough to carry over the sound of the operation, "what makes you think I won't do the same thing? Can a tomb robber be trusted any further than a slaver?"

Verley thought about it. "You're in a fix without your ship, so you can be an ally until you're safe."

He laughed. Not only at her pragmatism, but also at the opening he drilled in the wall. He examined the cooling hole with his goggles off. From a pocket of his backpack he drew out a long, thin plastic tube. Slipping it into the hole, he fed through over a meter of its length.

He reached around to pull out the rest of the device. For several seconds he waited while the analysis ran.

"Breathable. Good." He took off the backpack. "You might want to stand a little farther back. I'm in a hurry now, thanks to the good captain."

Verley stood farther back.

Boosting the output of the laser, he aimed in and began beaming. He cut the bottom at a slant, then the left and rightward sides. After a few minutes, he finished off with the top. Satisfied with his adjustments, he fastened the cutter to his backpack and called to Verley.

"As long as you're a hostage, get over here and help me push."

Face impassive, she walked over and put her bare shoulder to the stone, following Marekallian's example. They pushed together.

The slab gave way immediately. With a scraping sound it slid down the angled cut and into the other chamber. Verley and Eks fell to the ground. For an instant they heard nothing. Then the block crashed to the floor of the chamber with shattering force.

Eks peered over the edge and shone his light inside. "Ten meter drop." He smiled weakly at Verley before turning back to play his beam about the floor of the chamber.

Crawling close enough to him that their thighs were forced into undesired intimacy, Verley peered with him into the dim interior. "What's in there?" she asked.

"Wonderful things," he told her, repeating an ancient blessing.

Worming his way back, he pulled out another piton and shot it into the ledge. He hooked a karabiner to the piton and threaded the monofilament cord through. He tested its tension with a couple of tugs, and nodded.

"I'll go first, then you follow." He pulled the backpack on, fastened it, and slid backwards to the edge.

"Aren't you afraid I'll release the line and strand you?" Her smile glinted wickedly in the low light.

"Why, I trust you implicitly, love." *And I always carry a second line.*

With a grin at her, he pushed off and played the line out.

"Aren't you afraid of traps?" she called to him as he slid down without so much as a rappel.

He hit the ground and called back up. "If I were, I'd have sent you first!"

The volunteer had second thoughts.

He floated twenty meters from the surface of the spinning hulk of the derelict and watched the dizzying blur of detail speed past him. His name was Rashni Jumbaru, his age was twenty-four, and his knees were shaking. Not that they had any need to give support in freefall. They shook, nonetheless.

"I suggest you act soon, Corporal." The voice in his helmet was cool but deliberate. *"It's spin won't stop accelerating until you deactivate the thrusters or until they run out of fuel. And they have a lot of fuel, Corporal."*

Corporal Jumbaru was securely attached to the massive harpoon gun. He positioned it before him to aim at a portion of the ship's leading edge. Hitting there, the gripper harpoon—which would bond instantly to cyprium or to plasteel in the same way as a lamprey—stood a much better chance of bonding completely before the spin of the craft yanked the launcher and Jumbaru into their rendezvous with the surface.

Rashni felt a dryness in his throat. The freighter was so large and near that it blocked any view of the sky beyond it. All he could see was a constantly repeating landscape that rushed from the top of the faceplate to the bottom. He experienced a vertiginous feeling of falling—or rising, he wasn't sure which. The view began to mesmerize him.

"Fire, dammit!" a gravelly voice demanded.

Jumbaru looked "up" to see a black line of space over the edge of the spacer. Squinting at the telit on the harpoon launcher, he zeroed in on a point a few degrees below the ship's "horizon." Low enough to avoid any irregularties in the hull that might allow the harpoon to shoot past its target, but high enough to assure a hard impact.

Or so Gheraka had instructed him.

Jumbaru had no time to think about the mysterious man who could apparently order a TGW major with near impunity. The corporal merely made sure the exit tube of the rocket launcher extended far beyond the back of his bright orange spacesuit. He pressed the firing stud.

The hiss of the harpoon rocket's shooting out of its tube vibrated through him. The monomolecular cable it towed played out with a sickening rumble that shook the launcher and with it Corporal Jumbaru.

He hoped the cable had some give to it. He soon found out.

It took less than a second for the rocket to cross the fifty meters or so to the spacer's approaching edge. Jumbaru didn't see or feel the impact. All he saw was an instant in which the cable—wrapped in a braided unipolymer plasteel cuff and dyed orange for visibility—seemed to go slack and begin coiling up. Then the impact point slid past its midcourse, twenty meters away from the sweat-soaked corporal. The cable began to straighten.

Jumbaru gritted his teeth and tried to mutter a quick prayer. He'd got out precisely two words when a powerful tug jerked at the launcher.

He had been strapped to it with dozens of belts and cords, carefully arranged so that he could unfasten them all with one hand—fast—and all stuffed with plenty of padding. Rashni had no time to be reassured. All he saw was the surface of the spacer rushing at him with sickening speed. All he could feel was the stomach-wrenching pull of acceleration.

The surface of the derelict loomed impossibly huge and sprawling before his eyes. It seemed to slow in its rotation as the launcher and the man it hauled were jarringly accelerated. The cable winch quickly played out more slack, trying to bring Jumbaru up to the rotational speed of the spacer without slamming him into the hull with the force of a cracking whip.

The sharp curve of the dorsal strut moved over the horizon.

Jumbaru screamed.

The gripper held. The cable held. The straps held. Rashni Jumbaru's grip on sanity slipped for only a moment.

He came within five meters of the hull—ten meters away from the dorsal strut that would have swatted him as a paddle would a ball.

Rashni whimpered bravely, watching the surface fall away from him. Dragging him up to the rotational speed of the spacer, the physics involved now sought to fling Jumbaru out to the maximum length of the cable. At that distance the centrifugal force would be equivalent to nearly 20 G. Jumbaru's shipmates had cheerfully assured him that at that G-force, he would flow between the straps that bound him as if he were soggy clay.

Corporal Jumbaru felt the click and whine of the cable's being drawn back into the launcher. He thanked Musla, Booda, Gri, and a score of other gods—even Theba of Outreach, just in case—for their benevolence (or lack of malevolence).

The winch pulled the cable in, taking Jumbaru to lower and lower orbits of force. Even so, the G-force would be nearly four at the surface.

"Your vital signs show all clear, Corporal." a voice said in his pounding ears. *"How do you feel?"*

Jumbaru felt terrible. "I'm fine. They don't make rides like this anymore." He gritted his teeth so hard his gums throbbed.

"Just remember to deploy your grippers before you unstrap."

Jumbaru made a sort of gurgling sound in agreement. The grippers were made for maneuvering on the outside of spacers. They bonded at the molecular level, yet could unbond just as easily at the flip of a switch. Theoretically, they should be able to hold to the ship as long as the ship itself held together.

Theoretically.

The harpoon launcher thudded against the hull. The gripper had narrowly missed hitting the rough surface of some radiator vanes to which it would never have held. As it was, the ball of the gripper had hit and flattened against a wide expanse of cyprium.

Jumbaru lay against the restraining straps and gazed "up" at the hulk to which he clung with a lover's fervor. He could see nothing beyond a few meters, which was just as well. Had he seen how the planet and stars whirled madly about him, he'd have been unable to function.

He flung his right leg as hard as he could against the hull. The centrifugal force fought him, dragged at his foot. He tried again.

The gripper on his toe caught and held.

He swung his left foot up and made contact. Controlling the grippers from microswitches inside his left glove, he stretched his legs until the soles of his boots made contact.

The reassuring snap of molecular bonding conducted through his bones. Now came the test of both the molecular bonding on his boots and the tensile strength of the mlss itself.

His right hand undid the straps holding him to the launcher. By the time he reached the last one, he felt threatened to be cut in two by it. It snapped before he could release its fastening and he was flung outward.

Rashni gasped. He hung from his feet at four G force. The Stand-up he'd taken had never been formulated to compensate for such a situation. Feeling every muscle in his body strain, he twisted his arms up and grabbed his thigh. Blood thundered in his skull, blackening his vision. Sweat dripped from his cold feet and legs, ran across his torso and pooled in the top of his helmet.

He edged up his leg, gripping at the braided cable wrapped around it for that purpose. The structure of his mobile life support system—spacesuit—held against the strain. He had feared that he would tear right out of his mlss and die of decompression. He still feared losing grip on all but one appendage and being torn apart by four gravities.

He reached his ankle. Holding himself with his left hand, he rammed his right palm against the plating. It held. His left palm followed.

He hung there like a Ghanji slothtiger, blood rushing from his head to his stomach. It cleared his thoughts. *My back will never survive,* he thought, sliding his left foot away from the bulk of the launcher. His right foot followed. The knee-grippers caught and fastened, followed by the grippers on his forearms. Last, he pulled his chest against the hull and attached the largest gripper.

He clung like a fly to the hull of the whirling ship. He was safe. At last he had time to think. He did.

Now what?

16

The chamber was larger than he'd thought.

Eks stuck the fourth lamp against the rock wall and watched—with amusement—Verley's struggle to descend. She let go to drop the last three meters to the floor—amid a ripping sound. Most of the impact she absorbed by flexing her legs. The sound of her boots hitting the stone floor echoed through the enclosure. Unfortunately her ripped halter dangled from the little burr of rock that had caught it, above.

Not bad, he thought, and watched her turn to look back up at the blue bandeau. "Leave it," he said, and turned to face the treasure chamber.

A mighty impressive thirty meters at its widest, the roughly circular vault housed hundreds of pedestals supporting cups, daggers, idols, necklaces, and . . . things. Wrought things, in gold and silver, bronze and precious stones and something that resembled ivory.

The center of the chamber was dominated by a sphere three meters in diameter. Its white surface reflected the lights softly. Marekallian saw that part of the floor had been excavated to support it in place.

He shook open a large sack and handed it to Verley. "Hold this. It is *not* to cover your warheads. Follow me."

Calling him swine is insulting pigs everywhere, she thought, and obeyed.

He paced past each of the pedestals, examining the pieces displayed. Gold and silver objects he slipped into the sack. Necklaces, rings, and bracelets went into a pouch on his backpack.

"What about this?" Verley asked, pointing to a lifesized golden skull.

"You want to carry it?"

She picked it up with both hands, grunting, and set it down heavily amid a great jiggling of bare breasts. She straightened and shook her head.

"All right then. Collectors don't care a jinkle for what something's made out of—it's what the artisan's done with it that counts. Some of the most expensive art in the Galaxy is nothing more than cloth with colored grease smeared on it."

He pointed at a small white object. "There—that one." He pulled out a small protekpak bag and held the carving over it. "It's carved from an animal's tusk. Look at the delicate toolwork! It—never mind."

He slid the artifact into the padded bag and sealed it. It went into another pouch of the backpack. Briefly he admired a sheathed ornamental dagger and slipped it into his boot. Looking up, he pointed at Verley.

"Those go in the bag."

Verley removed the large silver and turquoise earrings, dropping them in the bag with a pouty *"Hmph!"*

"You're not much fun on a date, are you?" He moved on to grab filigreed cups crusted with jewels.

"You don't exactly go to the liveliest spots."

Eks smiled. "Don't you like mysteries? Such as how did so primitive a society build this shrine tower? Where did all these beautiful artifacts come from when the natives have almost no knowledge of metalworking?"

"You tell me."

She waited for the Mindrunner to turn his back, then slipped a gold star disk into the back of her tights. It was heavy enough to slide past her buttocks—with the help of some pushing—down her leg and into her boot, safely out of sight.

"A previous age. A forgotten race on this planet. It rose to power and wealth, grew decadent, and collapsed. Probably before our ancestors left Homeworld. Think of it! A history lost even to the Areps. Here—just for us."

"Just for you to sell."

He tossed a few more metal items into Verley's sack.

She took to dragging it, holding the mouth open to catch Marekallian's pitches.

"I intend to study them for some time before I sell them. No worry there."

"I wasn't really worried."

"I take numerous holos of each item, compare them with similar items from other worlds . . ." He picked up a jeweled mask, glanced it over and set it down. Reconsidering, he took up the mask again and pried the largest ruby from its setting. He slipped it into one of his pockets.

"I'm trying to come up with a theory of art by cataloging familiar themes in races that evolved seperately from Galac–" He paused. "Is it getting cold in here?"

Verley felt the hairs on her flesh rise. "That sphere–" The words caught in her throat and she finished by pointing.

Eks peered at the large object dominating the center of the vault. A layer of frost was steadily accumulating on its surface. His eyes widened in shock when he realized what it was.

"Theba's kiss!" he whispered.

Jonuta barely heard Kenowa's loudspeaker warning. Listening carefully, he made out enough of the words to explain the shouting and thrashing noises he heard from the depths of the forest. He held up his hand.

Sakyo stopped.

"Back to the tower," his captain said. "They're expecting gods and we'd better give them a couple."

"Couldn't we just sneak out the other way?"

Jonuta shook his head. "They know the island better than we do, Sak. And have you ever known anyone to give up searching for gods?" He slapped the Terasak on the shoulder. "Come on, jacko—when have we ever been outmaneuvered?"

Sakyo looked at the clone of his dead captain and merely smiled. *Someday,* he thought, *I'll give him a list.*

They charged back to the clearing and ducked behind a large outcropping of aquamarine boulders.

"Set your stopper at Two," Jonuta said. "Be ready to beam at my command. *Stay hidden.*"

Sakyo nodded. "Always glad to have the easy jobs, Cap'n. I'll lie down while you deliver the sermon. Knock 'em dead."

"I'll be happy to keep them from knocking *me* dead."

"Here's your chance," Sak pointed from behind the rocks.

At a sprint, the fastest of the pilgrims sped into the clearing. They heeled to a stop at the sight of Jonuta leaning against the shrine tower. He idly picked at the last few bits of vegetation that still clung to his long scarlet coat. He looked up.

The Areps formed a tight red semicircle around the tower. Some of them stared with curiosity, some with impatience, a few with anger.

Jonuta straightened. Though shorter than most of the crowd of lanky red folk, he stood on high ground and assumed his most imposing stance. Godlike wrath showed in his black eyes and dark face.

"So!" he thundered, his deep voice rolling like the waves. "You want to dance? Then dance!"

The ruddy faces stared at him without comprehension. None of them understood Erts.

Throwing his hands in the air, Jonuta intoned a mystical incantation.

"Oh mighty Sakyo, terror of Terasaki! He that squatteth in the rocks! If your stopper be setteth in Two, zappeth thou the big one who standeth directly on mine way!"

Sak peered between the rocks and pointed the stopper beam as directed. The tall, husky Arep male in front of Jonuta began a spasmodic, ridiculous dance.

The others watched for a few seconds. A young man began to chant. An older woman joined him. Others quickly took up the same chant, their sound echoing through the clearing.

The man in the stopper beam was not at all in time with the song. He danced to the random jolts that sparked through his nervous system.

A woman chanting near him happened to grab his hand. The stopper field conducted through him to envelop her.

She joined him in his jerking and shaking, her eyes staring blankly in neurological shock.

Instead of retreating in fear, the others scrambled to touch the dancers. The field spread to them on contact, bringing even more dancers into the frenzy. All sought to join the mystic hysteria.

Jonuta raised an eyebrow in bemused speculation. *Wonder how many people it can handle before the field effect disperses?* Noting that everyone's attention had strayed from him to the dancers, he drew his own stopper and directed its beam at the far end of the crowd. Several members of the mob broke into a wild rictus. Those nearby immediately dived to seize any extremity they could catch flying by.

In less than a minute, nearly every Arep pilgrim was dancing in senseless twists and jumps.

"I hope you've got the next part of the plan, Boss." Sak's amusement showed in his voice.

Jonuta grinned and moved closer to the outcropping. "Why don't we sit this one out and think about it?"

Marekallian Eks stared at the icy sphere, his flash bouncing softly off the frosty surface. In its sealed vault for centuries—*millennia, perhaps,* he thought—the sphere had been protected from the humid ocean air. When Eks entered the chamber, the wet atmosphere had flowed in, condensing water and freezing it on the sphere. He reached up to touch its icy exterior with awe.

"Do you know what this is?" he asked, not caring whether he heard an answer or not.

"It's cold," Verley replied. She had seen ice only in drinks.

"It's a cryosphere!"

His heart pounded. He searched the surface of the globe, running his hands over the smooth surface until they stung in numb protest. He found a bump on the far side, near the base.

"Quick—give me a hand before the frost thickens." The cloudy vapor of his breath seemed almost to flow from his mouth straight to the surface of the sphere— where it froze.

"Even with the insulation these things have–" He grunted as he chipped at the ice with a piton. "Even with it, enough cold is leaking out to do this. What a power source it must have!"

"Well, what is it?" Verley watched, enthralled. Every time Eks chipped the ice, it seemed to heal. "Use your laser?"

He shook his head violently. "Can't. Can't risk piercing the shell. I guess you wouldn't know what this is."

He clenched his hands into a double fist and swung with all his might at the bump. The ice popped; something in his wrist made a cracking sound. Lips twisted in a snarl, Eks removed his backpack and lay on his back. He kicked savagely at the disappearing protrusion. The ice cracked, this time. He kicked again, less powerfully.

The bump collapsed into the sphere, breaking a large chunk of ice away to reveal a hole glowing in dim yellow hues.

Eks scrambled about and shoved his hand into the hole.

"It only stays open a few minutes. Then the cylinder slides out. It's an intelligence test. If the sphere happens to hit a meteor or land on the bump, nothing will happen." He felt around the freezing hole. "But if—ungh—an intelligent being opened it–"

"Shall I go find one?"

"–it'd be able to do *this*."

Marek jammed his fingers into narrow slots in the hole. He felt about with the cold digits until a series of studs slid back. The yellow light winked out.

The ball of ice stopped growing. Eks pulled his hand out and warmed it under his armpit. A loud crack caused Verley to jump in fright.

"What's happening?"

Eks smiled and stood, straightening his hat. "I just set it to defrost."

"In Musla's name, *why?*"

"For the surprise inside."

Verley stood back, almost to the wall. The cracking noises came more frequently. The sphere lost its frosty appearance and the ice on it grew shiny, sweaty. Verley stepped backward into the wall when a curved sheet of ice fell from the underside of the sphere to shatter against the stone floor. Another piece slid from the equator. It landed with the sound of breaking bones. Verley clenched her teeth to keep them from chattering.

Marekallian Eks began to speak in rapid, enthusiastic tones. He circled around the defrosting cryosphere, crunching through the broken shards of ice like a youth on his first trip through the snow.

"You see? It's working. Of course you wouldn't know what this is. Of course not! I only found out because my people once allied themselves—briefly—with a group of ex-slaves. One of them, a thief named . . . Oh, named something or other—I forget. I called him Demon Cat. He found one of these once. What a surprise. What a coup!" He turned to Verley and eyed her seriously. "I really do have a degree in sentenology, you know."

Verley grinned and nodded. *He's gone insane and I'm half a room away from the rope. Shit.* She kept the smile plastered on.

"I can see it all." He leaned both hands on a pedestal supporting a single small coin. "Years of study. A new race. Demon Cat tried to keep knowledge of the Akil from the rest of the Galaxy. But too many people saw her, too many knew. Not all ex-slaves are as tight-lipped as they could be, especially around allies. The alliance never came off, of course—they wanted to hide, not fight. They had nothing to offer the–" He stumbled over a word and instantly recovered. "–to offer us."

He turned to see a large fragment of the ice shell slide off the globe and crumble against the other pieces. The floor glistened with water.

The sphere stood fully exposed. It was an opalescent white, pure and milky in its depths. Silence returned again to the chamber.

"What happens next?" asked a breathless voice.

Marekallian shrugged. "I have no diea."

Unsteadily, he leaned an elbow against the pedestal. The small coin rolled from its stand and fell to the floor. He picked it up and turned it over in his fingers, lost in thought.

How that stupid thief could keep secret the discovery of

a new race—an old race, probably long dead but for these
cryospheres. The fool has no sense of history. Keep it out
of the hands of TGO—that I can understand. But to keep it
as simply a lover, a companion! He flipped the coin and
caught it. *How many fools have destroyed our past and*
clouded our future with their stu—

"Did you hear that?" Verley ran to the hole where they
had entered the vault.

"What?"

"That moaning," she said, listening for sound from the
hole eight meters above her head.

Eks looked up, listened. "It's outside. We'll worry
about it later." He stared at the coin in his hand. "Let's
make one more round before the thing defrosts complete—"
He blinked and looked at the coin again.

Though struck from silver, the disk contained some
alloy that prevented tarnish. On its obverse was the head
of an Arep, struck in high relief. The side view revealed a
long mane of hair braided down his back and tied with
narrow bands. Eks fingered his own queue, marvelling
at how some things never changed. He turned the coin
over.

On its reverse, in letters as crisp as the day they were
struck, centuries upon centuries ago, were the words

FIRST LAUNCH

NATIVE AMERICAN SPACE AUTHORITY

AUGUST, MMCCCLIV

Marekallian Eks recognized the ancient alphabet. He began to tremble.

Verley watched in astonished silence as the Mindrunner
clutched the coin, a distant fire in his eyes.

"Urth," he whispered. "Homeworld!" he cried, lurching about to stare at Verley with wild eyes. "They're a
lost race of *Urth!*"

Verley looked from Eks to the sphere. He saw her gaze
dart back.

"Not the Akil," he said. "The Areps! They came from

Urth! They must have crashed here, lost their technology! Reverted to savagery.''

"So?"

Eks threw up his hands in defeat. The need to talk ate at him. He wanted to share his discovery with someone who understood. Right now! Instead, he carefully wrapped the coin in a kerchief of tan Terasak grixsilk and deposited it inside a double pocket over his left breast. Sealing both flaps shut, he stepped up to the sphere. It was cool to the touch, but not painfully so.

"Come on, come on." He began to pace like an expectant father, water splashing away from the soles of his boots with every step.

Verley took the opportunity to pick up some bracelets and a necklace he had overlooked. She slipped them on.

Three breaks suddenly appeared in the sphere. They did not pop open or dilate or blow out. They just . . . appeared. Large enough to put a fist through, the holes were spaced equidistant around the sphere on a latitude that was not parallel with the floor. The instant the holes appeared, three streams of gas and vapor punched out like angry fists.

Eks jumped back in wordless alarm.

Verley clambered for the cord hanging behind her.

"I guess this is what happens next!" Eks shouted over the roar. He edged closer to Verley, ready to join her in making for the exit.

17

Major Zahrad watched helplessly from the con of *Paraida*. Ahead of his ship hung the tiny shape of the boarding vessel. Beyond it, the rotating bulk of the derelict. Corporal Jumbaru would have been invisible at that distance even if the rapid spin of the freighter had not blurred everything on its surface into a uniform gray.

The destrier's tractor field held the other spacer motionless, but could do nothing to abate its roll. That would be up to Jumbaru.

The corporal worked his way across the hull toward the first spin thruster, a red-glowing tube fifteen meters away. He moved one limb at a time, killing the individual bond, pushing his limb against the force trying to throw it away from the ship, and rebonding the gripper to the hull.

He covered a meter in just over a minute.

Every movement chafed him against the back of his mlss. Sweat puddled there in the suit. It wetted his shoulders and back, squished with each motion. And every moment that passed increased the force seeking to cast him into space.

He grunted with effort. *It must be over four Gs by now*, he thought, keeping his gaze locked on the thruster ahead.

Another minute of travel brought him faceplate-close to a problem.

A transverse brace lay between him and any further progress. Only ten sems high, it stretched for hundreds of meters in either direction. He considered climbing over it—and realized that his chest gripper would be useless at some point in the crossover.

He didn't waste any breath comming his shipmates.

Blinking the sweat and tears that pooled in his eyes, he

cut the bond on his right hand. Instantly, it flew away from the hull as if pulled by a vicious puppeteer. He flung it over the brace and bonded. The suit scraped against the beam. He repeated the act with his left arm.

He paused to take a breath. His contorted, ragdoll posture made the action difficult.

Now comes the hard part.

To place his right leg over the brace, he must also release his chest gripper, leaving him without his major bond. *But I held by my boots alone,* he reminded himself. *At only* three *Gs.*

He killed the bond on his right foot, fighting the urge to let it hang away from the ship. He swung it toward the hull over the brace, at the same instant killing the bond on his chest gripper.

It didn't work.

Freed from contact with the hull, his torso tried to swing out. It was restrained by his left leg. The torque was transferred to his right leg. It was thrown clear of its target. The gripper missed making contact with the hull and swung back outward.

Jumbaru hung by two hands and his left leg. Panicked, he killed the bond on his right hand and sought to drag his leg into position. His mistake was instantly apparent.

He screamed in agony.

The right side of his body, hanging free, tried to tear away from the bonded left side. From groin to throat, muscles stretched and ripped. Joints popped, dislocated. Bones strained to the breaking point. His head lolled outward, strangling him.

Through the shrieking pain racking his body, one final command reached his left hand. The fingers clamped against the microswitches with a force that drove the nails backward into his flesh.

Corporal Rashni Jumbaru—unbound—flew away from the spacecraft at a dizzying velocity. Suddenly weightless and free of stresses, his body collapsed into convulsions.

Onboard *Paraida,* Major Hataan Zahrad stared in silence at the telit. It displayed a green dot flying away from the surface of the derelict.

"Retrieve him," he said, and lowered the comm-mike.

The tiny mote that was the boarding craft rotated on its thrusters and surged toward an interception course with the corporal.

"Sensors show life functions erratic," the lieutenant said, her voice terse and hushed. "Since he was thrown in a direction away from the planet, the boat should be able to catch him."

The major wiped briskly at his moustache and flipped the comm-switch. "*Paraida* to *Zinja*. Our attempt to disable your thrusters has failed. Have you made any progress for your side?"

You've got to be kidding! Shig thought, fighting to remain conscious. *Even if I really wanted you to board, what could I do?*

The telit read 6 G. Maximum. The creaking of cyprium and unipolymer plasteel groaned through the struts and beams of the ship.

Shig wondered if—at this speed of rotation—even SIPACUM could perform the function he'd programmed into the DS. Certainly no human could do it. He flipped on the microswitch that controlled the comm. Scarcely able to breathe, he transmitted the (convincing) sounds of a man being crushed into unconsciousness. He didn't have to try too hard.

"Systems damaged beyond re–repai–" he choked out, dropping his head to one side and moving his fingers toward the DS controls.

He realized then that he'd strapped his arm too tightly. The fingers had gone numb. *BOOPFAITU!* Presumably, Booda's Plan For All In The Universe included cruel jests.

He twisted his wrist, tried flexing his fingers. They stayed in place, crushed rigidly against the armrest. He nudged the comm off.

"Vark!" he said, his throat nearly collapsing under the centrifugal force. "Jacko—I need you."

"Vug?"

"Reach over here. Hit the middle button. My hand's dead."

The Bleaker grinned. The G-force distorted it into a hideous grimace. His yellow teeth sported flecks of dark red foam. ''Stupid—flainer. Wants—me—to—break—mine.''

Like a shot, though, Vark's arm flew across the narrow gap between their chairs. The armored glove landed on the back of Shig's hand as if it had been dropped from three stories.

''Feel that?'' Vark's smile leaked blood.

Shig sucked air through clenched teeth.

''Then it ain't dead.''

Vark edged his hand across Shig's fingers and punched the center button.

SIPACUM reacted with the speed of light.

Paraida's DS officer responded to the arming of *Zinja*'s weaponry by initiating her own warmup. She was a fraction of a second too late.

The spinning ship fired three shots at the TGW destrier. Three well-placed, computer-aimed plasma bolts blasted *Paraida*'s tractor nodes. The field was instantly cancelled.

At the same instant, the ''derelict'' ship's engines fired just hard enough to kick it into a tumbling, unstable attitude.

''Spacer is falling out of orbit, sir.'' The lieutenant checked the red trajectory line SIPACUM had plotted on her screen. ''Its path will take it into the atmosphere.''

Something chittered for her attention. Consulting a telit, she twisted about to look at Zahrad.

''*Zinja*'s SIPACUM has just broadcast an alarm. The ship's engine dampers have withdrawn. Power source is in overload.''

Zahrad's dark skin paled noticably. He gripped the comm-mike with knuckles the color of weak tea.

''Zahrad to Gheraka. Proceed with recovery. I am pulling *Paraida* out of orbit. You may intercept us at—'' he paused to check the coordinates the lieutenant was punching in, ''—at twenty-seven, three-forty eight, ninety-six, attitude seventeen at forty thousand kloms.''

''*You're staying in orbit and following that wreck to its impact point!*''

''She won't have an impact point, Gheraka! She's going to *blow*. And I don't want to be within a megaklom of her when she does. The electromagnetic pulse alone would knock out—''

"I'm ordering you to track that ship!"

Zahrad stroked his beard. He had been a cautious man all his life. That he stood within grasping distance of his pension made him even more cautious. Facing what he considered to be sure death on one hand and a possible court-martial on the other, he made his choice.

"*Myrzha* Gheraka, I respectfully refuse on the following grounds. *Zinja* is almost certainly lost to us. It did not have a tailer on it when we arrived, so we can't be sure it is the ship we want. I am under no obligation to put my ship and crew in danger under orders received for a mission of mere surveillance."

"By the book, Major?" The gravel in the voice had been replaced by a smooth, stony coolness.

"When my ship and crew are at stake, yes."

"I have the authority to—"

"Not according to the book." Zahrad nodded to the lieutenant.

Giving the major a confirming nod, she ordered SIPACUM to bring *Paraida* out of orbit. The ship reacted slowly.

"If," Major Zahrad continued, "you can get a comm from your central command authorizing you to seize control of this ship within the time it takes *Zinja* to blow, you may. Otherwise, I am ordering the boarding party to retrieve Corporal Jumbaru, intercept *Paraida* at the stated coordinates, and prepare for tachyon conversion." He paused for dramatic effect. "If you prevent the crew from complying, I shall have no recourse but to abandon the boarding vessel and return to Sekhar."

The comm remained silent for more than a minute.

Finally, a tired voice said, *"Corporal Jumbaru secured. Returning to* Paraida."

Major Hataan Zahrad exhaled slowly. Punching up the ship's log, he spoke clearly. "Day three. The freighter *Zinja* of Terasaki encountered and engaged in battle with slave vessel presumed to be the target spacer. Fragment of debris detected with ion tailer still functioning. Target spacer presumed destroyed. *Zinja* mortally disabled, deorbiting with undamped drive. *Paraida* preparing to depart vicinity of blast." He thought for a moment. "Captain

Hoyuko of *Zinja* battled valiantly to save his ship and is to be commended."

The last was a mere formality. TGW never handed out commendations.

"The derelict is hitting upper atmosphere, sir." The lieutenant watched her telit in fascination. She had never seen a spacer incinerated.

Marekallian stuck his gas spectrometer into the stream of vapor issuing from the sphere.

"Just helium." His voice squeaked from inhaling the lighter gas. "It's venting out." He rubbed his arms against the chill filling the room. Water vapor condensed around his feet.

Verley shivered and drew toward him.

He wrapped his arms around her and tried to warm her exposed skin. "It shouldn't take too long to vent," he said.

"There's something inside it."

Eks looked at the sphere. The shell had become translucent. The lamp he had set on the far side of the vault shone through the sphere, faintly outlining a dark shape at its center.

"Akil," he breathed.

The chill in the vault abated with the escape of the lighter helium through the entry hole high in the wall. Eks felt something more, though. Approaching the sphere, he felt a definite warmth radiating from the object. From somewhere in its depths, a low humming commenced.

He ran his hands over the warming shell. *An Akil. And a lost race of Urth! More than any explorer could hope to find. Marek, my jacko, you've hit the all-time high stakes!*

For a moment, he rode on a wave of excitement. Research, tracing the course of the Homeworlder's flight to Arepien. Study, communicating with the Akil. Lectures, revealing his accumulated knowledge of–

Of what?

The thought stunned him. *Of Protected planets?* He ran a hand across his head. Catching his fingers in the thong tying his queue, he ripped it savagely from his hair and threw it to the floor.

"Damn them!" he shouted.

They'll never let me reveal what I've learned from any planet. They'll want the Akil. They'll revise operations for Arepien. Damn them! And damn TGO too! He was trapped from both sides. His allies and his enemies both had their reasons for suppressing his discoveries. *They'll never let me breach security and TGO would never let me admit I openly flouted Protection, that I sacked temples and robbed graves.*

He kicked at shards of ice and fumed.

They'd never let a rogue become a hero. I made my choice years ago. I'll be a rogue to my death. He stopped and listened. *Which may be sooner than I want.*

The noise outside the tower had increased.

Like a lightning flash, his old smile returned. *Then to hell with them!*

The sphere cracked. Seven fissures radiated from a point at the top of the globe and raced downwards. Hitting the antipodal point, the cracks widened, splitting the shell into seven petals that fell open like a lotus in bloom.

Marekallian jumped back, narrowly avoiding being flattened by one of the pieces. Almost as quickly, he pounced forward to stare at the figure slumped at the center of the device.

A transparent sack clung to its body like wet tissue. It stood, more or less, in a crouching, lopsided position. Mists swirled around it, evaporating in the returning warmth. Its size was less than that of either Eks or Verley.

The Mindrunner grabbed a section of the shell and pulled it out of the way. He wrinkled his nose at the whiff of a horrible, wet odor. For a moment he feared that the Akil was dead. Climbing up the squat cylinder that supported the humanoid, Eks reached out and tenderly put his arms around its waist and back.

He lifted.

Part of the sack remained attached to the column. It ripped along a seam, spilling a few liters of clear liquid around Eks's feet.

The body twitched in his arms.

"It's alive!" he cried to Verley. "Help me."

Verley stepped carefully over the wreckage of the

cryosphere and offered an arm. She supported his load while he sat down on the column and swung his legs to the floor.

The body in his arms clawed at the sack. Long, lemur-like fingers poked through the membrane, blindly seeking escape. Gurgling sounds issued from inside.

"Lay it down. Over there."

They carried the Akil between their clasped arms and lowered it to a dry portion of floor. Stripping his jacket off, he laid it on the polished stone and lowered their burden on top of it.

"It's like a sandbaby breaking out of its pouch," Verley said in a whisper.

The Akil tore at the sack until its head poked out. Thick, gold-white hair lay wet and matted against its head. Fur, as fine as silky down and pale as platinum, clung to its skin everywhere else. Its eyes opened slowly. A hand wiped away sticky fluids from them.

Verley stared at the Akil's eyes. Larger and rounder even than a Jarp's, they stared blankly. The irises were the color of metallic gold—like twin pools of shimmering gold flake, stirred by hidden winds. Verley gazed fixedly at them, her own eyes locked in mesmerized fascination.

The Akil looked around the room while still struggling with the remains of the sack. Its hands—delicate, yet apparently strong—tore the bag from its chest, revealing more of the fine fur and a flat, smooth chest. Using its slender legs, it kicked the rest of the sack off and lay on Eks's jacket, breathing shallowly and staring at its rescuers.

"Male," Eks said, looking the wet being up and down. A tone of disappointment betrayed his true hopes concerning the Akil's gender. "Well, I'm sure we'll find *something* to talk about."

The Akil blinked, uncomprehending.

Eks stood, lifting the creature gently. It allowed the Galactic to lift it, then smiled and said, "Lasht'miyek shashleel?"

"Uh, couldn't agree more," Marekallian said, grinning. "Hold him while I get my pack, Verley."

Depositing the Akil in the woman's arms, he noted with mild annoyance that the alien immediately seemed happier.

His lithe body snuggled firmly against the womanly one. His arms wrapped around her, ostensibly for support. She felt strength in his grasp, though. His golden eyes peered into hers of dark brown. She smiled warmly. Wet white-gold fur pressed to warm bare breasts. Neither the owner of the former nor of the latter minded a bit.

Frozen for a couple dozen centuries and he can't even wait till we're out of this mess. Speaking of which–

Marekallian picked up his jacket and wrung out as much of the thick fluids as he could before he bundled it up and shoved it into his backpack. With a grunt, he threw it on and fastened the straps.

"Get the bag. We're cutting our way out of here." He scanned the walls of the vault.

"This way," he said, walking to the far wall. *"Get the bag."*

He scanned the wall a second time. It *sounded* hollow. At least, the sonar indicated something less dense than rock. Unlimbering the laser, he clicked the dial up to high output and pointed at the rocky surface.

The beam punched through the meter of stone in seconds and hit what lay beyond.

The jet of water that spouted from the fist-sized hole almost knocked Marekallian's feet from under him. He sidestepped and looked back at Verley.

"Let's not go this way."

"I thought you weren't worried about traps." She led the Akil away from the stream of cold ocean water and hoisted the bag of plunder over her shoulder.

"I'm not," he said while water pooled around the soles of his boots. "I can swim."

Verley, who had never seen even a tubfull of water on Sekhar, eyed the leak with growing apprehension. The Akil watched with interest, not realizing his danger.

"They're all like that." Eks stood quietly checking the readings on each section of the wall with the sonar.

"Shouldn't we be getting out of here?" Verley asked, backing farther away from the water.

"It's a big room. Won't fill up that quick. Now, where would they put an exit?" He played the beam of his flash over the walls.

"Marek–"

"The frost on the sphere proves that the vault was sealed and never entered."

"The wall–"

"This must have been built after the Urth ship landed or crashed or whatever. They built this and then something happened to their technology. Probably just not enough resources to maintain their level, and they slipped back. Or maybe there was some plague. . ."

"*Musla.*" Verley cursed, and ran for the dangling cord. She dropped the bag and seized the line, climbing up as fast as she could.

The Akil looked from her to Eks to the cracks forming around the recently lased hole. His golden eyes widened beyond their already formidable diameters. Though weak and disoriented, he gained a quick awareness of the danger. Emitting a hiss of alarm, he crouched and squinted at the cord leading to the hole overhead.

Eks spun around in time to see a wet, pale figure leap four meters up and clutch at the cord. It landed above a very startled Verley. The creature clambered up the line and into the passageway. There he paused to look down at the woman.

Eks was about to shout when a splintering noise caught his attention.

The rock surrounding the waterspout crumbled. Shooting through with tremendous force, a river of sea water roared into the vault. White foam spewed about in the light from the lamps.

"Oh shit!"

Eks ran to the cord. It rose up quickly, out of reach. *One Dam' Thing After Another*, he thought in anguish, watching the Akil pull Verley up. Unaccustomed to rope-climbing, she gratefully allowed the small alien to pull her to safety.

"What about me?" Eks shouted, with water up to his knees. He leaned into the current that threatened to knock him to one side.

"I thought you could swim!" Verley looked down at him, her face flanked by dark hair stringy from exertion.

Marekallian dragged the bag of treasure from underwater and held it up with a grunt. "I can't with all this ballast!" The water had climbed to his waist. But for that ballast, he'd have been afloat.

The Akil, understanding not a word of the exchange, threw the cord's end down and waited. Watching the Mindrunner.

"Thanks, runt!"

Eks tried the cord to the eyelets in the bag. Waving back the pair above him, he scampered up. Water poured from his clothing and backpack. That extra weight slowed him in the last few meters, but he pulled himself over the ledge with a huff of triumph.

Verley and the Akil dragged him through the narrow opening and into the dark hall. Eks felt around for his hat, then peered back into the chamber. Nine or ten gallons of wide-brimmed hat floated in the swirling waters that filled the vault. Its band-light still glowed.

He sighed and began hauling up the bag. Getting a firm grip on the cord, he backed into the passage. He positioned his legs against the wall, and pulled.

"I'm not doing this for the exercise," he yelled. "Help me!"

Verley stood still, watching with serenely arched brows.

"Look," he told her, "if I leave without this bag, I won't be able to overlook that jewelry and whatever's in your boot."

Verley sneered. She also took a section of cord, and pulled. In a moment the top of the sack peeked over the ledge.

Even as Eks reached for it he saw that the lights he'd set on the walls were now underwater. Wet hair straggled in his face. The straps from his backpack chewed at his chest. And the dripping sack resisted like some limp corpse. Marekallian snarled a curse and stretched his muscles to their fullest. Reaching halfway down the sack with one hand, he used the other to jockey the top end into the hole.

Gold and silver scattered like cheap toys as he dragged the bag into the hallway. He took a moment to find his handflash and flip it on.

"You take care of the Akil. And this!" He shoved the

clanky bag in Verley's direction and concentrated on finding the correct way out.

Wearing a look of disgust, Verley hefted the load without a word. Something touched her feet and she twitched.

The Akil yelped. His feet splashed water. Water that flowed over the edge of the vault, now, to join them in the hallway.

"The whole damned ocean's coming in here!" Verley cried, and her voice rose to a squeal.

"Right," the Outreacher said. "We must still be below sea level. I guess we'd, ah, better head upwards."

"Did you think this clearly before you got your degree?"

"Cute."

He ran up the slopping passage, boots squishing and pants still dripping. The lightbeam bounced ahead of him, reflecting off meters and meters of featureless rock. Verley followed, toting the bag. The Akil kept pace with her. His huge round eyes adapted quite easily to the low light.

"I don't think that water was a trap," Eks said to relieve the silence. "It was probably a few millennia of seepage and bad engineering. Most tomb builders don't design their traps to destroy the treasures as well as the thieves." He stopped and raised his hand. The other two padded to a halt behind him.

"Dead end."

"With the water behind us?" Verley turned around as if expecting waves to be lapping at her heels.

Eks turned around and walked past the Akil, heading back down the slope. "There's no need to get all panicky," he said. "The water can't have risen that high." He turned a corner.

Verley stayed where she was, watching the light diminish. For a moment she was in total darkness with the Akil.

He pulled closer to her. His fur had almost dried, leaving him sticky and cool. Verley didn't mind the friendly contact.

The light from Eks's flash returned, bouncing up the tunnel.

"Panic," he said, turning the corner and running past them. He unstrapped the laser and set the output at maximum.

Verley held the flash while Eks considered where to cut. "I thought you wanted to swim," she said.

"The passage is filled with water. We're in an air pocket. It won't fill up, but we won't last long if we don't blast our way out of here."

"You seem to be pretty good at blasting your way *into* problems." Verley laid the sack down and sat beside it. The Akil knelt beside her. Its attention was on the man.

"Listen, sister, I've never been in a situation I couldn't talk or shoot my way out of."

He switched on the cutter. The exit optics glowed green— for an instant. They sputtered out.

"Better start talking," Verley muttered.

"Oh shit." Eks shook water out of the device and opened up its power source. He closed it just as quickly. He gave Verley a look. "I think it would be better if we didn't talk at all. We'll need all the air we can get." He turned the laser over and commenced dismantling it.

Verley fingered her new jewelry. *There are worse ways to be buried,* she mused.

Then she tried to think of one.

18

They danced without rhythm, without grace, without awareness. Caught in the stopper beams, the pilgrims to Round Island jerked, quivered and stumbled in random motion. Overhead, the light of the first rising star of Arepien's binary shone down.

The light reflected brightly off the twin rows of prass buttons on Kislar Jonuta's coat. He stood on a rock, casually pointing his stopper at the crowd. He smiled with theatrical broadness.

"Think'st thou, oh mighty Sakyo, that thou canst lock thy beam on yon pack of flaining Sainvituses and get thee down into the jungle, that we may runneth and saveth our arses?"

"Firm," Sak whispered loudly, with no desire to reveal his existence if he could avoid it.

"Then sneakest thou back and out," Jonuta said, stomping about in a burlesque of shamanic invocation. He strode away from Sak's hiding place, drawing the attention of the few clan members not involved in the holy frenzy. *Hangback bastards!*

Sak wedged his stopper between two rocks and jammed the switch in the On position so as to keep it trained on the right flank of the mob. *That ought to hold them till the charge fades*, he thought, wondering whether the wide dispersion of the beam would use up the power faster. He hoped so. Having one's nervous system jangled by a stopper beam for too long could lead to permanent damage. And if damage were his intent, the Fry setting would have been more merciful.

At the moment, though, Sak was more concerned about

getting away with his skin. The ancient phrase was Save Thine Ass.

He backed away from the outcropping, keeping it blocking the line-of-sight between the crowd and him until he reached the tower. He ducked behind it quickly and waited. Hearing no approaching footsteps, he redshifted into the forest.

The vines swallowed him up and he crouched quietly. A wood cony scampered away from him, chittering with disapproval.

"Kenowa?" he said into his wristlink. He waited a few seconds. Receiving no reply, he said, "Captain?"

"Speakest thou up, oh mighty Sakyo. It be loud and crazy out here." The voice on the commlink sounded loud and distant, as if Jonuta were shouting into the comm at arm's length.

"Coronet must still be under comm-silence. Maybe our guests *have* shown up."

"That," Jonuta intoned, *"wouldst be the capper on a long and unpleasant day. Booda's eyes! Runnest thou back to thine lander and get it ready, if Kenny hath not. Firm?"*

"Pos."

Sak circled around the periphery of the clearing, keeping an eye on the crowd. Jonuta stood above them like the Great Brown Hope. With one last look, Sak darted into the jungle. He soon found the path they had blazed through the foliage. In his haste, roots and puddles and vines sped by too quickly even to be noticed as obstacles.

"Didn't you say this was an air pocket?" Verley pushed the bag up another few sems and followed it. The Akil had already retired to the highest portion of the passage.

Eks watched the advancing water.

"At least that proves we're near the surface—the air's got to be escaping somewhere." He pounded his fist on the laser's rear panel. "Damn these cutters and damn Franji equipment and *damn oceans!"*

Verley's eyes widened. "Didn't you have a pulsar beamer?"

Eks glared at her. "Yes. Want me to put you out of your misery?"

"You could use–"

"If I fired that off in here we'd be roasted. Plasma against rock would spatter melted slag all over the place. Lava, firm it?" He moved his feet up out of the water. They had two meters of air space left, less than that of floor space.

Verley spoke quietly, without anger. "And what if we were underwater when you beamed?"

Eks looked at her long enough to break into a wide grin. He reached out and kissed her.

She returned the kiss with a fervor that shocked both of them.

"Jackobabe, you just saved the day!" Laughing, he lifted her by the arm and tossed her into the rising waters. The Akil watched silently.

"You too, furface." He reached out for the Akil's slim waist.

("M-Musla!" Verley squeaked. "M-my *breasts float!*")

A delicate hand whipped about to grasp the Mindrunner's wrist in a surprisingly strong grip. Golden *alien* eyes shimmered in the glow of the flash. Marekallian Eks spoke silently.

"Hey—I'm trying to save your life, friend." He turned to Verley. "Of *course* they float, desert brat. Call him over to you."

"He's not a grat! He just doesn't understand–"

"I do not need a lecture on epistemology, thanks. Just get this li'l flainer in the double-damned water!"

Verley held out a hand to the alien. His golden eyes regarded her, looked at Eks, at the dark advancing water. That lovely soft fur stood out from his body in a white-gold aura. Slowly, he slid down the incline and into the water beside her. He hardly splashed.

She smiled and ran a wet hand over his tangled hair. It was almost embarrassing that even under the circumstances this non-Galactic was disturbingly sensuous. (He was also interestedly watching her floating breasts.)

Eks pulled the pulsar beamer out of one of those many pockets. He edged into the water and dragged the heavy sack to plop in after him. Setting the beam for maximum discharge, he settled back in the water. Only his arms and head lay exposed, gently bobbing.

"Breathe twice, take a deep one and stay under till—"

"Ohgod!"

"—till I kick you. Then get up and out, *fast*. I think the water level won't get any higher, but . . ." He looked behind him at that slow, menacingly steady rise. "I've been wrong before. Now—down!"

Kick me, huh, Verley thought—and took a deep breath. She made a big show of it for the benefit of the Akil. Then, for the first time in her life, the woman from desert-sprawling Sekhar ducked her head under water.

After pulling a breath, the furred humanoid watched Marekallian slowly treading water all the while. Verley's hand shot up splashily, found and pressed the top of his head, and pulled the surprised Akil down.

Marekallian Eks slipped back into the water and actuated the beamer.

Shiganu of Terasaki and *Coronet* had no time to consider the wisdom of his actions. It was far too late to wonder whether the orders he had given SIPACUM had covered every contingency. *Coronet* dropped inexorably toward Arepien's atmosphere. The outer hull (designed for deep space and definitely not for planetary excursions) began to heat despite the meteor shields.

The crushing weight of rotation at six gravities combined with the thrust of the main engines contorted his inner ear's balance to the point of nausea; disorientation.

"Vaarrkhhh. . ."

His teeth remained gritted in pain. He had to fight to keep his tongue from dropping back into his throat. Centrifugal force held him immobile and elevated his weight past 46O kilograms.* His heart labored. His lungs fought the dreadful weight of his ribcage while the crushing pressure against his skin did hideous and painful things to his eyes and mouth. Shig was unable to do anything save try to stay alive while SIPACUM strove to save the ship.

He had programmed the computer to propel *Coronet* into a

---

*Over a thousand *pounds*, Old Style; Sakyo's weight at 6G.

trajectory that would skip it through Arepien's atmosphere like a flat stone skimmed over a lake. If the crew of *Paraida* calculated his descent—and assumed that his drive was out of control—they would project an impact point on the far side of the planet, out of their view.

Shig hoped they wouldn't hang around to make sure. SIPACUM would alter the spacer's course at the low point of a hundred kloms from Arepien's surface. He hoped that the fear of an undamped double-p drive's overload would get them out of orbit and far away by the time *Coronet* reappeared over the opposite horizon.

Spacefarer Shiganu also hoped that the ship would survive the screaming skip through the planetary atmosphere. And that *he* would!

He was not all that optimistic.

The hull temp was above the thousand-degree mark. Creaks and groans filtered through the pounding in Shig's ears. The strain of the ship's spin and the buffeting of the atmosphere attempted to twist and flatten the hull; at the same time, the friction of the upper atmosphere threatened to roast *Coronet* and its crew of two. Both helpless.

"At . . . least," Shig gritted through a haze of fading awareness, "We'll app . . . reciate M-us-la's Cold Helll . . . when we–get–there . . ."

Vark, unconscious, said nothing.

19

Kislar Jonuta of Qalara took a step to the side. The portion of the crowd of Areps not caught in the grip of either his or Sak's stopper beams moved toward him. Meanwhile, he kept talking—and thinking.

They're going to keep me here until the dam' dance is over. They want their own signs of divinity and they aren't about to let me leave until I've given it to them. Tao's testes—what do they want? A Nirvanan dance band?

He continued to talk while he edged toward one side of the tower. Tracing great circles with his arms, he strode back and forth as if delivering a classroom lecture—intoned mightily in his resonant voice.

"Thou hast me cornered, oh lanky disciples of The Mother and Her lover. Thou makest it severely difficult for me to redshift and saveth my ass from thee." He leaned back and shouted to the heavens. "All I do ask, by Booda's omnipotent balls and Sak's genuis, is a diversion! Something to draggeth this most unwelcome attention off me!"

Promptly the ground behind him shrieked and exploded.

His reflexes acted instantly to throw him forward. His shoulder hit the ground and he rolled so as to bring himself fully about. He faced the source of the commotion with his stopper ready.

Of course that freed half the gaggle of worshipers of the weapon's effect. They recovered weakly to gaze dully at the events at the tower's base.

Blinding light flared from the soil a few meters from the base of the shrine tower. The air shrieked again and dirt flew upward as if thrown from a volcano. A blob of nearly molten stone hit Jonuta's coat and sizzled.

"Uh! Booda's balls!" He shook it from him and slapped at his coat before crawling to the side. Away from the crowd and the tower. The black cylinder of his stopper he kept pointed at the crater.

Again light flared from it. The Areps able to do so covered their eyes. Some dancers, still under the spell of Sak's beam, happened randomly to stare into the actinic flash. They were dazzled into temporary blindness. That failed to stop their frantic chorea in the least. No one fled.

Slag formed a brim around the circumference of the hole. Steam wafted from it, obscuring its depth. The odor of ozone and burning vegetation rode the air heavily. From somewhere within the fuming caldera arose the sounds of struggle, accompanied by the sound of water surging and dripping.

"Whee-ooo!" The shout came in a familiar voice.

On his stomach, Jonuta moved slowly toward the jumbly outcropping of reddish, pearly, and tan rock. He could guess what was coming next.

The more curious worshipers walked silently toward the cooling channel. They heard the sound of a muffled metallic jangling, somewhere inside the slanting tunnel into their planet. Since their god was standardly associated with the planetary sun, Jonuta wondered if they had added the ridiculous aspect of old Persian dualism; an antigod that lived within the planet.

No, he reflected, *else surely they'd be* red*shifting, not* blue–!

A human grunt issued from the hole. A large green-and-brown sack came flying forth to land in the dirt with a wet sloshing sound mingled with a lot of jingle-jangle. It listed to one side like a drunken Booda and capsized, at last coming to rest with a tired rattle and clink.

Next a hand grasping a pulsar beamer reached for the edge of the hole. It started to grasp a large piece of slag.

"Yeeowch!" The hand retracted, fast.

Moments later, Marekallian Eks jumped out of the channel cut by his beamer. He was followed by Verley and the Akil. The Mindrunner rubbed his burned fingers as he turned around . . . to face nearly two hundred tall, staring descendants of the "Amerinds" of Homeworld. His eyes went wide.

"Oops. Wrong party."

(As quietly as possible, Jonuta slid behind the big outcrop, then rose. He ran, crouching as he raced to the jungle.)

Members of the Arepienese crowd moved toward the newcomers. Some still displayed an awed, inquisitive look. Others realized that the man before them, though he might behave as a god, was taking up a suspiciously heavy sack. And it jingle-clinked.

Marekallian Eks smiled graciously. He held the bag in one hand while his other covered the crowd with the beamer. Wet hair hung in his eyes, but he dared not reach up to brush it aside.

I may have only one chance to get my hands on this, he thought, lifting the bag halfway off the ground. "Uh!" *How'd Verley ever carry the damned thing?*

Noting the scores of shuffle-dancing natives, he no longer had to force a smile. "That dam' slaver has style," he muttered.

The Elder, her head still buzzy from the number Two beam, approached him angrily. She addressed him in T'gitish.

"What's she saying?" Verley asked, drawing the furry alien under a protective arm. She could still hardly believe all that underwater pawing she'd received.

"I'm not too sure, but I assume she's not too pleased with our shopping spree."

"Wh-at do we do?"

"Think they'd believe us if we told them we'd lost our tour guide?"

Verley gave him a look—while Rakhin Ndyanda Q'gita reached for the bag. Righteous anger lit her eyes so that they shone like polished jasper.

Eks spoke over his shoulder. "Back away from me toward the forest."

He maintained a strong grip on sack and plasmer while failing to notice that they'd been surrounded almost completely. He twitched the bag of loot out of the woman's reach and pointed the plasmer at her face. (Verley shuddered.)

"Uh-uh, stalecake. Rights of salvage and all that."

The Elder failed to recognize the awful threat of a plasma weapon. She reached up to knock his hand away.

"Theba's thighs!" Marekallian muttered, realizing that he couldn't do it. Turning the device aside, he zapped a nearby stone outcrop. A bolt of white-hot ions sizzled out to vaporize the center of the mass of gray/red/tan stone. Boulders fell in on one another with a satisfying crash. Something cracked loudly.

And the rest of the pilgrims stopped dancing.

They stood about or collapsed for a few moments, woozily regaining their senses. One by one, they joined the crowd now totally surrounding the aliens to their world. They eyed the furry one, but showed little fear.

"What was that?" Verley asked.

Eks regarded the pile of rubble that had concealed Sak's stopper. "I think I just shot my way into more trouble."

Kunda vines slapped against Jonuta's face like whips. Insects, too slow to avoid his hurtling form, bounced off his chest and extremities. His lungs sucked in air and pushed it out, fighting to provide his muscles with the energy to keep up his alarming pace. An upraised arm shielded his face.

He crashed through flora he had thought impassable on the way into the forest, back when there wasn't so much rush. Wood conies scampered out of his way. Greenwings fluttered into panicked flight, screaming to their nestlings and scolding the scarlet-carapaced creature disturbing them in its headlong race through their domain.

The muggy air of the forest combined with sweat to turn his equhyde boots into a clinging second skin that creaked with every movement. Beams of sunlight pierced the foliage to provide illumination, but Jonuta wished fervently that the forest were dark and cool instead. From the thickness of the plant growth he estimated that he was over halfway through.

That was when he heard the shouts behind him.

He had never realized how difficult it was to look over his shoulder while he was running full tilt. He tried only once. Regaining his stride, he jumped a decaying tree trunk and splashed through calf-deep water. Meanwhile he tried to recall whether he'd ever seen weapons on any Arep. Deciding that he had not, he slowed to a trot and drew his stopper. He made a sharp turn at a curtain of kunda vines and checked the cylinder's setting Oh Two. He didn't have to wait.

The pair of followers halted short of his hiding place and turned to split up. Too late. A low hum filled the forest silence. In the dim lighting, a faint violet glow emanated from behind a stringy veil of vines.

Both Areps collapsed, neurologically frozen by the Two-beam. The humus surrounding a fallen tree cushioned their impact.

"So much for that dynamic duo," Jonuta muttered, and ran.

After long minutes of extremely difficult running, he broke out of the woods and sped down a gradual slope toward the shore—and the landers. *Coronet*'s in-grav boat waited on the beach, powering up. With a tight grin and a final burst of exertion, he forced his powerful legs into a sprint. In a matter of seconds he pounded over sand and soil and slammed up the ramp into the lander.

He took in Sak's presence at a glance. "Zip us up! Redshift!" He popped into the chair beside Kenowa, pausing long enough to wink at his aide: "Mind if I drive?"

"You can drive it anytime, anywhere you want," she said, running her tongue over her lower lip. Relief left her weak but could not overwhelm her sensuousness. Especially since the aroma of her recent lovemaking still clung to her.

"Still can't raise *Coronet*, Cap'n," Sak snapped. "Shig must—"

"What's that?" Yarala—entirely naked and still less fetching than Kenowa—pointed out the starboard viewing port.

"Booda, *no!*" Jonuta saw the glowing dot above the ocean's horizon seem to drop down out of view, growing brighter and larger with every millisecond. He knew what it had to be. A sick helplessness washed over him.

"*Coronet*," Kenowa whispered.

Sakyo's mouth refused to move, even to breathe. He watched in tortured silence while the object disappeared beneath the horizon. With it, he felt something die inside him. His compact body slumped back in the chair.

Quiet, endless seconds dragged by unnoticed. The four stared blankly at the featureless junction of ocean and sky. Thinking, remembering. . .

Sak was the first to shout.

"There!"

Appearing to rise over the horizon like a sun, a blazing teardrop soared almost lazily across the southern quadrant of the sky. A glowing trail of ionized air followed it, shimmering and sparkling and breaking up behind the flaring swirl of flame.

No one dared say a word. As if their hopes could lift the artificial meteor, they watched in silent vigil. The pure white flames seemed to tumble and spin in unstable gyrations. Almost directly overhead, it swerved slowly and ceased to grow in size.

When it began to shrink—losing its tail—Sakyo whooped.

"It's rising! It's skipping out of the atmosphere!" He pounded the arms of his chair, and only the startled Yarala noted the wetness of his eyes.

The tail of ionized air—heated to glowing by friction—shortened to nothingness. Almost immediately, the head of the meteor lost its glow. It vanished into the lazulite-blue sky.

Kenowa jumped as if goosed. She had been leaning on the commsender when a burst of static cracked from its squeaker.

"*Coronet to lander. We made it!*"

"Out of what?" Jonuta demanded, seizing the swingaway comm-mike.

Shig's voice filled them in on the confrontation between *Paraida* and "*Zinja*." Jonuta listened without comment, his dark eyes steady and intense. When Shig had finished the report, Jonuta asked several questions about the ship. Satisfied with the information, he leaned back in his chair and prepared the lander for boostoff.

"Do you have rotation and thrust vectors under control, Shig?"

"*Pos, Boss. We're lifting to thousand-klom orbit to await your arrival and docking.*"

"Uh. Shig . . . where's that damned destrier now?"

"*The last report from* SIPACUM *before we hit the atmosphere shows it pulling out of orbit, rush. I had them convinced that we'd be a minor nova, Captain.*"

Shiganu sounded justifiably proud of his skill at bluff and deceit. A smiling Jonuta threw SIPACUM into control.

"Then prepare to receive boarders, *Coronet!*" He flashed his smile at Kenowa and squeezed her bare thigh as the engines whined to life. Turning to Yarala, he said, "If you want to remain here on Arepien, you still have a few seconds to unstrap and get out."

"I . . . think I won't be welcome in my clan when word spreads of my collaboration with the sky-gods." She snuggled back in the conforming shape of the chair's cushioning. The soft equhyde felt warm and luxurious against her unclothed skin.

"Besides, Captain—I have to take my revenge on Mayekalliah for his treatment of me."

"If he ever catches up with us. And—" Jonuta initiated the launch cycle—"we'd better catch up to *Coronet,* or *we*'ll be left behind."

"All in all," Kenowa said, "I'd rather be in Norcross."

Jonuta's squeeze, high on her thigh, was hard. Meanwhile the engines screamed into full power and flung the boat into the sky. Acceleration pressed Yarala into the cushions and stuffed her gasp back down her throat. In amazement she watched the ground dropping away. A glance down at herself afforded her the ego-shaking sight of her breasts flattened against her chest by the G-force. Feelings of dizziness, elation, and tingling pleasure flowed through her long, lean nakedness. Even her abrasions and contusions felt like badges of victory, now. She wore them proudly, first marveling at seeing tree*tops,* then watching the sky around them turn from blue indigo to a deep amethystine.

The first Arep into space! Her eyes sparkled even as the stars that appeared, sharp and bright. They did not twinkle, she noted with puzzlement; instead they shone with a naked brilliance in colors and hues she'd never seen before. Air no longer lay between them and her. Only . . . space.

I'm a spaceborn Arep—the first! I'm a spacefarer!

She toyed with the term, the imagery, the memories her brainboosted mind called up and displayed for her. She would travel *everywhere,* she mused. *I will run through the* tunnels *of gigantic* spacers, *climb through the maze of passages on* space stations, *float in space! I will even wear* clothes!

She tried to imagine the feel of fabric enveloping her—soft weaves as different from the coarse fibers of her clan's looms as the two cultures' modes of travel. She looked at the big woman who was so clearly the woman of this tall, rumbly-voiced space captain.

The shorter Kenowa's voluptuous body was clothed—and seemed to reveal as much as Yarala's. *And she carries herself so proudly!* Yarala gazed on in dreamy admiration.

Her thoughts were interrupted by a sudden decrease in the invisible weight clamping her down. The sky outside had become black. Blacker than any night on Arepien.

"I have you onscreen and on visual, *Coronet,*" Jonuta said.

He fed new information to the computer. The boat shifted altitude, matching courses to an intercept point farther along in the orbit. At this distance, *Coronet* glimmered like a diamond among the other gems strewn across the "sky." It was the only jewel that twinkled. The flickering of the attitude jets saw to that—and the slight rotation Shig had retained to ensure an even cooling of the spacer's surface after its flaming plunge in and out of Arepien's atmosphere.

Yarala felt lighter than a feather. Her skin seemed barely to touch the chair. But for the drug she had taken—Stand-up—her stomach would not have let her enjoy the new sensation. As it was, she floated happily against the restraining straps with her hair flowing about her as if she were swimming in the sea. Hoding her arms out, she relaxed—and watched them refuse to drop.

I can't even tell which way is down anymore! It looks as if I'm at the top of everything!

"Slow that spin," Jonuta rumbled, concentrating.

They neared the spacer. Since she had no sense of proportion for the craft, Yarala watched amazed as it grew and grew—and grew. Its bulk filled the lander's viewport.

Still it expanded. A sensation of falling overwhelmed her. The weightless sensation added to her alarm.

In the side of that wall of cyprium and plasteel lay a small, lighted hole. It grew. Yarala stared wordlessly, watching it widen with every second of their approach. She knew her life would change when she passed through that aperture—a yawning door into another existence. Not another world—other *worlds*.

It occurred to her that her life had changed irrevocably quite a while back, when she'd first seen Marekallian's lander descend from the sky and disappear into the blue-leafed forest.

I am a Ga-lac-tic *now*. She savored the word. Citizen of the Galaxy.

"Abate the roll so we can line up, Shig. Good. As soon as we've docked, prepare to redshift. Inslot course to Qarala and move out to sufficient distance for tachyon conversion."

"*Firm, Cap'n. Program* SIPACUM *to begin seeking entry point?*"

"Program SIPACUM as you said, Shig."

Again Jonuta glanced at the ruddy-skinned, entirely naked young woman behind him. He didn't bother giving her a reassuring smile. Nor would he mention that he'd be making another memory deposit with Fumiko Kita-daktari. Captain Cautious intended to remain both cautious and a captain.

"*Firm,*" Shig's voice said, with distinct ebullience.

Jonuta eased the lander into a direct line with the open docking bay and matched velocities to the computer's optimum range. The rim of the hull passed the side viewing ports, swallowing the boat. It slid into *Coronet*. Hissing jets eased the smaller craft to a stop in front of the shock cushions. Armatures extended to lay hold of the lander and tug it gently into its berth within *Coronet*.

The captain of *Coronet* terminated the docking procedure and unstrapped.

"It's great to be home," he said, sliding an arm around Kenowa and pulling her close.

20

Gheraka showed no outward evidence of the anger boiling in him. He stood with Major Zahrad in the major's quarters.

"You understand that this will probably mean the end of your career," Gheraka said equably.

Haatan Zahrad allowed the slightest trace of a smile to change the set of his lips. "I think not," he said just as civilly. "All I have done is on record and follows procedures. TransGalactic Watch has a tradition of supporting commanding officers in their field decisions."

Gheraka smiled without looking at him. "A tradition is only that."

The lapis lazuli surface of Arepien was hardly visible beyond *Paraida*'s rearward viewport. To the telepresence senses of SIPACUM, however, the planet was still very close indeed. At twenty megakloms distance, the destrier's sensors continued to scan the Protected world.

A chime sounded.

"If you please, *Myrzha* Gheraka—that was the two-minute warning for tachyon conversion. I'd like to be alone."

Gheraka's sour, knowing smile had barely surfaced when a voice spoke courteously from the inship comm.

"Major Zahrad, sir: we show a localized neutrino flux coming around the limb of the planet."

Zahrad maintained his calm demeanor. "Localized? Not a ship-drive explosion?" He hoped not to hear the answer the second lieutenant was about to give him.

"Localized to spacer configuration, sir. Adjusting for redshift time dilation, we backtrack it to a probable course for Zinja."

"They survived." Zahrad stated the fact with a flat simplicity.

Gheraka was more emphatic. "They escaped, you mean. *Almost*." He grinned with a feral intensity that deepened the cleft in his chin. "Bring the helm around." He turned to go, then looked down at the major. "That is, *with* your permission, *Major*."

Zahrad sighed quietly. ODTAA, he mused. Resisting the urge to have Gheraka put in irons regardless of the consequences, he faced the commsender.

"Abort tachyon conversion. Return to the planet at intrasystem flank speed."

He enjoyed the use of archaic terminology. He was certain that Gheraka had no capacity to appreciate its irony. (*Paraida* yawed about, its engines increasing their thrust to full speed.)

"Activate Defense Systemry. Prepare to engage target spacer."

"I don't want a battle," Gheraka reminded.

"We may not be able to avoid it."

Gheraka's voice regained its gravelly edges. "That depends on your skill as a tactician, Major."

So does handling you, you puffed-up glorified clerk! Really think I'm going to lose my temper, don't you?!

In an equable tone Zahrad said, "Umm."

21

Shig had already engaged DS by the time Jonuta and Kenowa reached the con-cabin. Yarala followed, unconcernedly naked. She padded along with grace, marveling at her ability to recognize things she had never seen.

Thanks to the encephaloboost Eks had given her, she understood that a spacer was a closed system, protected from the vacuum all around it by walls of incredibly strong stuff called cyprium, beyond iron and even steel. She had a vague grasp of the method of travel between the stars, though the concept of light's having a *speed* was something she barely comprehended. With difficulty.

She took the time to look at and appreciate from a distance the *prettiness* of all the console lights and controls. The crew were busying themselves. Yarala could think of nothing she had to do anymore. She decided to remain well back and try to be silent and invisible.

"Spacer approaching at full speed," Sakyo announced, and strapped in at the forward DS station. He checked the TP monitoring systemry and used computer simulation to track the return of the destrier.

"Pos," his captain said expressionlessly. "Spooks don't usually stick around an undamped engine. These jackos are either brave or slow-witted."

Jonuta stood before the con, within the curve of the multi-lighted console. Proud of the physical condition he exercised twice daily to maintain, he never sat when he was oncon. *Coronet* had been designed to leave controls within easy reach of his fingers while standing his full 180-sem height.

He stood now with grim intent, Kenowa seated beside

him. He had been about to tell her to take Yarala back for something to wear. That would keep.

"Inslot cassette six-three-bee, Kenny, but don't actuate it yet. We should have time. Keep a grip on 63C. We *may* need to jam-cram."

Jonuta trusted no one but Jonuta to prepare course guidance cassettes. The one marked 63B ordered SIPACUM to prepare the ship for subspace transition with only a single *ping* as twenty seconds' warning. Number 63C contained the program for the last-ditch escape effort called jam-cram. Sixty-three-Cee took control of the spacer and *rammed* it without warning into transition phase, within ten seconds of actuation. That action was worse than dangerous and spacefarers referred to it obliquely as Forty Per Cent City.

The probability of ship—and crew—surviving a jam-cram intact was 59.7731-etcetera-to-infinity per cent. That left a probability of 40.2269 per cent of . . . something else. Simply put, forty per cent of the spacers that jam-crammed were never seen again. Whether they reappeared somewhere else in space or time was a question pondered by theoreticians and theologists. No one knew for sure.*

Among others, pirates Artisune Muzuni and Corundum had gone Forty Per Cent City—the latter facing the assured destruction of his ship by his enemy, Kislar Jonuta. Corundum and his ship *Firedancer* had vanished from the spaceways. They had not been seen again. Or missed.

Kenowa had glanced sharply up at her captain, then obeyed. "Six-three-Bee inslotted and ready. Six-three-Cee standing by." She looked up at Jonuta again with a loving gaze that complemented her efficiency and concealed her apprehension.

Shig filled Jonuta in quickly on details of "*Zinja*'s" encounter with *Paraida*. His fingers deftly operated the keyboard before him, running systems check while he spoke.

"Someone seemed mighty insistent on boarding. So I decided to beg for what he wanted. And made sure neither of us was satisfied!" He checked a telit, nodded, and

---

*Except, perhaps, Carnadyne—of whom almost no one had ever heard. See *Spaceways* #11, *The Iceworld Connection*.

grinned. "I think someone wants something from us, and that we won't be attacked because of . . . that something."

"Maybe not," Jonuta said, watching the other ship close in. "At any rate, sounds as if it isn't poor old Jonuta, specifically, they're after. Why don't we follow the Tao and head out their way?"

Shig grinned in wicked delight.

The usual reaction to the sight of a TGW destrier closing in was to make neutrino tracks in the opposite direction. Jonuta knew a wiser way, if the spooks were truly intent on seizing *Coronet*. To set course away from the pursuing ship would permit it to overtake, simply because acceleration increased geometrically. *Paraida* had been boosting toward them for several minutes. *Coronet* could never hope to out-accelerate the policer craft. Short on choices, Jonuta took the unobvious path of escape.

He ordered the ship to fix directly on *Paraida*, and accelerate.

The master of the other spacer, Jonuta knew, would be unable to match velocities simply by altering course a few degrees. In space, changes of direction required the cancellation of momentum in the original direction, and *then* acceleration in the new vector. Turns of a few degrees needed only little shift in momentum. Turning around demanded the complete rotation of a massive ship one hundred eighty degrees, all the while it was rushing on, followed by total deceleration and acceleration in the reverse direction. The ship either covered thousands of kloms in the maneuver—or its human component would be splattered all over its walls. Zip-spurt-whizz turns were for holomovies devoted to thrills rather than accuracy/authenticity.

Too, *Paraida* would hardly seek to use a tractor field to pull in a ship already slingshotting straight toward it. The only choice open to the master of *Paraida* would be to fight or get or haul tail out of the way.

Ship's master Jonuta was gambling on the other captain's not wanting to fight.

Onboard *Paraida*, ship's master Zahrad overcame the urge to flinch.

He assessed the situation with admirable calm. The man standing behind him, virtually breathing against the back of his head, did not improve matters.

"Pretty energetic for an undamped engine overload, wouldn't you say?"

"Um." Zahrad pursed his lips and checked a turquoise telit. "It could be operating on SIPACUM commands without anyone oncon. A cassette left inslotted; fried circuits. Or maybe Captain Hoyuko survived. If he did, he'd be on his way to dock with us just as he said he wished—just as he'd doing."

"That's not docking speed! That's hostility. Their DS is up."

"Could be on autom–" *Oh to the Fourth Hell with it!* "Then we engage them?"

Gheraka mulled the question over—taking into consideration the fact that while TGO was hardly military, these gray-and-maroon uniformed TGWers were, and that the Mission Recorder was certainly turning, turning, recording . . . Just what did he wish to say—on tape?

What he wanted would probably be intact after a fight. That is, if the other ship surrendered or was disabled. Regrettable if he destroyed that flaining Hoyuko's ship and lost what he sought! On the other hand . . . *if they want to play Narjeelan roobaball with steep shot, I can play just as hard.*

"Do not fire unless attacked," he said, feeling an unfamiliar sense of control and restraint possessing him.

"Ac-knowledged," Zahrad said, dragging it out. "Cut drive and rotate the ship a full one-eighty, Lieutenant." He watched the star field shift laterally before him. "Maximum acceleration along the target craft's vector."

Though many megakloms ahead of *Coronet,* the spacer strove to attain a matching velocity. Its engines fired back at Arepien to slow its approach. It would nevertheless be some time before *Paraida* was moving away from the planet rather than toward it.

Ass-backwards into the unknown, Zahrad thought, quietly observing three telits. The pallid green showed the distance between *Paraida* and Arepien. The figure was still decreasing, though at a slower rate as the drive fought to cancel its previous acceleration. The off-white telit displayed the distance between the two spacecraft, toy ships against the dark immensity of the abyss between the stars. Those numbers came down even more rapidly, since the supposed derelict was gaining on the destrier. The eye-eez blue, as always, showed *Paraida*'s rate of acceleration.

Zahrad actuated the ship-to-ship.

"TransGalactic Watch ship *Paraida* to freighter *Zinja*. We congratulate you on your successful effort at damping your engine overload and surviving your fall through *Protected* planet Arepien's atmosphere. Now that your spin has abated, we shall send over a rescue party to take you onboard. Do you firm, *Zinja*—Captain Hoyuko?"

There . . . that ought to tell us what he's up to!

Spacefarer Shiganu looked at his captain. Jonuta nodded. "You answer," he said. "Audio only. Visual's on the fob, of course."

"Zinja to *Paraida,"* Shig said in a casual voice, leaning in to the comm-mike. "My thanks for waiting for us! We were afraid you would redshift when our engines undamped." *And why didn't you, you flainin' blue-balled grat's ass?!* "Atmospheric drag managed to disable our spin thrusters. The drive held long enough for us to insert the damper rods manually. We are slowly putting 'er back together. Thanks for your help, *Paraida!* I think we can limp back to Terasaki."

Gheraka snapped the sender from Zahrad's grasp. "We'd be more than willing to send a detachment onboard to help put your ship into proper condition for flight. We are not just policers, you know."

Shig took a deep breath and covered the commsender. He looked to Jonuta for guidance. Jonuta chuckled quietly, enjoying the Terasak's plight.

Realizing he'd get no help from the boss (unless the situation deteriorated dangerously), Shig took his hand away from the mike.

"No need for you to worry or trouble yourselves with us, *Paraida*. I have one crewmember left. He's got most of the problems under control. I know TGW has more important things to do. . . ."

"Perhaps. But since you managed to destroy the ship we were assigned to follow, you have obviated our mission here. And since that ship managed to to cripple yours, I think it's only fair that we render assistance, *Zinja*." Gheraka bent in while he tucked the mike into his armpit. "Lieutenant! Prepare a boarding party. Stoppers on setting Three. I'll head up the operation. And have a computer traumatizer ready."

(The Lieutenant looked to the major for confirmation. Zahrad scratched at his mustache and nodded gently. Now that they had an opportunity to fulfill their mission, he had no grounds for defying this Gheraka person. And if Gheraka wanted to disable the merchanter with a traumatizer . . . well, that endangered *Paraida* not at all.

(Furthermore, the fart had given orders on Zahrad's bridge, and that was on record. Setting Three, was it? Bloody idiot!)

Shig was meanwhile wondering what to do next. The exchange of cordial offers and polite demurrers would not last long. *Coronet* was fast gaining on *Paraida* and would soon pass it. The destrier—already accelerating in the same direction—would not stay behind for long. Its more powerful engines would soon enable it to overhaul its . . . prey?

He ordered SIPACUM to plot intercept point within a few thousand meters. SIPACUM acknowledged. Imperceptible course corrections followed, constantly updating and altering the flight path to bring the ships alarmingly close. (SIPACUM duly warned about that, in red.)

Paraida's engine glare was visible now as a tiny white glimmering dead ahead against a field of sharp, steady stars in several hues. Shig looked up at Jonuta and grinned.

"I'm going to make them think we're on a collision course, then actuate Sixty-three-Bee just before we intersect. We'll hit transition phase while they're trying to get out of our way."

"Difficult to judge when SIPACUM will find an entry into subspace," Jonuta reminded, and it was all the advice he bothered to give. So far, everything Shig had done had followed his captain's philosophy. The destrier's master wanted the freighter? Fine—he'd get the freighter—in abundance!

Paraida's computer was meanwhile displaying its best calculation of the other ship's course on the lieutenant's screen.

"Showing *Zinja* on collision course, sir. Interception in eight mins from my mark . . . *Mark*." She looked up. "Our velocity differential will be more than fifteen hundred kloms per second, Major."

Zahrad took the news calmly. He knew tactics when they stared him in the face.

"Stand ready to alter course by twelve degrees ventral starboard on my command. Until then, we sit tight. Route all shield power aft and be ready to shift fields to maintain maximum protection when we cross."

He stared at her display and tapped on the armrest of his chair at con. And watched Gheraka, who was looking over the lieutenant's shoulder, either at her telits or the minimally interesting bulges within her gray tunic. He gave no outward indication of such interest. His emotional reaction was nil. He merely logged an observation.

"Lieutenant: have the boarding craft outfitted with two deep-thrust engine modules. I'm heading down to suit up." He turned. "With the major's permission, of course."

"Uh." Zahrad's attention remained fixed on the approaching freighter. "Damage control stand by. DS stand by. All: stand by for evasion maneuvers."

He took a deep breath and let it out slowly. *If Gheraka doesn't make this my last flight, I will!*

On the supposed freighter, Shig watched the eye-eez turquoise numbers of the telit decrease with *Coronet*'s ever-increasing proximity to *Paraida*. When the ships neared one minute to crossover, he actuated cassette 63B.

"They expect some action," Sak said from the forward DS station. *"Their shields are up max to cover their arses."*

Jonuta stared at the viewing point. The glow that was *Paraida* grew steadily brighter. "They'll be torn between running away and dropping their shields to fight, Shig. I take it you're counting on their belief that cowardice is the better part of employment."

Shig grinned. "At just the time they have to make a decision, we vanish on the Tachyon Trail."

"Uh. A fine plan, except that it hinges on your guess as to when SIPACUM will find a safe conversion point. We're less than a minute away from intercept and there's been no warning."

Shig looked down at his telit. His epicanthic eyes narrowed. For a few seconds he thought furiously. His finger flicked the commsender switch—audio only.

"Ah, *Zinja* to *Paraida*. Why haven't you matched our velocity? You can't board us at this differential." *That ought to keep 'em off-balance. Always make it the other guy's fault.*

"*Uh, Zinja . . .*" The voice spoke from the commbox with an unsure slowness. "*We won't be up to your speed until several minutes after we've passed each other. Suggest you cut your drive so that we may overtake you more easily at that time. Also, please alter course. Our computer shows a collision intersection in thirty seconds.*"

"But my engines *are* cut off. Stand by." Shig made tapping noises on the edge of the console and bent forward to broadcast his gasp of alarm. "Grabbles! My telits are feeding me bad scrute. My drive's at full thrust and I thought . . . Let's see if I can . . . Did you say collision intersection?" Shig practically shouted the last—and bit at the inside of his cheek to prevent a laugh from escaping.

"Pos! Double-firm!"

"Then I ought to . . ." He paused to tap the console again. "Hmm. Helm doesn't seem to respond. Are you *sure* we're going to collide?"

"Evasive action!" the commbox squawked, as the TGW craft's master doubtless felt a terribly chill.

Thrusters slammed the destrier "down" and away in a way that Shig and the tightly smiling Jonuta sincerely hoped worse than discommoded *Paraida*'s uniformed crew.

Coronet passed the TGW craft so swiftly that only the TPs caught and recorded its sidewise view. To anyone unconcerned enough about death in space to be gazing out a viewport, the "freighter" grew from a rapidly expanding patch of light to a mountain that passed *Paraida* in a blur at a mere few kloms, and pulled ahead of it. An instant later only the glow of the spacer's drive marked its rapidly diminishing form.

In that instant a boarding craft shot away from *Paraida*, hurled by the two high acceleration thrusters supplementing the boat's standard engines. The crew, crushed into their couch-like chairs, strove to disguise any outward signs of discomfort. The earlier example of Corporal Jumbaru emboldened them.

Gheraka revealed no hint of a plan. Under his gloved left hand lay the controls for the grappling field. Under his right gleamed the firing key for the computer traumatizer. He watched 'puter simulation of their approach to *Zinja* through acceleration-flattened eyes.

"Here comes a boat!" Sak bellowed, and commanded DS to command that little craft while he awaited orders to destroy it.

"If they don't try anything for a minute or two," Jonuta said, at last getting rid of his long coat, "maybe we'll get out of this with no casualties—on either side, Sak."

"Uh. I have shields up, Cap'n."

"Just remember what happened last time before transition!" Shig said, and a bright red telit caught his attention. "They've turned on their grapplers."

"Get ready, Sak," Jonuta said. "We don't want them dragged along with us." He glanced around to see something he'd almost forgotten—an entirely naked woman whose skin looked as if she'd been dipped in paprika. "Good g—*sit down!*" And he tossed her his piratic coat of scarlet.

He didn't bother to watch her obey. He swung back to stare at the simulation. The boarding craft lagged hundreds of kloms behind him. An electromagnetic web emanating from it tied both vessels together invisibly. If *Coronet* converted to tachyons with the boat thus invisibly attached, no one could predict how badly the entry onto the Tachyon Trail would be affected. SIPACUM had made its calculations based on the mass of *Coronet* alone. Leeway was allowed—a few hundred tons. And the boarding craft massed over three thousand tons.

Jonuta avoided taking lives needlessly, and he was most

definitely opposed to any kind of firefight with policers—especially the super spooks of TGW. Bluff and trickery were his weapons, and they usually worked. On the other hand a threat to *Coronet* was a threat to Jonuta of Qalara.

Kenowa looked up at the man she loved. Though he appeared calm, she knew the signs: the taut-set jawline, the tension in the fingers he moved over the console. She sighed. *And I've been thinking about little more than getting his singed coat repaired!*

Abruptly Sak reported plasma flaring on the pursuer's hull. *"Can't be attitude jets. Too bright. Ho! The boat's falling back!"*

"Field's been cut!" Kenowa said.

Jonuta and Shig exchanged a look. Jonuta flipped five. Shiganu looked back to the telits, perplexed. . .

And SIPACUM *ping*ged. Twenty seconds to tachyon conversion and entry into "subspace"—that nonexistent non-place where movement was faster than faster than light. Jonuta flexed hands that were tight with tension.

He did not even notice when Kenowa eased up the aircon. To hell with the nekkid red cake's bare tail on the floor—Kenowa's man was sweating!

"Something's been launched from that boat!" Sak called excitedly. *"Closing in."*

"Fire."

Sak ordered DS to blast the bogey.

"Ten seconds," Kenowa warned.

"Impact on the hull!"

"Impossible! I hit that sisterslicer! DS computer firms!"

"If they slung a lamprey at us this time, you can bet it's no mere tailer—" Jonuta's words seized up in his throat and the Arep behind him made a gasp-squeal sound.

Coronet, its crew, and the object clinging to its hull converted into tachyons and vanished from the system of the (not-so) Protected planet Arepien.

"*Zinja* did not fire on the lander, Captain."

"I know, I know, Lieutenant. *Zinja* fired afterward—got Gheraka's lamprey, I presume."

"But . . . something got the lander."

"Uh." Zahrad stood, stretched wearily. "Well, we'll

run it all back later and see what we can deduce—or have computer deduce for us. Take it, Sayda. I'm going back to see what sort of shape Gheraka's in.''

Pleased at hearing her name rather than rank, the lieutenant nodded and saw to transfer of controls. The major departed the con-cabin.

Gheraka and the surviving members of the boarding party were floating or being carried onboard *Paraida* still, Zahrad saw, in their mobile life support systems. Several of those left alive after the boat had been disabled by (something/someone) suffered wounds more severe than Gheraka's. Zahrad soon knew that the overbearing man had been blinded, by a plasma beam's piercing the hull. Zahrad didn't even indulge the natural served-the-bastard-right thought. Gheraka was a man, a Galactic, and Zahrad pitied him.

Molten slag had also peppered Gheraka's right arm; at least his suit had sealed automatically before losing too much pressure. He had lost a fair amount of blood.

He babbled deliriously about an attack from nowhere while medical crew sought to strip him and lower his body into the cybernetic daktari.

Major Haatan Zahrad watched the operation in silent meditation, hands clasped behind his gray-uniformed back. His eyes were flat, contemplative.

If I'm lucky, he'll die or turn up with brain damage from decompression. (Maybe that would be lucky for him, too.) If I'm not, I'll have to face him and and his new optic implants, his bitterness, and his condemnations at an inquiry.

Zahrad heaved a sigh, then flipped his fingers philosophically. *Pensions aren't what they used to be, anyway. Maybe that little gal on Eagle can use another partner on her farm.*

22

Spacer *Coronet* dropped out of "subspace."

Jonuta had endured several hours of tense waiting before ordering his Mate, SIPACUM, to return them to normal. Whatever had impacted on the hull had not behaved in the manner of a computer traumatizer—or anything else. Maybe it had failed. Maybe it was set on time delay. Jonuta had to know what it was—and how to remove it.

Shig and Vark suited up in the airlock to starboard. What few sensors remained reliable on *Coronet*'s hull after its hurtling passage through Arepien's atmosphere reported the object's location. Just aft of the airlock. The TPs provided no further information.

"This slicin' well better not be some grat-humpin' charge waitin' out there to blow our flainin' faces off," Vark grumbled, while he sealed the molecular bindings on his mlss/spacesuit and connected its helmet.

Shig reached out to cycle the airlock. He didn't feel up to conversation. The prospect of another repair expedition after being nearly crushed and vaporized seemed almost worse than being stuck on Vark's home planet. Almost.

Pumps sucked the air out of the chamber. Shig looked over at Vark's helmet and saw his own mlss reflected in the coated faceplate.

"*Firm whether it's a lamprey,*" Jonuta deep-voiced in their helmets. "If it is, we'll have to determine its exact position on the hull."

"What if it's a bomb?" Vark sounded almost subdued.

"*Don't discuss philosophy with it,*" Sakyo advised.

"Thanks." *Motherhumpin' sisterslicin' slant-eyed short-fart!*

210

The outer hatch unsealed noiselessly. Vark and Shig prepared to push out into space.

They faced three pressure-suited figures, afloat just outside. While they considered their unarmed situation, the one in the middle raised its right hand.

"Take me to your leader."

"And what," Jonuta commed, *"will you do when brought to me?"*

"Give you your thirty per cent, of course." Marekallian Eks laughed triumphantly.

"Thirty? Seal the hatch, Shig. Lock the double-crossing flainer out!"

"You seemed ready to leave without anything." Eks pushed the other two bodies inside the airlock and reached past Vark to cycle the hatches. *"Although,"* he added over the roar of inrushing air. *"I must applaud the great idea of turning your spaceship into a fireball to distract the Areps. Fantastic diversion! We got away before any of them managed to pick up their jaws. You shouldn't have, just for me!"*

"I didn't!" Shig glowered and his hand moved in the direction of the stopper he was not wearing. The sound of Jonuta's hearty laughter interrupted the angry gesture, anyhow.

"I suppose I did agree to let you onboard if you caught up to us. And I always keep my word. Almost. If the price is right. Welcome, Myrzha Eks. I look forward to picking out my forty per cent of the . . . loot, lootrunner."

"Didn't we agree on thirty-five?"

Jonuta's voice was absent from their suitcomms as the five trooped into *Coronet's* tan tunnel. Eks removed his helmet to face Captain Jonuta, who looked as tall and very nearly as big in soft cotton clingshirt and tight pants of linden green. Eks nodded a greeting and fingerflipped at the same time.

"I tried to be reasonable, Captain J. And after the way I helped you by placidating that boarding vessel! Those scum didn't even know what hit them."

"They weren't about to catch up to us."

"Maybe not, but I like to be sure. Always kick a man when he's down, you know."

"Ugh," a voice said, and the Mindrunner turned to see Kenowa's head, peering around from a side-tunnel. She looked past him. "Qalaratini?"

Jonuta smiled. "Make it two. We'll see if Eks is man enough for a Qalaratini."

"Ah—you have Qalara Passion dry gin onboard?" Eks smiled. "Wonderful!"

Jonuta stared—and then stared at the third member of the party as Verley got its helmet off. It was not a head or a face Jonuta had ever seen. Nor had he even seen one like it. Alien! (After unsealing the Akil's overlarge mlss and checking that the transfer from lander to airlock had not affected him adversely, she removed her own suit.

(That was interesting, too.)

"What the vug is that?" Vark was staring, looking the Akil three times over. Though about the same height, the Bleaker outmassed the alien by a factor of at least two.

"Been calling him Phoenix. Came out of an egg." Eks threw this suit back into the airlock. "Just a new race I happened to discover. Like him?"

"Pos!" Jonuta nodded without hesitation. "How do I claim forty per cent of him? *Kenny!*"

Marekallian Eks grinned. Brushing back his length of black hair, he stretched and swung his arms. "Ahhh. Well, Cap'n, that's just something we'll have to work out before we part company."

"Oh—oh, my." Kenowa had reappeared, and was gazing at the golden-furred alien.

"Another refugee for you to find some clothing for," Jonuta smiled.

Kenowa looked from the Akil to her man, and back to the Akil. Then she dropped Jonuta a sly grin. "Why bother?"

Later, propped up beside Jonuta in his bed—he naked, she more or less wearing something so soft and loose that he had left it on and merely disarranged it thoroughly while he sliced her halfway up the wall—Kenowa gazed at the screen he had flicked on. She smiled lasciviously and rubbed Jonuta's thigh, high up. Both watched the image of the Akil—"Phoenix," for now. He had preened that absolutely beautiful fur the color of an F-class star, and he looked absolutely deliciously intriguingly sensual.

Definitely, Kenowa thought. *We'll have to work something out before we part company.*

"Jone," she said, low and musically, "d'you have a hankering for that beautifully colored Arep girl?"

Reading her like a simulscreen book, Captain Jonuta laughed.

Geb ran the computer simulation one more time. *That's the trouble with undetectable landers—you can never find 'em!* He had scanned Arepien four times with no luck. Yet how could Marekallian Eks be gone?

"No answer on any of our frequencies." Ashtaru set the hailing message to repeat automatically. She tapped her green nails nervously against the commbox. "I . . . don't think he's down there."

"Where could he have gone without us?—without a ship?"

"You're the one who detected all those ionized trails when we came into the Alkoman system, Geb. Someone's been through here and maybe down on Arepien too—someone messy. I'd say Marek's been nipped, or worse." She moved her hand but continued her tapping, against the armrest of *Eris*'s second chair.

"He could be onplanet with a dead lander. We know where he made planetfall. If he's not there . . ." Geg hopped down from the chair and moved before her. Looking up at the seated woman. "If he can get back to us, he will. If he makes it to Sekhar, he'll guess we've returned here."

She rolled her eyes. "So we . . . stay?"

"We stay. Powered down till we're undetectable."

A few moments later, *Eris* resembled a non-reflecting asteroid. Cool, dark, radiating nothing, the black hulk silently orbited Arepien, awaiting the return of its master.

Geb practiced quick-draws with a deactivated minibeamer. Ashtaru sprawled watching a holodrama—a quick-draw thriller supposedly set on Macho where men were men and women weren't much.

They waited.